# Mary's Daring Demand

## A Pride and Prejudice Variation

Jaime Marie Lang

IDLE MUSINGS PUBLISHING

# Contents

# Chapter One

Never before had Gabriel Goulding hurt so much from watching someone else suffer.  It was an odd sensation that he was unfamiliar with. Living his life on firm principles, he tried to always be good to those around him. In school, he had bullied no one and tried to help those who were. He even volunteered at Mrs. Darcy's charity when he was in town. Until that point, he would have considered himself empathetic to others' suffering, and yet he had never felt the way he did at this moment.

He had come with Darcy and Miss Mary to look over Longbourn, the estate previously managed, albeit poorly, by the late Mr. Bennet. Gabriel liked Darcy and though he did not see how he could help, he was more than willing to come, especially if it meant being in the company of Miss Mary. However, he hadn't anticipated that such a simple task would be so painful.

He wandered the property, his footsteps quiet as he tried to stay close to Miss Mary without making his presence too obvious. Gabriel knew Miss Mary well enough that he could see her pain despite her attempt to remain stoic. It dawned on him that he had never seen her suffer before. He had witnessed her joy when her sister Kitty married and whenever she played with her niece and nephew. He had even seen her protective side rear its head when Kitty had been the butt of all the malicious gossip in London. Her own pain, however, was new to him and it shook him to the core.

"Careful, Miss Bennet," Gabriel said and reached out as she attempted to step over a pile of rubble. He was very careful to address her as Miss Bennet aloud, it was after all what she should be called as the oldest unmarried Bennet daughter. In his heart and mind, he knew she would remain Miss Mary no matter what was proper. It was, after all, how he addressed her the day he had begun to fall in love.

With a sad smile, Miss Mary took his offered hand to help steady her as she walked over the random bits of wreckage and broken parts of her past. "Thank you, Mr. Goulding. There seems to be rather more debris than I would have thought."

Longbourn had been her home for nineteen years and he knew on some level that those nineteen years had not been happy ones. Gabriel could tell when she recognized some broken bit of a chair or porcelain shepherdess. Her shoulders would droop, and her chin would wrinkle before she tightened her lips and moved on. His heart sank each time it happened, as if the weight of Miss Mary's memories were weighing on him as well.

Stopping to look at a wall that had been smashed through, Gabriel contemplated the sorrow he felt. He had known for some time that he loved Miss Mary, but he was unprepared for the other emotions love brought with it. Was it possible that the difference between a fleeting infatuation and true love was the pain that he now felt? Did true love mean that you would willingly take on more pain if it meant the one you loved would suffer less?

To say that he was having a morning of revelations was an understatement. What truly stymied him was the feeling of not being able to do anything about it. If they were engaged or even courting, he could try to comfort her. Instead, he had painted himself into a corner, letting himself fall so deeply in love before he could offer any kind of relationship. He was not in a place in his life where he could provide for a wife. In fact, it would be quite some time before he could.

So all he could do was watch her suffer while looking for little ways he could help her without crossing any lines. Miss Mary had quietly moved to a door at the end of the hallway on the ground floor, and despite her determined attempts to enter the room, the door would not budge. Gabriel immediately went to help her and upon further inspection, it seemed that the frame of the door had warped, and the door had become stuck. Putting his shoulder to it, he pushed against the door's resistance, only to have it pop open unexpectedly.

Without the resistance to hold them up, he and Miss Mary both fell into the room. Moving to protect Miss Mary from the fall, Gabriel twisted and grabbed her around the waist, causing her to fall on top of him instead of against the hard floor. He lay there, momentarily stunned by the impact before slowly coming to the realization that he was clutching Miss Mary to him.

Removing his hand reluctantly from around her waist, he smiled to see a single tendril of her hair had broken free to caress her forehead. She blinked owlishly at him as he asked, "Are you all right?"

"Um, yes, I seem all right, but you saved me from hitting the floor. Are *you* all right?" Awkwardly, Miss Mary tried to find a way to get off his supine form.

Clasping Miss Mary to him once more, Gabriel sat up and, bringing her with him, helped her sit up as well. As soon as she was upright, Miss Mary moved to kneel in front of him, her face full of concern. Reaching out, she looked as if she wanted to check his head for damage. Smiling softly, he clasped her hand and said, "I have a hard head. Do not worry, I assure you I am fine."

FINDING HERSELF SPRAWLED ON top of Mr. Goulding had wiped Mary's mind of all thought. The first thought that finally coalesced into being was surprise at his unexpected strength when he effortlessly caught her to soften her fall. The next thought was how green his eyes were up close. Their vibrant color resembled fresh spring leaves, full of energy and strength. Had she never been close enough to spot the flecks of gold hidden among the green?

She managed to respond to Mr. Goulding despite trying to find a way to crawl out of sight and die of embarrassment. Realizing that he might be hurt, Mary said, "Um, yes, I seem all right, but you saved me from hitting the floor. Are *you* all right?"

Somehow she found herself sitting next to him as he continued to reassure her that he was fine before helping her to her feet. Clearing her throat, Mary struggled to get rid of the tightness that gripped her. She offered a shaky, "Thank you," and stepped away from him, forcing herself to look around the room. There was no way she could dwell on what had happened and still maintain her composure. She would think of it later when she had the chance to be alone.

Focusing on her father's room was difficult, but she managed. She had wondered halfheartedly if her father would leave his room free from destruction. Her father had loved his books more than anything else in the world and yet it seemed that when he left Longbourn, he had not been able to bring them all. He had, however, not left those remaining in good stead. The remnants of an untold number of books lay in torn and shredded remains around the room. Piles of ripped pages were scattered, the worlds they contained unceremoniously discarded.

It looked as if a large fire had once roared in the fireplace, fed by any number of books. The ashes long cold were piled high, and it hurt Mary to see them. Her father had loved his books to such an extent, but he had cast them aside with as much cruelty as he had his family. Reaching out, she ran her hand along the dust-coated shelf nearest to her. The shelf had once held so many tomes, a testament to mankind and the power of the written word, and her father had destroyed them all because he could not get his way.

Once the Bennet ladies had been freed of his tyranny, the servants and tenants who had stayed due to the hardworking women abandoned Longbourn. No one would put up with Mr. Bennet for any length of time. Without rents to fill his coffers, Mr. Bennet had quickly gone bankrupt. That is when the clause in the entail had allowed Mr. Collins to have Mr. Bennet evicted and took possession of the property. Only Mr. Bennet had so utterly ruined it all that Longbourn was unlivable. Mr. Collins did not have the money to do anything with Longbourn and for a time, he left it to ruin.

Eventually, Mr. Collins was approached by a buyer. The entail allowed him to sell the home as it ended with him. What he did not know or understand was that the man who approached him represented the husbands of Elizabeth, Jane and Catherine. They had come up with the idea of returning the property to the Bennet ladies as it should have been. So Mary was there, fighting the demons of her past and facing the devastation her father left behind.

Did it make her a terrible daughter and a bad Christian to not regret the fact that her father had passed not long after abandoning Longbourn? Whatever her label, she could be nothing but relieved to know that she would never have to face the man again. Though she had rarely cowered before her father as Kitty had, she had allowed him to assume she was moralizing and simple in order to avoid the worst of his barbs. She never had the fortitude to confront him, as Elizabeth did in so many ways.

Shaking her head, Mary walked over to the desk that her father had relished sitting behind. Having rarely been allowed into his study, she had few memories of seeing him there at his desk, though the few memories she had still made her shudder. It was only as she drew closer that she spotted the knife. It was an eerie sight that left Mary feeling unsettled. There on the table lay a book splayed open in surrender with a knife plunged through its pages and into the hard wood of the desk below.

Creeping closer, she looked at the book, trying to decipher what tome her father had found so enraging. It was a book on floriography—the language of flowers with illustrations and descriptions all in French. If you did not know her family, it might have been startling and confusing, but knowing what she did, Mary somehow found it hilarious.

Unlikely as it seemed, Mary burst out laughing. Her father, it appeared, had finally deciphered why his youngest daughter was constantly gifting him flowers. His reaction had been rather extreme. How hard had it been to stab straight through the book and into the table? Her laugh was a great hysterical thing that got the attention of not only Mr. Goulding who looked at her with worry, but also William who had been in the next room.

"Are you all right, Mary?" Fitzwilliam Darcy approached her, his wide eyes full of concern as he entered the study through the open door.

Mr. Goulding approached as well, looking almost as if he wanted to embrace her or possibly, he was simply afraid of her uninhibited laughter. "Yes, Miss Bennet, are you well?"

Sobering with effort, Mary pointed at the book and replied, "The book." Her father had never once considered that his wife and daughters were capable of finding a way to defy him. He had thought that Lydia was entirely stupid, giving him flowers all the time, instead of viewing her as a clever young woman who was cunning in her own right. Lydia was quite fond of floriography and used the flowers that she loved so much as a way of showing her spite and hatred for the man. While Mr. Bennet had thought his daughter foolishly loved him, she had been telling him on a regular basis what she truly thought.

"It seems he finally read the book that Theodore gave him before we left," William commented as he yanked the knife out of the book and set it aside to check the marred wood beneath.

"I had always wondered if he would ever decipher the hidden meanings. I know he thought that Lydia had a terrible eye for color and composition when she gave him bouquets or paintings of flowers. She spent quite a lot of time in her garden whenever he was being horrible." Accepting the handkerchief from Mr. Goulding, she wiped at her eyes that had begun to water. She would not admit to crying, not at that juncture. "She always had the perfect flower to give him and he, the man who thought he knew so much, could not understand the language she spoke."

Looking up from the desk, William asked, "Will you tell your sister of her success and his apparent understanding?"

"I think I will write to Lydia this afternoon. As much as I would like to have her here with me for this, I am glad she is with Mother back in Derbyshire." Reaching out, Mary gathered up the book and fingered its ragged scar. The hole in the book was a reminder of the damage her father had left on his family. "Mama spent too much of her life trapped here with that man and now she has finally found true happiness with her new husband and son. I am glad she is not here. And as for Lydia, I am glad to be able to protect her from the darkness of this place."

"Yes, there will be a lot of work returning Longbourn to any sort of grandeur." William tried to pick up a small table that had once held a chess set, only for it to fall to pieces in his hands.

Putting down the book with a sigh, she wiped her soiled hands against the apron she had worn to protect her dress from the grime of the home. Mary wrinkled her nose to see the gray streaks left there. "I am less concerned about the manor house than I am about all the tenant cottages and farms. While I doubt my father ransacked them as he did his home, they will still need repair."

Mr. Goulding went back to the doorway and inspected the door frame, inspecting it for whatever sorts of things people who studied design and structure did. "I have not seen any major structural damage. There is, of course, a lot of damage to the items within the home and a few problems from the damp and broken windows."

Pushing some of the debris into a pile with his foot, William shook his head. "Mary, what say you of getting people into the house to remove the rubble and seeing what can be salvaged? We can assess the home itself and see what repairs need to be done."

Nodding her head, Mary agreed. "I am not opposed to that, though we should probably ask Lizzie if she has any other ideas. I do hope she is feeling better when we return to Netherfield."

"Yes, I do hope so." Despite William's claims, Mary noticed that he could not get rid of his smile. This helped to cement her suspicion that her sister was once again with child.

"Why don't we go and check the servants' quarters and the kitchen? We can easily leave rooms without furniture and what not, but we will need to make sure there is a way to feed everyone." Turning her back on her father's domain, she forced herself to put it out of her mind for at least the moment. She would probably think about it in the small hours of the night when she could not sleep.

As she walked through the empty halls, she wondered if it would ever be possible to make Longbourn feel like the home it had never been. A crunch underfoot caused her to halt her steps and she looked down, spotting the remnants of a broken figurine. Leaning over, she carefully fingered the broken fragments. Part of a small, smiling face looked up at her, and she realized it was a piece of the figurine her mother had always kept on the mantel. The figurine was once a happy, dancing girl that would never dance again. Mary froze, lost in thought, remembering how her mother would smile as she turned it just so before company came. It had been a wedding gift to her mother from her parents. Unshed tears burned in her throat, but she stood and moved on down the hallway. There was too much pain in the house to focus on the loss of one small figurine.

Squaring her shoulders, Mary continued on with the echo of the heavier steps behind her. At least one of the gentlemen was behind her, following her to the kitchens. She wondered what they might think of the domain that was typically run by women. Had either of them ever spent much time in the kitchens of their childhood homes?

As she entered the kitchen, she was comforted to see that the destruction was less evident. Looking through the various cabinets and drawers, she realized that though everything would need a thorough cleaning, most of it was salvageable. Yes, there was some kind of nest in one of the cabinets that would need to have its inhabitants evicted, but despite that, it would be fairly easy to resume using the space.

The sudden skittering of something running across the floor behind her had Mary gathering her skirts closer to herself and drawing them away from the floor. Wrinkling her nose in disgust, Mary mentally upped the amount of lye she would be bringing over to clean with. It would take quite a lot before she would feel comfortable eating anything that came from this room. Everything would be thoroughly scrubbed with hot water and lye before anything else. More sounds of small, unwelcome inhabitants had Mary deciding that she would also be needing a cat—perhaps several cats—to comb through the building while they were working on repairs. Based on the unsettling noises she had heard so far, the cats would certainly eat like kings or queens.

Noticing William and Mr. Goulding looking around the kitchen with slight looks of confusion, Mary managed to smile. She expected that neither of them had spent much time at all in the kitchens of their homes in their childhoods. Beyond the need to pilfer biscuits, it seemed that men and boys left the kitchen to the woman folk of their lives. "Besides several furry tenants that I have plans of evicting with several large cats, the kitchen looks to be in a good state. Or at least a better state than the rest of the house."

Mr. Goulding nodded in agreement, though his eyes grew wide when he spotted her skirts gathered up above her ankles. Then, quickly looking away, he said, "I can ask around and see if anyone knows of any kittens in the area that need a new home, or of someone with some extra barn cats. I am sure it is something we can take care of quite easily."

Blushing at his reaction, Mary considered dropping her skirts, but then the continued sounds of mice skittering out of sight left her unable to do so. "I would be appreciative of that, thank you. We will need to scrub everything thoroughly." Looking around once more, Mary took note of the layer of grime and dust that had been interspersed with tiny footprints, showing more evidence of the pests that had made the kitchen their home. "Very thoroughly, but it will be easier to take in hand than the rest of the house."

Mr. Goulding managed to maintain eye contact with her, though this time his expression was one of concern. "We? Are you planning on helping? I am sure—"

"That I would be completely capable of rolling up my sleeves and cleaning." Looking at Mr. Goulding with raised eyebrows, Mary waited to see if he would catch his error. She knew that many men thought women of certain status should follow certain patterns of behavior, but she had long ago decided not to let someone else stop her from doing what she could—and should—do to aid others.

Looking rather chagrined, Mr. Goulding rubbed at the back of his neck while seemingly trying to formulate a response. "Yes, I am sure you will do what you wish to see the house returned to a livable state."

Mary glanced at William, who seemed to be smiling at Mr. Goulding's befuddlement. She remembered how often William had found himself in a similar situation when trying to speak with Elizabeth early on in their relationship. Was he happy to be the one not with his foot in his mouth for once? Clearing his throat and relaxing his smile with apparent difficulty, William said, "I am sure that we can round up several willing maids from Netherfield to help get the kitchen in order. Though I will be trying to keep Elizabeth at home with her health being so unreliable at the moment."

"Yes, I will encourage her to stay at Netherfield as well." Mary smiled to herself, thinking of the possibility of having another niece or nephew in the coming summer. Until she had her own children, she was happy to spoil her sister's children and even her new little brother. She was content enough to wait, at least for now. Looking over at the still contrite Mr. Goulding, she offered him a forgiving smile.

If she could council Lizzie to be forgiving of all of Mr. Darcy's errors in speech back when she met him, then it was only fair that she would attempt to forgive Mr. Goulding. William had turned out quite well despite his propensity for misspeaking, so perhaps there was hope for Mr. Goulding. With skirts still in hand, she turned and left the room. She had no desire to stay with the mice and their friends any longer than necessary.

Once they returned to the broken sitting room, William looked around one last time in disgust at their surroundings before turning to Mary. "I think we have seen as much as we wish to this morning. Why don't we go back to Netherfield? We can discuss matters, and I would like to check on Elizabeth."

"I think that is a splendid idea." Mary smiled, grateful that someone else had suggested they leave the ruins of her childhood.

# Chapter Two

Gabriel watched Darcy fiddle with his glass of brandy. He appeared happily lost in thought, given the smile on his face. Darcy had been quite eager to get home and check on his wife. It seemed that she was well enough because he had reappeared fairly quickly and had yet to lose the besotted look since his return. Gabriel acknowledged that he wanted the same thing for himself and repressed a sigh. His love for Mary had cemented itself into his heart long ago, but for now, it would have to wait. As a second son his options were quite limited.

Even though Miss Mary had given enough signs of encouragement to make him believe she would gladly enter into a courtship with him, he felt he had nothing to offer her. She was the sister of an earl now—she could reach as high as she wished. He had no estate and, so far, no profession. His parents had told him he needed to find a way to support himself because, of course, all the family's wealth was going to his older brother and his younger sister's dowry. He had decided early on that he was not meant for the military or for the church, despite his mother's hints that he would look nice in a red coat. All he really had to work with was his training at Oxford. While he could easily get a job as a clerk at a law firm and work at becoming a barrister, he found it an unappealing prospect. At one point, he had been interested in design and architecture, but found his skill was not great enough for it to offer gainful employment.

It was a pity that he was not the firstborn, really; he had much more interest and knowledge on running an estate than either his father or his older brother. Where they were content to let things progress as they had always been and spend more than they should on the trappings of gentility, he was not. Gabriel had found learning about crop rotation and other methods of diversifying holdings to be fascinating. He had learned much about it from Mr. and Mrs. Darcy, not that his father ever listened to his suggestions. His father was firmly of the camp that held with tradition. According to him, the way his grandfather had run things was good enough and there was no questioning that. Why spend the family's money on more diverse crops and better equipment for the workers when they needed it to keep up appearances?

Gabriel had never been all that fond of the current fads in fashion. Looking down at his waistcoat, he gave it a tug. It was perfectly serviceable, and he liked the color; he did not care if it was two seasons out of date. Rubbing at his face in frustration, Gabriel decided he could do with some conversation. "How is Mrs. Darcy faring?"

Coming out of his thoughtful state, Darcy said, "Well enough. I will always worry, but she reassures me she is well, and with Mary tending to her I am sure she is as well as may be. What did you think of the state of Longbourn?"

"Frankly, I thought you exaggerated when you said you feared the condition of the estate. What gentleman would behave so poorly and destroy his family home out of spite? I had always known Mr. Bennet was not a gentleman I cared to get along with, but I had never suspected the depth of his insolence and depravity." Looking into the cheery fire for a moment, he pondered what Mary must have experienced under the power of such a man. She had not confided in him beyond saying that Longbourn was not somewhere they could safely stay. "I am grateful you freed the Bennet ladies of him when you did. Why was he so horrible, do you think? I never truly spoke with the man and was only vaguely aware that he had financial troubles."

His face twisting into an angry grimace, Darcy replied, "From what my Elizabeth tells me, he was angry that after his parents' and older brother's deaths, he had been forced to leave academia to take control of Longbourn. Instead of seeing the property and his family as the boons that they were, he was furious he had been deprived of what he had wanted for his life. So, like a child, he tried to make everyone as miserable as he saw himself."

Sitting with the information for a moment, Gabriel considered how a man could sink so low, all the while vowing to never descend down a similar path. Seeing the destruction of Longbourn had come as quite a shock. He had never expected to see such evidence of wrath. "I can understand now why Mr. Collins chose to not take control of the property and sold it instead. He would have to have a great deal of money to make the manor livable, not to mention the work needed to rebuild the tenant cottages. I doubt Mr. Collins has that kind of money."

"No, he does not. The current condition of Longbourn necessitates another prosperous property to fund its renovations." Darcy looked at Gabriel, something curious in his eyes, before adding, "Mary often speaks of your interest in design and agricultural reform. She said that you enjoyed Oxford, but you have finished your course of study."

The way that Darcy left off made Gabriel feel it was more of a question than a statement. Looking at the slightly older man, he felt that Darcy wanted to know something about him. They had spoken often, but he had never felt such an intent from him before. What was it he wanted to know? "Yes, it is a pity that I am a second son because I do not have the calling for the church or the military. Nor do I have the head for trade. I almost feel as if I am a man of the land, or maybe the people."

Nodding, Darcy leaned back in his chair, his fingers steepled. "What would you do with Longbourn if it was yours to repair? I could see your mind working while we were there."

Gabriel sat for a moment wondering if the illustrious Mr. Darcy was testing him. Through Miss Mary and her sisters, he had become acquainted with Mr. Darcy and Mr. Bingley, and more recently Theodore Fitzwilliam, the new earl of Matlock, though he would have never thought he would be developing friendships with such prestigious people. If he had his wish, he would be their brother-in-law. It was a very sobering thought.

Did Darcy want his help? He could not know without forging forward. "Yes, well, I did see some places where adjustments to the layout would be of benefit. For example, instead of trying to repair the damaged wall with the gaping hole, it would be better to leave an open space or doorway to help with the flow of the home. I am also concerned about the condition of some of the flooring and woodwork in the rooms where the windows had been smashed. The wet and damp can cause all kinds of problems." Noticing that he still had Darcy's undivided attention, he continued, "I am actually more interested in the tenant cottages. I took some time this morning to check a few over before I met up with you. Several might need major restructures. I saw two that needed new roofs and there was one that had been partially knocked in from a fallen tree."

Eyes widening slightly at the news of the damage to the tenant cottages, Darcy inquired, "What would you suggest we start with first?"

"The main house mostly needs to be cleared out and cleaned, which does not need the full attention of anyone. With several workers given a daily task, it would be fairly simple to get what needs done effectively. Then a carpenter could assess the remaining problems." Taking a sip of the brandy in his glass, Gabriel allowed himself to think of what he would do if Longbourn was his own property. There was a lot there that could be used. It was like starting fresh instead of having to worry about the generations of habits that you would need to overcome to implement wiser strategies. "The tenant cottages could be worked at in turn, saving the worst cases for last, and enabling people to move in as they become livable. Winter is approaching and I would focus on getting cottages ready if you want tenants in place beforehand. Also, I would select tenants who were willing to try new agricultural practices. The soil here is good for more than just the typical wheat crops. I have heard of those not much farther south doing quite well growing hops and barley, selling it to the breweries, and making quite a tidy profit." Stopping, he looked back at Mr. Darcy and flushed in embarrassment. He had let his mind run away with him. He had no intention of talking as much as he did. Pemberley was a huge estate—much larger and more profitable than Longbourn ever was, or any of the properties hereabout for that matter. Mr. Darcy would know so much more than himself.

Smiling kindly, Mr. Darcy saluted Gabriel with his glass. "Here is to not ever being embarrassed by admitting to know things. I like your ideas. While I can tell you are thinking that I have experience with my estate in Derbyshire, what you do not understand is that you are from this area and will know things that I do not. I think introducing hops or barley in the spring is a brilliant idea." Pausing, he looked as though he was debating something. Then with a bob of his head, he shrugged his shoulders and said, "I was going to wait until Bingley arrived next week, but he is delayed for some reason or another and so I will just say this now. We have discussed it and those of us who put up the funds to purchase Longbourn would like to offer you a position. It may not be something you were thinking of, but it would provide you with a nest egg should you choose to accept it."

Narrowing his eyes in confusion, Gabriel asked, "Position? What are you needing help with?"

Without hesitation, Darcy replied, "I am wondering if you would be willing to be a steward of sorts. Longbourn is going to need attention—much more than Bingley or I can provide. We both have our own estates that need attention." Reaching out, he took a sip of his amber colored drink. Then letting what was left in his glass swirl around for a bit, he watched it glow in the light of the fire. "We cannot stay here as long as it would take to return Longbourn to the state it should be in, which brings me to my proposal. Would you be willing to oversee things now and when we eventually need to return to our own estates?"

Gabriel sat for a moment, shocked at the proposition. Mr. Darcy was giving him the opportunity to work on an estate from the ground up and if he did not miss his guess, he would have the opportunity to determine the buildings and structure of how Longbourn would operate going forward. "Would I be getting all the instructions from you, or would I be allowed to make decisions?"

Downing the last of his brandy, Darcy put his glass down and nodded. "At first I would appreciate hearing what you would like to do, but eventually yes, you would take the lead on decisions. For the most part, I merely want Longbourn to become as great as it could be. I have been watching you for some time and I think that you have a good eye, and you have the drive to accomplish all that needs to be done."

Gabriel could not help but grin. This was an amazing opportunity. He knew it was a huge undertaking, but it would give him the ability to put his learning to use and feel useful at the same time. He had never before considered becoming a steward, but it was possible that Darcy was giving him the opportunity to find his way into a profession. "I am honored that you would offer me such a position and I would love to accept it."

Though he was thrilled, he briefly wondered if Mary would mind being married to a steward. It would be more than a step down from her sisters' marriages so far. Shaking his head, Gabriel realized that this did not mean he had to become a steward, but it would give him a sizeable chunk of money that he could put towards his savings. He had been saving every spare coin he had from his allowance since the moment he realized he was falling in love with Miss Mary. She deserved so much, and he wanted to give it to her. First things first, he would work to earn enough to support her. Eventually, he could propose to her as they both wished.

Maintaining his analytical gaze, Darcy finally smiled and said, "I am glad. I truly think this plan will be of benefit to you and Longbourn. Where would you like to start work?"

Gabriel only pondered for a moment before responding, "That depends on whether you have plans to get any tenants this year."

"I only have one family that I know of who would like to come to Longbourn. A young couple from Pemberley who would like to try their hand at a new place further south. They will wait until early spring. Actually, they are planning on marrying in February and hope to come down soon after." Darcy smiled as he spoke, and it was obvious to Gabriel that he knew the young couple and wanted only the best for them.

"Well then, I think the very first task would be to organize some workers to clear Longbourn. We can move any salvageable pieces to the attics or servants' quarters for now, and then clear everything that is broken or beyond saving." Sitting forward in his chair, Gabriel's mind raced, spinning all sorts of plans. Putting down his still half-full glass, he rubbed his hands against the fabric of his trousers. "Once that is done, I can survey the tenant cottages. I will evaluate which home can be finished the quickest so that work can start there."

Darcy nodded and offered an affable smile. "I can see that you are full of ideas and that this will be just the task for you. My only caveat to your work is that I would like for you to ask for advice from my wife and her sisters. Elizabeth and Mary are here already, and Mrs. Bingley should be arriving soon enough. The sisters are the ones who ran Longbourn, not their father." He paused briefly, a reminiscent look on his face as if remembering a different time. "They were all devastated they had to leave it behind when they were able to escape their father. They know much about the land and the people who lived here."

Gabriel's planning halted at that comment. He had seen that sorrow on Mary's face that morning, and how affected she had been by the state of the home. On some level, he had known the sisters had worked hard to keep Longbourn afloat without Mr. Bennet's support, but he hadn't thought of what it would do to them to leave behind what they had worked so hard on. What would it do to a person to see all of their hard work undone by an evil man? Their father, no less.

He had not thought about speaking to the sisters about his plans, but looking at it from Darcy's perspective, he could not leave them out of the process. "You are right. I will consult with them as things progress." He grinned, thinking back to the comments Miss Mary had made and the way she had looked at him as she spoke. "I know Mary will insist on being at Longbourn as much as possible, working to improve it all."

Standing up, Darcy put away his glass, went over to his desk, and pulled out a file from a stack of several others. "I am glad you understand. Now to get to the financial arrangements. I am sure you would like to know how you will be paid, as well as what the budget for the project is."

DARCY WATCHED THE YOUNGER man leave the study. Had he ever been that age? Somehow the five-year age difference felt like a wide gap. Then again, at twenty-three, he had already been responsible for Pemberley, several satellite estates, and his much younger sister for two years. Gabriel was not exactly timid, but he had not seemed to have found his place in the world or gain the confidence that came with it. Darcy hoped their plan would be the making of him.

He was happy Gabriel had been so eager to take part in the plan that Theodore had suggested to him and Bingley. While having Longbourn was all well and good, it would need quite a lot of work in order to become a profitable estate once more. He had enough to handle without adding a struggling estate that needed major repairs. Frankly, he would much rather spend time with his wife and son than oversee yet another project. When Theodore had suggested having Gabriel oversee the work, it had been a stroke of genius. It was always nice to take care of two problems at once.

Both Theodore and Darcy knew that Goulding and Mary were more than quite fond of one another. They were hoping this would give the young couple the opportunity to work together and perhaps Goulding would get to the point. Elizabeth was very vocal about her frustration over the fact that the young man had not even asked for a courtship when it was obvious that he was smitten with Mary.

Sighing, Darcy played with his quill pen absentmindedly, the feathered tip twirling around as he thought. The things he did for his love for Elizabeth. Here he was, taking on the role of matchmaker. With a chuckle, he looked at the clock on the mantel and smiled. Artie should be up from his nap by now. Maybe he could take his son out to the stables and spend some time with the horses. Cadmus would be more than happy to get a carrot and Artie so loved feeding him. Putting down his quill, he stood and wondered if Elizabeth would feel up to joining them.

# Chapter Three

Mary hurried to return to her sister's room, eager to be there for Elizabeth. Her poor sister had never been this sick with her last pregnancy. Elizabeth might not have admitted what was ailing her, but that did not prevent Mary from knowing. Here it was almost noon and her maid said she had not been able to hold anything down. Mary had sent instructions to the kitchen staff to brew a stronger ginger tea, hoping it would help quell her sister's nausea.

Entering the room, she approached the bed where Elizabeth was lying and said softly, "The maid will bring up some more ginger tea as soon as may be."

Elizabeth was leaning back against her pillows with her eyes closed, looking rather wan. "Thank you, Mary dear. I do not know what I would do without your help."

Looking her sister over with a critical eye, Mary wished Jane would get here soon. If they did not get the nausea under control, Elizabeth would start losing more weight than was safe for her or the babe she carried. "I would never leave you alone at a time like this with you feeling so poorly. Even with that great big cream puff you have claimed as a husband trying to cater to your every need, you still need a sister here to support you."

Opening her eyes, Elizabeth's emerald gaze found Mary's as she attempted a fleeting smile. "Someday soon you will have your own household to see to, and your own husband and children to care for. You will not always be by my side. Until then, however, I am happy to have you here."

Though Mary smiled in response, she doubted her sister's claims. She had once dreamed of the life her sister described, but after years of little progress, she wondered if perhaps she wasn't meant for married life. She had first danced with Mr. Goulding when Elizabeth had met William years ago. Her sister was now married and expecting her second child while Mary was still not even courting. Forcing her mind to a more pleasant avenue, she leaned over and rearranged the flowers in the vase on Elizabeth's bedside table. "These seem rather unlike the flowers you normally have arranged by your maid."

"Those were a gift from Artie. He has been worried about my being unwell. I know that most of them are weeds, but he was so happy to bring them to me." Speaking of her dear son seemed to help Elizabeth as she managed a wide smile that took up most of the space on her face.

When she attempted to sit up straighter in bed, Mary hurried to arrange the pillows to support her. Once positioned, Elizabeth closed her eyes again and took several slow breaths, apparently fighting off more nausea. Once she opened her eyes again, she had a more serious look on her face. "How was Longbourn?"

Shoulders drooping at the thought of Longbourn's condition, Mary sighed. Sitting in the chair near the bed, Mary looked at Elizabeth sadly. "It was quite bad, though thankfully, we do not think it was damaged beyond repair. Much of the furniture has been destroyed and several windows have been shattered." Mary paused when her time in their father's study came to mind. "Father's study was more of a mess than I would have thought. It seems that whatever books he was unable to bring with him, he destroyed."

At the knock at the door, the maid was called in and Mary got up, helping the maid to settle the tray and pour a cup of tea. The maid had also brought up some dry toast, but Mary set that to the side to wait until Elizabeth felt ready to venture beyond tea. Handing her sister the cup of fragrant tea, Mary said, "Here you go, my dear. This should help."

The maid watched it all with a look of concern before saying, "The cook said that she will start brewing the ginger tea on the regular, as Miss Bennet suggested. We will have some for you whenever you have need of it, you only need to ask. If you have anything else that you feel might help or anything that you might crave, please let us know. We are all eager to get you feeling more yourself, Mrs. Darcy." Blushing at her long speech, the maid bobbed a curtsey and looked to the floor.

"Thank you, Ellen. You are being so kind," Elizabeth said with a warm smile. "Though I wish I was not such a bother, it is reassuring to know that you—that everyone—is so willing to offer their support." After the maid left, Elizabeth closed her eyes and took a tiny sip of the tea. She seemed apprehensive about drinking any more until she knew it would stay down.

Mary went back to her chair and watched Elizabeth with a careful eye, ready to grab for the nearby bowl if needed. They sat in silents for a few minutes while Elizabeth tested her ability to stomach the tea. Eventually, it seemed that Elizabeth was able to drink at will with no issue and she asked for a piece of toast. Once she had managed a few bites and was looking less green, she asked, "What were you saying about father's study?"

With a grim tightening of her lips, Mary looked at Elizabeth and told her the last bit of their trip to Longbourn. "It seems that father read the book on floriography before he left Longbourn. He had struck a knife into the book, stabbing straight through it and into his desk."

Elizabeth's eyes widened at the news and her already pale face grew paler still. Then, with a shake of her head, she seemed to grow in strength from somewhere within herself. "It may be wrong of me to say, but I am glad that he is no longer able to torment us and others with his horrible presence."

"I know the bible tells us not to judge others, so I will simply say I agree, and I am reassured that we no longer have to worry about him." It was very hard for Mary to get the image of the knife stuck in the book out of her mind. Over time, remembering life at Longbourn had become a hazy, distant memory, like a long-ago pain of a broken arm that was remembered but not felt. Mary had always tried to look at the good things in life and she had so many good things. Remembering her father's tendency toward cruelty was hard. She was especially grateful that Lydia had not been around him when he discovered that she had been poking fun at his ignorance the entire time.

With a final shudder at her morose thoughts, Mary was glad for the distraction when there was a small knock at the door, followed by the small voice that would always bring smiles to faces.

"I come in?" Artie's voice was muffled through the door but was still quite dear.

Elizabeth put her teacup on the side table and grinned as she responded to the little voice. "Yes, dear, please come in."

In a flurry of movement, a small body rushed into the room, followed by a much larger body traveling at a much more sedate pace. A wooden toy horse flopped onto the bed with childlike abandon, then little hands gripped at the bedclothes and, after a few grunts, pulled a little person up onto the bed. Crawling across the bed, little Artie flung himself against his mother and gave her a rather sloppy kiss on the cheek. "Ello Mama!"

Holding his small body to herself, Elizabeth kissed his tousled dark hair and leaned back to study his cheerful face. "How are you this morning, my little gentleman?"

Sitting back on his heels in her lap, Artie smiled and nodded excitedly, his curly hair flopping into his eyes. "Good! Said ello to Crum with Papa."

Looking up at her husband, who had moved to the side of the bed and looked at her with concern, she reached out a hand and took one of his in her own. Turning back to her son, Elizabeth inquired, "And how was Crumpet this morning?"

"He did a happy neigh." Then, with an uncanny accuracy, Arthur Theodore Darcy imitated his favorite horse's behavior with a neighing shake of his head. The little toy horse that often accompanied him was retrieved from the edge of the bed and was used to better demonstrate.

"Very happy indeed." Looking up at William who was now busy smiling down at their rambunctious child, she said, "Poor Cadmus. He has gone from being a Greek king to Crumpet, and now to Crum. How will he ever live it down?"

"He is a strong and noble horse—he will manage. For all that, he absolutely adores Artie." Leaning down, William gave his wife a kiss on the cheek. "How are you faring, my love?"

"Well enough, I suppose. I am already feeling better this morning and I have managed to hold down some tea and toast. Thank you for bringing Artie to visit me. I would have managed to make my way up to the nursery eventually, but I was missing our time together." Leaning over, Elizabeth scooped up her boisterous boy and cuddled her child to her chest, inhaling the simple wonder of him. After helping care for her niece and nephew, Mary knew the smell well—that unique, clean scent that all babies and toddlers seemed to possess. Smiling at her husband, Elizabeth whispered, "You always know just what I need, Wills."

Mary watched the love that her sister had with no little envy. She wished the same for herself, but it was always just out of her reach. After a few moments of watching the blissful scene between her sister and her little family, Mary cleared her throat, gaining their attention. "Good morning, Artie and William."

Looking up with a jolt, as if surprised another person was in the room, Artie spotted his aunt with glee. "Aunt Mawy! Morning." Then with the lack of foresight and enthusiasm that all toddlers possessed, he flung himself off the bed and into Mary's waiting arms.

Nuzzling his crown of dark curls, Mary smiled and asked, "How are you, my little love?"

Artie grasped her face with both of his chubby little hands, gently forcing her to look him in the eye. "Good. You play with me today?"

"Yes, of course I will play with you later today. I have a few things I need to work on first, though."

Growing serious, Artie nodded. "Right, do you work first, then we play later."

Nodding her head within its constraint, Mary grinned at the serious little boy. Sometimes he was just like her sister—bold and full of life—and other times he had such a serious expression, just like his occasionally dour father.

William spoke up from next to Elizabeth. "Are you planning on visiting Longbourn tomorrow?"

Tickling her nephew until he released her face, she cuddled him before saying, "Yes, I have already spoken with the housekeeper, and we have arranged for two of the maids from Netherfield to go over with me so that we may begin on the kitchens. It is not even fit to boil tea at this point, but we will get it clean and workable in no time."

"I have employed young Mr. Goulding to oversee the repair work and whatnot for Longbourn and its lands. He will be there tomorrow morning with some workmen clearing out the rubble and refuse." William paused, watching Mary for a moment, almost as if he wanted to gauge how she took the news before continuing. "I have contacted a glazier about all the broken windows. We don't want rain and snow getting in any more than it already has. It is a wonder there have not been any rotten floorboards." William looked thoughtful despite the way his son had traveled back to him and started climbing all over him like a little monkey.

"I wish I was well enough to come with you," Elizabeth said, her voice filled with her normal vigor and frustration. Typically the first to take on a hard job, Elizabeth always found it difficult to stand back and let others do when she could not.

"I am perfectly capable of handling the cleaning of the kitchen at Longbourn. Besides, I would love to live there again one day. I think helping clean it will help me scrub it free of all the old memories from the past." Mary tried to smile but knew she had not been entirely successful.

"Live there?" came William's question.

"Yes, well, I know I would always be welcome at your home or Mother's, Jane's, or Kitty's, but I want my own home. I know I am by no means on the shelf, but I am tired of attending the season. I cannot like it in London." Stopping to gather her courage, Mary brushed nonexistent lint from her skirt. "I have been considering getting a companion and requesting to stay there. There are many people here that I could help, and I like it here despite the memories."

Elizabeth gave a sharp look, first at her husband and then her sister. Her concern was evident in the way her brows drew together. "What about Mr. Goulding?"

"What about him? I have given him as many hints as I can contrive that I would be open to furthering our relationship, but he is stubborn in his refusal to move forward. I will admit that my heart is engaged, and I could never try to enter into another relationship knowing that." Standing, Mary moved across the room. Elizabeth and William's bedroom was not so very large that it allowed her to pace as she would wish, but movement helped. Turning back to face her sister, brother-in-law, and confused little nephew, she stood her ground. "I am content knowing that I can do good here. I will find happiness how I can, even if it is as a single woman. I will just have to dote on all my nieces and nephews." Mary offered Elizabeth a wide smile while silently praying in her heart of hearts that her sister would not see the sorrow just below the surface. She could not fight her sister and her heart at the same time.

Elizabeth smiled at her younger sister and if she saw anything more than Mary wanted her to, she did not let on. "I can see that you have thought this through. I will only say do not rush things. Give it some time. You will be working closely with Mr. Goulding, trying to bring Longbourn back to its former glory. Who knows what can come of it?"

"Thank you. And I am glad you are feeling better, Lizzie." Going to her sister, she leaned down to kiss her on the cheek and ruffle Artie's hair. The little guy had once again transferred between parents. He never showed any fear during acrobatic stunts, always confident that someone would be there to catch him. "I am going to write to mother and Lydia and check in with the maids who will go over to Longbourn with me in the morning. I am uncertain how long we will end up working tomorrow and I want to make sure I am not keeping them from other responsibilities."

In a swirl of skirts and false smiles, Mary left the room and went into the hall, eager to be away before her smile broke. Rushing to her room, she closed the door behind her and leaned up against it, blinking rapidly to stem the flow of tears that fought to surface. In a way, life had been easier when she was younger. Before she had learned more about the world and saw the many colors that tinted the reality around her, it had been easier to deal with disappointment.

Once upon a time, she had focused so completely on the bible and Fordyce's sermons that it was easy to see what was best. At one point, everything was straightforward. Whether her father described her as plain or she was unnoticed at a dance, it simply exposed others' vanity. She valued herself beyond others' opinions. So, she had not tried to look her best.

It had taken time, but she had learned that her earlier reasoning had been flawed and she eventually saw the value of wanting to look pretty for yourself and on occasion others. It felt nice to be able to be more herself, but it created another problem. She was still sometimes overlooked and without the shield she used before it hurt. It hurt that she was being overlooked by Mr. Goulding. She did not know which would be worse though—being intentionally ignored by the man she loved or being simply overlooked for some unknown reason.

Moving away from the door she had been leaning on, she started to search through her things to find an outfit she could get grimy. It was going to be a messy and tedious job she was taking on, but she was determined. She would not dwell on the sadness that was trying to creep its way into her life. She would find a way to exist, even as the ache in her heart threatened to consume her.

WHEN THE DOOR SHUT behind Mary, Elizabeth looked at her husband with sorrow. "Oh, Wills, it is horrible to see her so sad when we are so happy. I know she would love her own husband and children, but it is more than that. I suspect she wants Mr. Goulding for her husband, and it is his children that she wishes to bear and raise."

Reaching out, William smoothed the hair away from her face before kissing her brow. "I fear he is hesitating because he wants better for her than what he can offer. Her sister is a countess, and he thinks that she could marry so much better than him. The foolish boy does not see that to Mary, he is better than any lord or duke."

With a twitch of her mouth, Elizabeth gritted her teeth in frustration. "If I know my sister, she thinks it is her looks or something of that sort keeping him from acting. What can we do to encourage the match? I will not have my sister sad for any longer than s be." Looking up at William, she allowed him to see the depths of her concern.

"I hope that if they work together, things will come to a head. Maybe they will argue and get all their problems out in the open," he said, smoothing a hand down her arm before taking her hand in his own. "I find arguments very enlightening on occasion."

Elizabeth beamed in response as she watched their son play on the bed with his small replica of Cadmus. "I wish my sisters were all as happy as I was. How did we have it so easy?"

Jerking back slightly, William looked down at Elizabeth. "Easy? Are you forgetting me constantly putting my boot in my mouth and Wickham trying to kill us both? Then there was your father. He was a whole problem."

"Yes, easy," Elizabeth laughed and leaned up to kiss the man responsible for so much of the happiness in her life. "If falling off a cliff made me see my love for you, it was easy in comparison to all the angst poor Mary is experiencing."

William moved to sit on the bed, settling in beside Elizabeth, before kissing her temple. "Oh, Lizziebet, sometimes your courage terrifies me," he confessed. They were silent for a moment, content watching their son as he abandoned his toy horse and joined them to play with the buttons on William's jacket. "Are you sure you are well? You were not this sick last time."

"I am well, I promise. Or if not well, I am well enough. Every pregnancy is different. Maybe this time we will get the girl I want." Leaning back, Elizabeth rested her head on her husband's broad shoulder, his warmth lulling her into a light doze.

# Chapter Four

Traveling by horse meant it did not take Gabriel long to arrive at his family's estate, and he nearly regretted not walking instead. He had been so excited thinking of all the possibilities at Longbourn that he had not stopped to think of his family's reaction to the news. He was quite uncertain of how his family would react. Or rather, he was fairly certain how they would react; he was uncertain how he would handle it.

He knew his brother and father would most likely belittle any ideas he had for improvements to Longbourn. They would laugh outright at his plan for growing hops. Neither of them had ever taken well to any of the ideas he had for their own property or the tenant homes. They had summarily refused even his suggestions about implementing crop rotation to increase profits. His family was quite stuck in its ways.

Looking over the building from where he sat atop his horse, Gabriel could see where things were starting to look shabby. He knew money was starting to become fairly tight, not that his father would ever mention it to him. It was clear in the way his father no longer saw to repairs and the smaller portions at dinner.

Dismounting, he gave his horse an affectionate pat and led him around to the stables. After handing him off to a happy stable boy, he took a deep breath, preparing himself to face his family. He entered the home through the kitchen, and stole a biscuit from the cook, Mrs. Humphrey. He had always loved the woman. She was the creator of wonderful things and had not run him out of the kitchen when he would come to watch.

"Only one biscuit, I won't have you ruining your dinner," she said by way of greeting, then smiled broadly as he took an extra biscuit. It was a routine that had been played out repeatedly since his childhood. "Young Master Gabriel, how are you today? Did I hear you were looking over Longbourn with that Mr. Darcy fellow?"

Snacking on the biscuit, he smiled at the wonderful, familiar flavor as it played on his tongue. He swallowed and said, "Yes, he offered me an amazing opportunity to help him renovate Longbourn. There is a lot of work that needs to be done—Mr. Bennet did not do right by his property at all."

Mrs. Humphrey shook her head, one of her rarely seen scowls firmly in place. "The way that man behaved is just deplorable. Treating his womenfolk poorly and his servants and tenants worse." Picking up a cleaver, she began chopping a large chunk of meat into much smaller bits. Then, pausing, she gestured with the knife and proclaimed, "I will say that it is good that the good Lord will be judging him and not myself. I am a Christian woman, but men like that try my patience, that is for certain." She resumed her chopping, then put the cleaver to the side to scoop up the meat and drop it into one of the simmering pans.

Gabriel was surprised to hear that Mr. Bennet was so poorly thought of by Mrs. Humphrey. She was the kindest woman he knew, and it startled him to hear her speak of Mr. Bennet so. More than that, watching her speak while chopping and waving the cleaver made him glad that he had never angered her. Shaking his head ruefully, he considered how society viewed Mr. Bennet. He knew there was sometimes talk about the man, but there was never a big to do about him. It was possible, however, that Gabriel had missed the bulk of the indignation about him while he was off at Oxford. "I never much knew the man, but he left the manor house destroyed and the tenant homes in bad condition."

Washing her hands after dealing with the meat, Mrs. Humphrey dried her hand on a towel before responding. "I am sure that you will set it all right in a trice. You are a good boy, Master Gabriel." Reaching up, she patted his cheek in an affectionate manner. It was a move she had done countless times over the years, and it brought back thoughts of his childhood.

He leaned down to kiss her wrinkled cheek before squaring his shoulders, ready to brave his family. "I will see you later, Mrs. Humphrey."

Mrs. Humphrey called out after him as he left the kitchen. "You come see me in the morning and I will get you something good to eat before you leave for Longbourn. I can't have a great big boy like you fainting away from hunger."

"Will do, Mrs. H," Gabriel called back, laughing at the mental image of him collapsing from hunger.

AFTER CHANGING, GABRIEL CHECKED his reflection in the hall mirror. If one hair was out of place, he knew he would hear it from his mother. He understood that he was postponing the inevitable, and yet his feet still did not move towards the stairs.

"Hello, brother. You were gone for quite a while." Looking up, Gabriel spotted his younger sister, Evaline. He was nearly ten years older than his sister. His parents had thought there would be no more children after he had been born and they had been content enough. Though when little Evaline had come along, they had been thrilled.

Her behavior seemed to be all that was proper, but somehow, there was no warmth to her. He had been sent off to Eton shortly after her birth, and he never managed to grow as close to her as he wished. Studying her, he realized she was growing to be pretty, with long brown hair that seemed to be brushed to a shine.

She offered him a smile, though it seemed to stop before it reached her eyes. It was as if she thought herself above such things, and he briefly wondered how a girl so young could have become so cold. "Hello, Lenie. I was visiting with Mr. Darcy and his family. They have taken Netherfield for the time being."

Huffing in frustration, Evaline said, "Please do not call me that. I am too old for such undignified nicknames."

Slightly taken aback by the venom that coated his sister's words, he tried another tactic. He truly wished to develop a better relationship with her but knew that he was fumbling the task. He cleared his throat and tried again. "How was your day, Evaline? Did you do anything of interest?"

With a delicate sniff, Evaline tilted her head. "I worked at my embroidery and practiced the piano and the harp."

Surprised, Gabriel smiled at his younger sister. "I did not know that you had taken up the harp. How is that going? Are you enjoying it?"

Evaline looked at him as if he had forgotten something important. She did not roll her eyes at him, but it looked to be a near thing. "Music is not a matter of enjoyment for me. As a lady, I will need to entertain. First for my suitors and then my husband's guests. If I am to become accomplished, I must become proficient at it."

Once again, Gabriel found himself worrying about Evaline. Perhaps he could introduce her to Miss Bennet and Mrs. Darcy. They were everything that was proper, and yet they managed to find a way to have joy in their lives. "I can appreciate your intentions, but I firmly believe the fundamental objective should be to create a pleasurable atmosphere for your guests with the music you provide. How can you do that if you are not enjoying yourself?"

"You, brother, are being purposely obtuse." Turning away with a swish of her skirts and a flash of her hair, she added over her shoulder,

"Do not forget that dinner will be soon. I may not be allowed to dine with the family yet, but you are expected to."

He watched her go before flicking at a piece of lint on his trousers. Resisting the urge to tug at his freshly tied cravat, he straightened his shoulders, hoping his parents would find his appearance—and his news—acceptable.

GABRIEL REMAINED STILL AS his father inspected him over his wineglass. "So you were spending time with Mr. Darcy? I approve. That is a favorable friendship to cultivate." Taking a large sip, he set the glass down to partake of his meal.

"Yes, I agree, dear. Brother-in-law to an earl, even if his sister-in-law and wife are Bennets. Do not be foolish enough to lose that connection." His mother, as usual, supported his father's every proclamation while still managing to interject her own points.

"I have confidence in young Gabriel. I believe he is working very hard to keep that connection." Jude's smarmy smile was on full display as he cut into his food and took a bite.

Had Gabriel not been seated so far away from his brother, he would have risked the consequences of kicking him under the table. Was it normal that his older brother annoyed him so? They were four years apart in age and his brother always acted as if he was so much better than Gabriel because of it. Jude was constantly calling him out in front of their parents for one thing or another. More than that, however, Gabriel knew that he suspected his feelings for Miss Mary, and Jude looked down on the idea of marrying a Bennet.

Not that Gabriel would let anything stop him. If he had half the chance to provide a decent life for her, he would propose to Miss Mary in a heartbeat. Stabbing at his supper with more force than necessary, Gabriel cut off a piece of his pheasant and took a bite. It was always better to keep his mouth busy when dealing with his family. Otherwise, he could offend them all.

As his father cleared his throat and took a sip of his wine, Gabriel braced himself for another round of questioning. "Have you given any more thought to your path in life? You are getting rather old to join the regulars or navy, but it is possible you could work at becoming a barrister. You know that as a second son, I will not continue to support your idle ways forever."

*Yes, but you will support Jude's useless ways until you die,* Gabriel thought, and looked down to keep himself from voicing those thoughts. Only looking up once he could force a smile, Gabriel responded calmly, "Actually, I received an offer to help Mr. Darcy oversee the reconstruction of Longbourn."

"Longbourn?" his father questioned, shaking his head in disbelief. "That mess of an estate. I will never understand why a wealthy man like Mr. Darcy would throw money away on a property like that."

A snide laugh came from his mother. "Sentiment most likely. He is in love with his wife, they say." Gabriel ignored the remark, knowing his parents did not suffer from, in their words, the plebeian notion of love. It was one reason he had wanted love for himself—he would never choose to live the way they did.

"Yes, Mr. Darcy is quite fond of his wife, doesn't even keep a mistress." Jude's snicker was quickly stopped at the sound of their mother's scandalized screech.

Clearly less bothered by the comment, Mr. Goulding said, "Jude, save talk of mistresses for port and cigars, not at the dinner table." Their father was always permissive and indulgent with his firstborn.

Gabriel had already decided he would not be joining his father and brother for cigars and port after dinner. He seldom enjoyed the pastime and knew they would find every opportunity to make a snide remark. Besides, he was eager to get to work in the morning knowing he now held the fate of Longbourn and its future tenants in his hands.

# Chapter Five

Turning her face up to catch the morning light, Mary savored the way the autumn breeze played with the wisps of hair that framed her face. After a good night's sleep, she felt that she was almost ready to face the disaster that was Longbourn. While most of her previous day had been spent seeing to Elizabeth's care, she had taken the time to play with Artie as well. There was something about the boy that always left her in a more positive frame of mind.

Though she worried still for her sister, Elizabeth had been insistent that Mary go to Longbourn as planned. In Elizabeth's mind, if she could not travel to Longbourn herself, the least she could do was send Mary with as much help as she could manage. So there was Mary, sitting in the wagon with the maids and supplies ready to tackle Longbourn's kitchen. They were bringing plenty of soap and scrub brushes and buckets. The maids talked softly as they traveled the few short miles to get to Longbourn, and though Mary did not know the girls who had volunteered to help, they both seemed pleasant and energetic.

While the rocking of the wagon was not as comfortable as a carriage would be, Mary was too practical to ask for a carriage to be brought just for her. They were already using so many of Netherfield's staff to work on Longbourn; she did not need to add to the burden. Mary told herself that the uneasy feeling in her stomach was just the rocking of the wagon and not anxiety about working with Mr. Goulding. There was really no reason for her to fret about running into him. It was not like he would be hanging about the kitchen.

It was one thing to see Mr. Goulding on occasion and share conversations as was allowed by society and propriety, but she had always managed to maintain a certain amount of distance from him before. How would she handle seeing him every day, all day while working at Longbourn? Could she pretend like she was not hurt when he spoke to her about insignificant topics? Did she have the strength to act like all was well when all she wanted to do was demand to know why he could not love her?

Biting her lip, Mary forced herself leave such miserable thoughts behind and concentrate on what was. She had the opportunity to face the ghosts of her past and make herself a home from the ground up. If Mr. Goulding would not push forward with their relationship, she would simply find a way to find a way to be happy, or at least stay busy. Surely if she was busy enough, she would not feel the ache in her heart so much.

She watched as Longbourn grew closer. The outline of the building was the same from her childhood, at least at this distance, and the destruction was not yet visible. Even as she grew closer, it was not that obvious unless you paid attention to the broken windows scattered around the building.

William was right—they would need to get the windows taken care of before inclement weather caused any more problems. After pulling up to the property, Mary gratefully accepted the help from the groom who had driven the wagon. Getting down, she shook out her skirts, squared her shoulders, and attempted to steady her nerves. The day would certainly be a challenge, but she felt up to the task. She was a Bennet lady after all, and they were stronger than they looked.

GABRIEL HAD MET UP with Darcy early that morning, when the sun was just beginning to rise, to make arrangements for the men who were coming to oversee the harder labor at Longbourn. They had worked for less than an hour before they heard a wagon arrive with the women who would take on the kitchen. He used their arrival as an opportunity to go outside and hefted a piece of broken furniture out into the open area next to the house they had been storing all the rubble. They would decide how to dispose of it all later.

He was glad of his heavy gloves. The work he had been doing was much more physical than he was used to, but he was quickly gaining acceptance from the men he worked with. Dusting himself off, he looked up and spotted Miss Mary as she was helped off the wagon. She was so different from his family. His mother and sister would both have refused to ride in a wagon, and never would they insist on helping clean up a kitchen. Yet here she was, a woman who could reach so far, stooping down to gather cleaning supplies and bring them into the kitchen.

Following her and the maids into the home, he fought his nervousness to greet her. Resisting the urge to rub his gloved hands against his pants, he moved them behind his back. Clearing his throat, he began, "Miss Bennet, it is good to see you this morning."

Looking up, Miss Bennet shifted the broom and bucket in her hands around before responding. "Good morning, Mr. Goulding. How are you on this fine day?"

Looking out over the yard that had once been the kitchen garden, he nodded in thought before looking back at her. "Well, I am well. Uhm..." Cringing inwardly, Gabriel moved on to the first topic that came to mind. "This weather had been very conducive to our work. The cooler weather has been helpful, and as long as the wetter weather holds off or, heaven forbid, snow, we should be able to get quite a bit done in short order." It had been some time since he had been this anxious around Miss Mary. Racking his brain, Gabriel tried to discern why his heart was suddenly beating so. He had known her for years. They had spoken at length a number of times. Could it be possible that catching her the day before had changed something? Or had it been the night full of thinking of her and his hopes for their future?

"I am glad to hear it. The cooler weather will make it easier for us ladies to scrub the kitchen free of grime." Looking over her shoulder at the long-neglected kitchen, Miss Mary wrinkled her nose.

"Hopefully within a day or so, I will not feel disgusted by the thought of brewing tea in the kitchen."

Rubbing at the back of his neck, Gabriel tried to find a way to extend their conversation. He could speak normally with her, he could. "Yes... Um...how is Mrs. Darcy faring? I know Mr. Darcy was quite concerned about her yesterday."

Smiling, Miss Bennet seemed to ponder something for a moment before responding. "She is improving, not entirely well, but better today at least. I spent time with her this morning making sure she was managing. I left her with a new book and some ginger tea. William, or rather Mr. Darcy, will see that she is well cared for in my absence."

Gabriel briefly wondered what it would be like to have such a close relationship with his own siblings, but it was too difficult to imagine. He was grateful Miss Mary was able to experience such relationships though, as well as to hear that Mrs. Darcy was doing better. She was a very kind woman, and he hated to hear that she was unwell. "That is good to hear. I have always envied their relationship. It is something I would aspire to should I ever have the opportunity to have such a love in my life—" Gabriel's eyes widened as he caught himself, and he felt his cheeks heat to what felt like a hot shade of vermilion. What had he just said? Sweat began trickling down the side of his hairline and down the back of his collar. "I... I should get back to removing the debris from the first floor. I will be sure to ask your advice about anything we find that we can hope to salvage. Miss Bennet." Giving a quick bow, he took off back to the main part of the house and looked for a room he could hide in to thoroughly castigate himself for his misbehaving tongue.

What had he just done? What had he just said? He was speaking of love and blushing like a schoolboy. How had he become so carried away? He knew he was not in a position to make any overtures to Miss Bennet, not yet at least. Maybe after he had helped with Longbourn. Mr. Darcy was being extremely generous, and he had been steadily saving whatever that he could. Perhaps in a year or two he would be in a place that he could suggest something.

Leaning against the wall, he allowed himself a small moment of despair. He let his head fall back and hit the wall behind him with a thud. No woman would want to wait that long to even begin courting, and Miss Bennet should not have to wait that long for him to become the man she deserved. What should he do? What *could* he do? If he was closer to Mr. Darcy, he might ask him for advice, but he did not feel comfortable with that idea. What if Darcy discouraged him from pursuing Miss Mary?

Stepping away from the wall, Gabriel began to pace hoping that movement might very well help put his thoughts in the proper order. After tripping over a broken piece of a chair, however, he realized there was too much on the floor to pace properly. He looked around the room with a heavy sigh. The space was not too dissimilar from his state of mind—nothing was fully formed or useful, just random pieces of disjointed frustration. On the one hand, his attachment to Miss Mary was so strong that it nearly consumed his every thought and feeling. Conversely, he felt compelled to hold off on advancing their relationship in order to protect her. The war within himself was becoming more difficult to deal with.

After realizing there was no immediate solution to his inner conflict, he begrudgingly turned his attention to the work at hand. Leaning over, he began picking up the pieces of a broken sideboard. It could have been lovely once, but now it was nothing more than kindling. Leaving the room with a hand full of what must have been something someone loved, he moved to discard it. Maybe he could think as he worked? Or at least distract himself from his worsening problems.

After he was done with his load, he went to check on the other workers and the various rooms they were clearing out. Hopefully, there were pieces of furniture that could be salvaged, though they had not gone upstairs much at all. He would work on that once they had cleared the main floor. Maybe there would be less destruction there. The notion that one man could annihilate all that had been painstakingly accumulated over generations was deplorable.

"Mr. Goulding, sir, I think you should see this."

Gabriel looked up from his mindless, repetitive work of gathering debris while pondering on better ways to do such a task. Maybe they should get a wheelbarrow for each room so there would be less walking around with armfuls of heavy items? Gabriel smiled at the man who had called out to him. "Yes, Jeremy? What is it that I need to see?"

"Most of the trinkets and whatnots are all smashed beyond use, but I think I found a chest that old Mr. Bennet missed." Jeremy stood expectantly in the doorway and appeared eager to show off his find.

Taking his armful to the hallway, Gabriel left it on a larger pile of rubble. "That is splendid, show me." Walking down the hallway behind the groom, Gabriel could see evidence that he had been working diligently all morning. Several rooms had been cleared of debris and were ready to be repaired or painted as needed. As they made their way to the last room in the hallway, Gabriel was hopeful that something might be saved from the disaster that was Longbourn.

Jeremy moved a ruined chair further out of the way so that Gabriel could more easily see a small chest. Looking at the chair, Gabriel shook his head at the stuffing that was falling out of it. It looked as if someone had taken a knife to the chair and ripped the cushions to pieces. "I don't think Mr. Bennet saw it on the ground behind the chair," Jeremy explained. "I think we might save the chair if we reupholster it, though. That Mr. Bennet was a bad 'un that is for certain."

"This is a wonderful find. Marvelous job, Jeremy. I am sure the Bennets will be so very happy to have something left from their home." Kneeling down, Gabriel opened the chest to find some sort of dish set. There were teacups and a teapot carefully preserved in hay to prevent breakage, and it seemed to be an entire set. "This seems old. It might have belonged to Mr. Bennet's mother or even someone before her. Miss Bennet and Mrs. Darcy will be thrilled to have such a find. Can you take the chair upstairs to the servants' quarters or maybe the attic, if there is no room there? If you spot any furniture we might reupholster or mend, move it up there as well. I would like to preserve as much as possible for the ladies."

"Good plan, sir." Jeremy picked up the chair and began to move to the doorway.

"Do you need help with that?" Gabriel questioned.

"I think I have this, sir, thank you. I will let you know if we find anything that I need help moving." Readjusting his grip, he turned to go, but paused. Looking back, he said, "You know, there might be some interesting finds in the attic already. I know I have heard of things being stored in the attic and forgotten about for generations."

Closing the lid on the chest, Gabriel gently picked it up. "Thank you, Jeremy. I will be sure to let the Bennet ladies know to look up there at some point." Gabriel moved towards the kitchen, eager to show the find to Miss Mary. She had been so sad to see the destruction, and he hoped that finding something that survived could bring a smile to her face.

"I think at least we have the cupboards clear of any more vermin," came Miss Mary's voice from the kitchen. Gabriel hastened to reach her and show her his find.

"You know they will come right back if we do not get a more permanent method in place. Clearing out their homes will only do so much," another feminine voice responded, most likely one of the maids.

"I am trying to see about getting a few mousers to keep things in check. So far, I have not made any headway, but if either of you hear of a cat or two we can set up here, be sure to let me know," Miss Mary replied.

The breathy reply of Miss Mary had Gabriel wondering what she was doing that left her so. Upon entering the room, he looked around with his arms full of the chest. "It may not be a cat or two, but I think I have found something you will be happy to see—" He knew he had heard Miss Mary's voice, but he could not see her.

"What?" From within the cupboard, there came a sudden thud, as if a maid had accidentally dropped a heavy object while cleaning. Scooting back on her heels, the woman's head came up, and she grimaced in pain as she rubbed the sore spot on her head. Only it was not a maid, it was a very dirty Miss Bennet. Her hair was wrapped with a kerchief, and she had the absolute cutest smudge of dirt on the bridge of her nose. "Oh, Mr. Goulding, I did not hear you come in. Was there something you needed me for?"

Gabriel waited while she stood and shook out her skirts. Swallowing convulsively, he found himself distracted by the smudge on her nose, but managed to say, "I found a chest that seems to be intact. I thought you might like to see it. Miraculously, I do not think anything inside was broken. Your father must have missed it." Placing the chest on a semi-clean table, he stepped back and allowed Miss Bennet to examine it.

Wiping her hands on a rag, Miss Mary stepped forward and opened the chest by lifting the latch. Her gasp when she saw the chest's contents made Gabriel offer a hopeful smile. Would the items bring her happy memories? The longer he had been at Longbourn, the more he realized the place must have many unhappy memories lurking about. But there had to be good memories, didn't there?

Hesitating only for a moment, Miss Mary extended her finger to trace the gentle curve of a teacup. Then, lifting it gently, she brought it to her chest as a little girl would a cherished doll. "I think this was Grandmother Catherine's tea set. When Lydia was little, she almost broke one of the cups and Mama put the set away. It was precious to her, and she did not want Lydia's little hands breaking anything. I do not remember ever seeing the set out again." It looked as though Miss Mary fought back tears as she clung to a teacup for comfort.

Happy memories then. Gabriel was glad. "Where would you like to keep the chest? I could have it moved to the attic for safekeeping, or you could take it back to Netherfield with you?"

Shaking her head slightly, Mary put the porcelain cup decorated with a spray of flowers back in the chest. She made sure everything would be safe before closing the lid. "I believe I would like to take it back to Netherfield. I would love to show Lizzie what you found." Gabriel couldn't help but notice the intensity in Miss Mary's gaze, her eyes shining with a flicker of regard that instilled in him a hopeful longing for the love he yearned for. "Thank you for finding this. It will mean so much to us all."

Gabriel felt a pang in his chest as he looked into her eyes, causing him to swallow hard. He quickly shifted his gaze to the chest for a moment before mustering the courage to look back up and lock gazes with her again. "There are a few pieces here and there that we are managing to salvage. Nothing as grand as what is in the chest, but we are moving what we find upstairs to the attic or servants' quarters as necessary."

A flicker of a smile graced Miss Mary's face as she said, "I have yet to find the courage to go upstairs and check over the rooms that I was most familiar with. I have a sinking feeling that it will be just as damaged, if not more so."

"I have not gone into the family wing, so I do not know for certain, but I would be careful if you go up there." The expression on Miss Mary's face started to harden, and Gabriel realized that he had made a blunder. Not that he knew what that blunder might be, of course, but desperate to change the subject, he turned to view the kitchen. It seemed mostly the same, but he was sure they had been working hard. "How are things progressing here in the kitchen?"

With a delicate shrug, Miss Mary looked around the room at all that still remained to do. "Well enough. We have disposed of all the nests that we have found, and we have begun cleaning out the stove so that we may boil water to clean with. It will take a while longer, but we are managing."

"Be sure to let us know if you need help with anything in here, ladies," Gabriel offered. "I am sure any of us gentlemen would be happy to oblige. Miss Bennet, ladies." With a bow to Miss Bennet and a nod to the maids with her, Gabriel turned to go back to his tasks. He had things to do, and he did not want to risk saying the wrong thing yet again.

***Mary put her foot on the first step. With her decision made, she firmed her stance and went up the stairs. She had lived in this house for nineteen years of her life. Why would Mr. Goulding ever think of insisting on her being careful? Why would she need to be careful?

Making it to the top of the stairs without incident or any sightings of vermin, Mary bit her lip and began down the hallway. Would she look in her room first, or would she be brave and explore her mother's sitting room? Maybe she should start in her bedroom. It was closer.

The door swung open with a creak that spoke of a need for grease. Taking a timid step forward, Mary looked around the room that she had spent so many hours of her life in. They had taken what they could when they had left Longbourn, but of course they could not take as much as they would have liked. Smaller items were taken where possible, but larger items like furniture was left behind.

Everything seemed to have been painted in a thin coat of dust. It only made sense no one had been in to clean in what was most likely years. Mary's childhood bed was still standing, but the side table with the mirror had been broken. Walking towards it, Mary looked for the stool that she had always sat on when she brushed her hair. She did not see it, or rather the pieces of it in the other broken bits.

Approaching the bed, she knelt but did not see it anywhere under the bed, though she did realize everything would certainly need to be washed. Once they had the kitchen clean, she would start work on the linens that needed cleaning and mended. Would it be more beneficial to bring it all back to Netherfield to wash or try to do it here? She would have to ask Elizabeth what she thought.

She walked to the broken window and looked out. Despite the fresh air blowing into the room, there was an odd musty smell that she could not place. Looking down at the yard below, Mary noticed that there in what was once one of her mother's beloved rose bushes was her stool. Long forgotten, it must have been the instrument of her father's wrath, used to break the window in his rage.

An odd snapping sound had Mary looking for the source of the sudden noise. Was there an animal in her old room? Startled, Mary froze in place. What was that sound? Before she could give it another thought, the floor beneath her feet gave way and she fell with a strangled scream.

# Chapter Six

Gabriel looked around the room he had been cleaning up. Most of the larger pieces were gone. It needed to be dusted and mopped, but that would come later. At least there were no holes in the walls of the room, unlike some of the others. Part of the ceiling was discolored, but he had not had time to investigate. A sudden snapping sound had Gabriel looking around in concern. That sounded like wood snapping. Was the structure less sound than he thought?

A sudden shower of wet plaster came from the ceiling by the outer wall. Taking a step back from the falling particles, concern growing, Gabriel turned to go investigate the problem. He hadn't gone two steps when a muffled shriek and a crashing sound stopped him dead in his tracks. Coughing at the particles of dust and loose particles in the air, Gabriel swung his gaze back to where the discolored plaster had once been. Blinking rapidly to get the grime out of his eyes, he focused on the fact that there was a foot sticking through the ceiling. It was a woman's foot stuck through the floor of the second floor and into the ceiling of the first. He knew that shoe; it was Miss Mary's shoe.

Turning in a rush, he fled the room, calling out as he went. "Jeremy, get one of the maids and hurry to the second floor. I think Miss Bennet has partially fallen through the floor and we need to get her free."

Jeremy's response from the next room was quick. "Yes, sir!" His footsteps took off at speed toward the kitchen.

Taking the stairs two at a time, Gabriel rushed to the room that Miss Bennet was in. Upon entering, as much as he wanted to rush to her side, Gabriel paused to look around the room. It would not do to rush to her side and bring the whole of the floor down. His gaze first narrowed in on Miss Bennet. She was sprawled haphazardly on the floor, her body partially splayed, and her forehead resting on her out flung arm prevented him from seeing much of her face. "Miss Bennet, are you well?"

Looking up, her eyes wide in a pale face, Miss Bennet gulped before responding. "I do believe the floor has been weakened by the elements getting in through the broken window."

"Yes, it appears that is the case." Gabriel felt a ghost of a smile flicker across his face at her so obvious statement. She had completely ignored his question about her wellbeing. "Are you injured?"

Biting her lip in a way that did something to his heart, she said, "Not that I can tell, though I am afraid to move too much and risk falling further through the floor."

Offering a smile that he hoped was not too grim, Gabriel glanced at the surrounding floor. It seemed that the floorboards were only discolored near the window where she had fallen through. The closer you were to the door, the more sturdy everything appeared. "Are you able to get your foot free?" Stepping cautiously closer, he tried to see how she was stuck, but all he could see was her skirts pooled around her prone form.

"I do not think so." Miss Bennet paused, seeming to try something but wincing, she stopped. "My ankle seems to be lodged against something and I am afraid that if I tug too hard, the entire floor may collapse."

"Oh, my goodness." The voice of the maid came from behind Gabriel. Turning, he saw that the young maid stood next to Jeremy, her hands clasped to her chest, her face creased with worry.

Looking at the grim-faced Jeremy and the frightened maid, he spoke. "Thank you for coming to help. Jeremy, do we have a ladder on the property?"

"Yes, sir, I think I saw one over by the stable. I will have Isaac fetch it. We will set it up downstairs. Just in case." Ducking out of the room, he rushed off.

Taking a few more careful steps, he knelt down outside the ring of oddly colored wood. He could reach out and grab Miss Bennet at this distance, but he did not want to injure her accidentally by tugging on her if her foot was stuck.

Turning back to the maid who stood by the door, he smiled. "I am sorry, but I do not remember your name." Gabriel tried to remember if he had ever been introduced to her, but came up blank.

Adopting a determined posture, she straightened her back and seemed to shake off her fright. Looking him in the eye, she said, "Nellie, sir. What can I do to help Miss Bennet?"

"I am going to try something, but if that does not work, I will need to go downstairs and free her foot from below. If that happens, I want you to stay up here with Miss Bennet." When he saw her nod, Gabriel turned back to Miss Bennet, who, despite her appearance of calm, was pale. Looking closer, he could see sweat beading along her brow. "It seems we are in an odd situation, Miss Bennet. What say you to reaching out and taking my hand and trying to use me as an anchor to pull yourself free?"

Nodding her head, Miss Mary reached out and grasped his hand. Despite the fright of the moment and the fact that her hand was trembling, Gabriel had to swallow at the strength of her grip. She was looking for him to help her. She trusted him, and he would not let her down. Feeling her pull herself towards him, he tried not to pull as well but instead tried to remain firm and allow her to make the progress on her own at her own speed.

Crying out, Mary stopped suddenly, pain etched deeply in the lines in her face. "I think there is something sticking the wrong way into my ankle." Putting her free hand down beside herself, she tried to gain a better angle, but suddenly things began to give way. Slipping further down, she screamed, but then clamped her mouth shut.

Biting her lip as she slowed and then stopped, Miss Bennet gripped at his hand, terror evident in the whites of her eyes.

"I do not think this is working." Miss Mary whispered. Closing her eyes, she seemed to focus on her breathing, steadying herself. The hand not wrapped around Gabriel's was pressed to her chest over her heart.

"Nellie, I want you to come over here and lie on your stomach. Once you are able, it would be best if you could hold Miss Bennet's hand to hold her steady. Miss Mary, you need to take Nellie's hand and I will work on getting you free." Looking at Miss Mary, he noticed her eyes were still closed, and she was still biting her lip. Her grip had only tightened. He tried to gently releasee her hand to allow Nellie to take it, but Miss Mary would not let go. Running his free hand over her the back of her hand where it gripped his own, he tried to soothe her. He could feel the pounding of her pulse in her wrist. Leaning down, he kissed her knuckles and then, lowering his voice, he cajoled. "Come now, Mary, you are going to have to let me go. I am going downstairs. I will try to see if I can free your foot so that you can pull yourself out."

When he used her first name, Mary's eyes popped open, and she searched for something in his expression. Whatever it was that she was looking for, she found because, though she still looked terrified, she loosened her grip. She let go in stages until only the tips of her fingers brushed against his and then, visibly shuddering, she was free of him. Only Gabriel knew he would be forever within her thrall.

Nellie, who lay on the floor next to him, reached out and took Mary's hands in both of hers. "There now Miss Bennet. Mr. Goulding will be going to get you free, and all will be will in no time."

"You have my word," he vowed, "I will have you free in no time." Dashing off, Gabriel raced down the hall and down the stairs. It seemed as if he was going so very slowly and yet in no time at all he was downstairs and in the room that had Mary's leg through the ceiling.

MARY ALLOWED THE SOOTHING nature of Nellie's voice to flow over her. Clinging to her hand, Mary locked her gaze on Nellie's. "Thank you for being here with me. I never get into scrapes like this. Normally, this is Elizabeth's job." Mary knew her laugh was hollow and would never fool anyone but if she tried to be serious at that moment, she would burst into tears.

Smiling soothingly, Nellie nodded before speaking, "I have often heard tails of your sister getting into scrapes. Didn't she fall off the edge of the path on the way up Oakham Mount? Broke her arm, I heard say."

"Yes, that she did." Of course, Lizzie had been helped off that edge by the weasel Wickham, but he was no longer anyone's worry. "Here I thought I would be safe if I stayed mostly indoors."

Squeezing Mary's hand in reassurance, Nellie grinned. "Well, despite everything, at least you have a handsome young man desperate to help you. Take it from me—that doesn't happen every day."

"He is rather handsome, I must admit." Mary remembered his wide green eyes regarding her with such concern. His eyes were not the green of her sister Lizzie's deep emerald, or of her own hazel eyes that could not decide whether they were mostly brown or muddy green, but rather the green of the first leaves of spring. He had always had the thickest of lashes. She knew any number of women would pay for lashes like his. His face had a strikingly chiseled appearance, and his dimpled chin added a touch of ruggedness. With light brown hair, the color of toasted wheat, and a ready smile, Mary always felt warm when she had his attention.

With a sigh and a giggle, Nellie said, "I wish I had a beau such as him, that is for certain."

"I wish I did too—" Mary grimaced at the peculiar sensation of a hand on her foot. That was really rather odd. She tried to interpret the feelings of wood poking into her leg from her knee down. Where originally just her foot was on the other side of the floor, now mostly her ankle was free while her foot floated upon nothing. With her left leg kneeling on the floor, she carefully distributed her weight, praying that it would prevent any additional damage and keep her from falling through.

Giving Mary's hand a pat, Nellie shook her head. "Oh, don't you doubt yourself! He might not have said anything to you yet, but his eyes speak volumes."

A loud knock from below them had both women looking at the oddly colored floor with concern. "Miss Bennet!" The voice was muffled, having come from the floor below, and while it was impossible to tell who spoke, Mary suspected it was Mr. Goulding.

"Yes?" Mary called, looking down at the floor that had swallowed her leg.

"A piece of wood is angled in such a way to prevent you from pulling your leg up. I am going to attempt to remove it. You must let me know if anything pains you."

"Do not worry, I will make sure you know." Mary managed to keep her voice steady, but anxiously bit her lip once more, oblivious to the fact that she was on the verge of drawing blood if she didn't cease worrying at it. She was not the best at dealing with pain and knew she would give herself away whether she tried to hide it. She would never have handled a broken arm and a fall down the side of Oakham Mount with as much grace as Lizzie had.

Drawing Mary's attention with a gentle squeeze of her hand, Nellie engaged her in conversation. "Miss Bennet, have I ever told you how much my family feels indebted to yours?"

Mary's attention jerked to her companion. "How ever have we helped you so? I remember you lived here before we moved away, but I do not remember doing something so significant that it would feel indebted."

Keeping a firm grip on Mary's hand, Nellie replied, "While you were here, you and your older sister taught the local children to read and write. My little brother was one of the children you taught."

Tilting her head, Mary's mind sifted through all the children that she had helped teach over the years. "Is your little brother Nathen?"

Nodding, Nellie chuckled, "Yes, he is."

"He was always the cutest little thing, all painted over with so many freckles." Mary grinned despite the odd felling of things at her foot and ankle moving around without her command of it. Blinking rapidly, Mary tried to keep from crying as the pain in her ankle increased with whatever was happening. She forced herself to pay attention to Nellie and gripped her hand ever tighter.

"That would be our little Nathen." Nellie got a far-off look on her face as if picturing the freckle-faced little scamp. "He took what you taught him and kept working at it. He has earned himself an apprenticeship with the town solicitor, and is on his way to becoming something. No one in our family has ever had much learning at all, and now young Nathen is learning and working at a solicitor's. He might even make clerk someday."

Giving a little shake of her head, Mary asked, "That is all splendid, but how is your family indebted to me and mine? All Elizabeth and I did was help to teach him what we could."

"He will go farther than any of us ever dreamed for him or ourselves. It is because of you, your family's kindness and compassion for those who could not offer more to their own." Nellie looked into Mary's eyes, seemingly happy that despite the unfortunate circumstances, she had the opportunity to explain her gratitude. Or possibly, Mary thought, she was simply glad she had distracted the woman whose hand she held from her parlous situation. "When the position became available to help at Netherfield with you coming back to the area, I knew I had to make myself available to help."

Mary studied the girl who held her hand so tightly. She had at first thought Nellie to be in her early twenties, but now that she was looking closer, maybe she had been off by several years. It was possible that she was only in her upper teens, possibly Lydia's age of eighteen or even nineteen. "While I would want no one to feel indebted to me, I am happy to hear that the work we did made a difference." Mary managed, grateful for the distraction as it felt like something was sawing against whatever poked against her leg. It was sending jolts of pain up her leg with every movement, and she hoped that whatever was happening would not cause her to fall through the floor entirely and land on whoever was trying to help. What a disaster would that be.

GABRIEL MADE IT DOWN the stairs in record time but stood frozen, looking up at Mary's poor, captured leg. He finally jerked free of his fearful trance when Jeremy and Daniel came into the room carrying the ladder between him. "Good timing, gentlemen. I was unable to help get Miss Bennet free from above, so we will have to work at it from down here. Let us set the ladder directly below her and see what we can do."

It was a simple task to get the ladder set up and for one of the men to hold it steady while he climbed closer to Mary's foot and ankle.

Gaining height on the problem at hand helped him to see exactly how she was stuck in the floor. A thick splinter of wood was pointing the wrong way for her to pull her leg out. It looked as if when she pulled up, it had started to dig into her skin just above the ankle.

Gabriel was glad that she had stopped moving because she had begun to bleed where the sharp edge of the splinter was digging into her. The sight of her blood trickling down her ankle and then soaking into the soft cloth of her shoe left him feeling slightly sickened. How could he remove the splinter without causing more damage? Drawing his gaze away from Mary's blood, Gabriel fixed his sight on the two men below him. "What tools do we have that might cut wood?"

Rubbing at the back of his neck, Jeremy suddenly looked up at him, his eyes alight with realization. "I think there is an assortment of tools in the stable. I am not sure what, though."

"Run and get what you can. We need something we can use to see or cut a bit of this away for her to be able to pull free."

Nodding, Jeremy took off, leaving Isaac to stay behind and help. Looking up at the foot coming through the ceiling, Isaac commented. "It looks like something is digging into her. You will need to get rid of that before she is free of the problem."

Looking at it carefully, Gabriel tried to best understand how to go about freeing her. "Yes, I think I will have to either whittle away at the wood sticking into her ankle or maybe saw it free of the rest." Gabriel hesitated, fully aware of the impropriety of looking at and touching her ankle, but he couldn't let it stop him from lending a hand when she needed it. Gritting his teeth against the shiver that ran through him when he touched her skin, he focused on what was important. He ran his hand along her ankle and felt around the splinter. It seemed that when she had pulled her leg up, she had lodged the wood into her skin.

"Is it stuck in her leg firm like?" Isaac asked from below him.

The splinter resisted his attempts to gently separate it from her leg. He quickly stopped when she seemed to wince as he struggled with the splinter, he growled under his breath saying, "It has cut her some on the sharp edge, and it seems to be lodged into her skin. I do not think it is cutting anything dangerous, though." Gabriel tried not to think of how delicate her ankle felt in his hand when he tried to see how close the wood was to her skin. This was not at all the time to realize that he had never seen her ankles up close. He had never seen any lady's ankles, or rather, ankle up close. Shaking his head at the direction of his thoughts, Gabriel forced himself to think of the danger to Mary if she fell through the ceiling.

Nodding, Isaac seemed to process the information. "I doubt it will be very comfortable for her to have it sawed on, but unless she wants to live the rest of her life stuck through the ceiling, we shall have to try what we can."

Gabriel nodded but did not feel capable of speaking at that moment. He was too fixated on the thought of possibly bringing Mary pain in order to free her. It was not an easy thought. Could he hurt her for her own good? Should he ask one of the others to do it if pain was unavoidable?

Coming in with an arm full of tools, Jeremy returned in a rush and out of breath. "I brought whatever I thought might have any chance of helping." Setting the tools on the floor with a thud, he sorted through what lay there, searching for something. Once found, he handed the tool up to Gabriel before returning to the base of the ladder. "I think this small hack saw might be of the most use if you are looking to break away a small piece of wood."

Gabriel swallowed convulsively. He could not leave a task that might hurt Mary to someone else. He had to stand up and do what he must. Deciding that he had to at least warn her of what was transpiring, he shouted through the floor. "Miss Bennet!"

"Yes?" came a very muffled reply.

Running his finger along the handle of the tool he had been handed he thought for a moment and then proceeded to say. "It appears that a piece of wood is angled in such a way to prevent you from pulling your leg up. I am going to attempt to remove it. You must let me know if anything pains you."

There was a slight pause, and then another muffled response. "Do not worry, I will make sure you know."

Grasping at the section of wood he had chosen with one hand and the small saw with the other hand, Gabriel set to work. He carefully positioned the saw, aiming to cut the wood as close to the remnants of the solid ceiling as possible. He could feel the friction and push and pull on the wood with the hand that was holding tight to the wood itself.

Glancing over, he took note that the wood was wobbling slightly as he sawed. It did not look like it was digging deeper into Mary, but it was moving around some, aggravating the wound. He knew that it must be hurting Mary, but she had yet to cry out. Continuing his efforts, he was frustrated at the speed at which he was making progress. To be fair, he was making progress, and he was trying to be careful so as not to hurt Mary unduly. The metal teeth of the saw bit into the wood and small traces of sawdust began to drift down into his hair and eyes. Blinking rapidly, he tried to keep his eyes free of the irritants floating down into his face.

After what seemed like too long, the largish splinter came free of the floor despite sticking out of Mary's leg. Normally he would leave it in to be better taken care of later, but he knew it could injure her if she tried to pull her leg up through the hole still lodged in her. Knowing it would hurt Mary Gabriel bit back a growl, and mouth in a hard line, he pulled out the splinter out as gently as possible. Her bleeding had been steadily increasing but was not heavy enough to be worrisome.

Gabriel dropped the bloody splinter to the floor, his hands trembling as he peered into the hole that still cradled Mary's leg. It appeared from this angle at least she would be able to pull her leg up without anything else stabbing her. Climbing down the ladder, he looked at the two men who were eager to help. "I am going to go upstairs to see if Miss Bennet can remove her leg now. Stay here and shout if it seems as if something, anything, is amiss."

Only waiting for their nods of agreement, Gabriel rushed back up the stairs. Rushing into the room where Mary patiently awaited her liberation, he couldn't help but notice the pained look on her face. She also had the remnants of tears on her lashes. As soon as he entered the room, her expression became hopeful, a hint of a smile appeared on her still pale countenance. Trying to reassure her, he spoke in a calming voice. "I think I have removed the impediments to removing your leg from the hole."

"Well, that is reassuring." Mary once again smiled, and it pained Gabriel to see that it did not reach her eyes. "What would you have me do?"

Coming closer, he took Nellie's place on the floor. Reaching out, he offered his hand and was relieved to see how quickly she took hold of him. "I want you to slowly try to pull your leg free. Just like before, use me as a fulcrum and try to put as little pressure on the floor as possible."

Nodding her head, she responded, "All right." Mary bit her lip again. Gabriel saw where her lip was starting to bruise and even split at her misuse of it. Closing her eyes, Mary began to pull against his hand and this time she seemed to be making progress. Then all of a sudden, she was free and falling into him from the force of her release.

Eager to get her away from the dangerous hole in the floor, Gabriel took her in his arms and scooted backwards towards the doorway. The first thing he noticed after his scramble away from the danger was the quiver that was running down the length of her body.

Everywhere she leaned against him, a fine tremor shook her small frame.

Mary was the smallest of her sisters, only shorter than Mrs. Darcy by an inch or so and every inch of her seemed to be affected by the recent experience. "It is all right. You are fine. You are free and everything is well." He crooned in her ear, smoothing back the hair from her face. Her hair was more straight than curly, and it seemed to be coming free if its many pins.

Having her so close, he saw just how damaged her bottom lip was. Bitten, bruised and bleeding, it looked painful. Had he caused her that much pain? Unable to stop himself, Gabriel ran his thumb softly along Mary's abused lip. Their eyes locked in a wordless conversation full of apology and forgiveness.

After their endless moment, Mary seemed to come to herself. She sat up, trying to move away from him and away from his support. Gabriel felt the loss of her warmth acutely. "Thank you ever so much for your aid. I was foolish in the extreme to think to come up here on my own." Looking away and around the destroyed room, she shook her head in derision. Her voice was a ragged whisper. "I only wanted to see what my father had done to my room."

Noticing Nellie standing in the hallway with an indulgent smile, Gabriel quickly stood and offered his hand to Mary to help her up. No matter what he may want for his future, this was not the time or place to indulge his wish to stay close to her. "It was a natural desire. Though in the future I would suggest avoiding any discolored floorboards."

Accepting his hand, Mary stood, but gave a visible wince when she put pressure on her injured foot. "Thank you for your aid and thank you for not lecturing me on my stupidity." Her wry smile did not hide the vivid blush that had begun to race across her face.

Turning, Mary made to limp away towards the stairs. How she meant to get anywhere in the condition she was in was perplexing. Though he could no longer see her ankle, he knew she must still be bleeding, and she was noticeably limping. Tilting his head, Gabriel watched her for a moment, confused by her behavior.

Rushing to Mary's side, Nellie tried to wrap her arm around her smaller frame. "Miss Bennet, let me help you."

Hair flying about Mary shook her in denial. "Oh, thank you Nellie, but I am fine. I am not so very injured. I can make my way back to the kitchen under my own power, I am sure of it." The limping continued.

Gabriel easily caught up with Mary. She was not moving quick. Leaning around, he observed her brightly colored cheeks. Their rosy hue was so vibrant, they seemed to have taken on a fiery glow. Was this denial due to embarrassment?

# Chapter Seven

Why, oh why, did she have to blush so fiercely and so easily? No matter what she did when she was truly embarrassed, Mary could not hide the vibrant blush that would erupt on her face. It did not even stop at just her cheeks, either. It spread to her ears and down her neck. Today it felt as if it had spread all the way to her toes.

She just wanted to get away and hide from how embarrassed she was. But it seemed to not be something she would be able to manage because no one was leaving her alone. Making it to the stairs, she plastered on a smile and looked at Mr. Goulding and Nellie. "I am fine, really, I can manage."

Mr. Goulding's eyes seemed to dance with some secret joy, but at least he did not laugh at her obvious stubbornness. "It seems that we have two options. You may take my arm and allow me to support you, you are injured after all, or I will carry you. I did not save you from falling through the floor to let you take a tumble down the stairs now that you are free." Offering her his arm, he waited.

Mary looked at his arm that hung there waiting for her compliance and struggled to make the decision she knew she should. The most rational part of her brain seemed to understand that she would feel even more embarrassed to be seen being carried like an invalid. A small part of her wanted to refuse in order to know what it would feel like for him to carry her. Swallowing her pride and frustration, Mary took his arm and allowed him to help her down the stairs.

Her leg did hurt, but she could tolerate it, albeit barely. Despite that, it would be foolish to take a tumble down the stairs because she refused to accept help. Through it all, her face was still aflame. She could feel it in the heat on her cheeks and even her ears.

Making it to the bottom of the stairs with Nellie trailing behind them, Mary tried to smile and hold her head up. "Thank you for your assistance. I am sure I can make it back to the kitchen and resume working. We have accomplished much, but we still have a long way to go. I do not know what I was thinking of trying to reminisce." Mary tried to remove her arm from Mr. Goulding's, but found that he was clasping her hand.

Eyes still dancing, Mr. Goulding did not release her. Smiling calmly, he said, "While you have an honorable idea, I believe we should return you to Netherfield at this juncture." Mr. Goulding's voice was gentle but left no room for debate.

Her smile growing artificially large, Mary tried to convince him she was fine. "I am sure that I can manage the few hours that we were going to remain here. There is no need for me to rush off." Giving a slight tug to her hand, Mary realized he was not letting her go.

Raising his eyebrows, Mr. Goulding smiled back at her. "What would you have me say to Mr. and Mrs. Darcy? That I not only allowed my lack of foresight to endanger you, but that I allowed your injury to wait and possibly become infected instead of having it seen to immediately?"

Mary pondered Lizzie's and William's reaction. Neither of them would be happy to hear that she waited to see to an injury, and she did not want them to discourage her from returning to Longbourn. Her shoulders drooping in defeat, Mary responded to his query. "It seems that you have the right idea of it."

In no time at all, Mary and Nellie were in the wagon and one of the grooms was directing the animal back to Netherfield. Conversation was scarce everyone either enjoying the nice autumn day or lost in thought. Mary's face had started to feel less fiery, or maybe that was just because of the cool breeze. Despite the time and distance that separated her from the escapade that had her stuck in a floor, Mary remained mortified.

Yes, that was the problem. It was not the impulse she had to throw propriety into the wind and lean up and kiss Gabriel Goulding on the mouth. What had she been thinking? She knew exactly what she had been thinking, and she shook her head at it. He had just saved her; she was in pain and frightened and he was comforting her and her sensibilities had run away with themselves. When he had run his thumb along her injured lip, it had been nearly too much for her to resist.

The entire situation was so unlike herself that Mary was perplexed. She was never the sister who got into binds or randomly kissed gentlemen. She was the plain one who enjoyed teaching children and offering council. Besides, if Mr. Goulding truly wanted to kiss her, would he not also want to at least court her? She felt so entirely foolish. She knew he hesitated to take that step, but what was it about her that made him hesitate?

Her mind wanting to shy away from the drama of the morning, Mary looked at Mr. Goulding. Not that she was sure it was a wise idea. He had insisted on accompanying them. He stated it was only because he wanted to discuss the latest issue with William, but Mary suspected he wanted to make sure that she arrived back to her family in one relatively uninjured piece. Did he think her incapable of riding back to Netherfield in a wagon? Even as a small child, she had never been the sort to fall out of a moving vehicle. That was more like Lizzie or Lydia.

Taking a breath, Mary released it slowly. She knew she was at risk of behaving like a petulant child if she did not stop that train of thought. The morning had put her out of sorts, and she had no right to become suspicious of Mr. Goulding's actions. Where had the normally logical woman that she was gone? Had she lost it when she fell through the floor?

She returned her gaze to Mr. Goulding, who was riding next to the wagon on his horse. While Mary was fond of the gelding, named Fox of all things, she preferred Cadmus, also known as Crumpet and Crumb by little Artie. Mr. Goulding's horse was less sleek lines and speed and more muscle and endurance, its reddish coat unassuming. He was more of a workhorse than a gentleman's steed, though somehow, he fit Mr. Goulding well.

Once they reached Netherfield, Mr. Goulding dismounted and after handing off his reins to a groom, he went over to the wagon and easily lifted her down. Mary tried to limp away from him and into the house but was stopped by his hand on her shoulder. When she looked up at him in surprise, Mr. Goulding leaned over and whispered to her, "I know you were embarrassed, but I must say I adore how lovely you look when you blush."

Eyes going wide at his comment, Mary felt herself being escorted away, but was utterly lost in thought. What kind of comment was that? He liked her blush? How did he have any right to express himself thusly? He had not asked to court her and though her sisters told her that he had strong feelings towards her, he had never acted on them. And here he was confessing that he thought her blush was lovely?

And there went her face again, giving her away as his words had her flushing scarlet. Looking at him over her shoulder as she was shepherded away, she saw his grin grow as he offered her a grand bow. Furious or flattered, she had no idea which she should be. Whatever she chose, she would have to do it away from him as he went with William and she was taken to her room to wash up and change out of her dirtied dress.

GABRIEL COULD NOT HELP but chuckle as he arrived at Longbourn. The way Mary had turned scarlet when he told her she looked lovely when she blushed had been spectacular. Then, after a moment, she looked like she did not know if she should thank him or hit him. He would remember it fondly for as long as he lived.

Not that he was happy that she had been injured. No, in fact, he still felt very guilty that he had been unable to prevent it. The first thing he was going to do was to inspect the second story for any other rotten flooring. He did not want anyone else to fall through the floor, not if he could help it. Dismounting from Fox, he brought him into the stable and settled him in. Then he went in search of the workers who had stayed behind.

The remaining maid was happily cleaning away in the kitchen. She had been relieved to learn that Miss Mary was being well cared for and that Nelle would be returning with the wagon and Jeremy shortly. He found  looking up at the ceiling in one of the rooms on the first floor. Walking up to him, he asked, "Did you find another problem?"

Pointing up at a discolored spot on the ceiling, Isaac said, "I suppose that depends on whether or not you look at finding more rotten boards is a problem."

Looking up to where he indicated Gabriel frowned. Why hadn't he noticed the discoloration before? He would have to contact a carpenter and get to work on the floors sooner than he had originally thought, otherwise it would not be safe. "I think finding out now before anyone has the chance to fall through another ceiling is a good thing. Will you help me look for other spots that we will need to fix? First and foremost, I want to make sure we are all safe working here."

"Sounds like a good plan to me. I wouldn't want to step wrong on some rotten wood. Man my size, I would be liable to fall all the way through. Better to fix things before something else happens," said Isaac. He left the room with a nod in Gabriel's direction.

Gabriel was glad to be working with such amiable people. Making a mental note of the room, he moved around the first floor looking at the ceiling searching out other water damaged spots. He wanted everything safe by the next time Miss Mary made her way back to Longbourn.

ELIZABETH CAME RUSHING INTO the room as Mary was just getting into bed. The housekeeper had come and tutted over her wildly bruising ankle and foot and smeared something over her bleeding cut before wrapping it. She was promptly commanded to get in bed and stay there with her foot propped up. The housekeeper's commanding voice rang through the air as she assured Mary that a cup of hot, sweet tea was en route to her room. She would drink it without protest.

Mary was still smiling at the housekeeper's dictates when Elizabeth settled on the bed next to her. Brushing the hair back from Mary's face, Elizabeth asked, "Are you certain you are well?" Elizabeth examined her ankle where the bruising was not covered by the bandage and grimaced. "I mean, you fell through the floor, Mary."

Mary offered a timid smile and shrugged. "Not all the way through the floor, just partially. I am fine, and frankly, I am more worried about you. How are you feeling?" Reaching out, she grabbed Elizabeth's hand and gave it a squeeze. She did not want to talk about her own folly. She would much rather change the subject.

"At the moment, I am managing. Who knows what later will bring?" Elizabeth smiled at Mary, but then raised her eyebrows and tilted her head. She had always been good at the scolding elder sister look. "I know you are trying to distract me with your concern for me. Only falling partially through the floor? One would think that we have changed places. This is the kind of scrape I was known to have found myself in."

Falling back against the pillows behind her, Mary sighed. "Yes, that thought did cross my mind as I was stuck there. It was certainly your sort of scrape. I am fine, really, more mortified than anything. I feel so foolish for exploring and not realizing there was something wrong with the floor before I fell through it."

Offering Mary a commiserating smile, Elizabeth appeared content to allow the conversation to move on. "Well, you are safe now. How was Longbourn before you were forced to leave?"

"Longbourn is going to be quite the project, though clearing it out is well under way. The kitchen at least was swept clean, and we had cleared all sorts of nastiness out. It still needs a good scrubbing and some cats before we ever bring any food there." Mary's nose wrinkled at the thought of the mice that they had evicted that morning potentially returning.

Elizabeth sat in the chair near the head of the bed and put her feet up on a footstool. "You know we can afford the workers to go there. You do not have to help. Especially now with your injured ankle, you will have to rest for a few days, or maybe a week. Beyond that, once the cleaning is done, there is not much you can do. Unless you are planning to learn how to patch walls and paint them."

"I know, but I wanted to be there myself." Mary began fiddling with the embroidery on the sleeve of the night clothes she had been changed into. "You know how bad I felt to abandon Longbourn to father when we left."

Elizabeth's lips twisted into a frown, and her eyes portrayed her sadness as they turned downward, as if haunted by the memory. "You also know that we could not have stayed. He would have found a way to destroy us all."

"Yes, I know. That does not mean I have to like what we were forced to do. I want to see Longbourn set to rights." Looking at her sister with a halfhearted grin, Mary said, "Who knows, maybe I will live there as an eccentric old maid, teaching the neighborhood children to read and write."

Elizabeth immediately shook her head in response. "I see many things for you, but I do not see you becoming an eccentric old maid."

"Do not fight me on this, Lizzie. One of the reasons I was relieved to leave Mother and Lydia behind in Derbyshire was their incessant cheerfulness, always hinting that I would be wedded in no time. I cannot take it from you as well." Mary looked away from Elizabeth, her voice dropping to a murmur. "It is simply too painful."

Elizabeth smiled gently at her wounded sister. "It is obvious that you will be confined to your room for at least this evening. I won't torment you as well, so I will leave you be on that subject. Since Artie is napping and cannot cheer you up, you will have to make do with me for now. What do you want to talk about instead? I am at your disposal."

ELIZABETH'S GUESS WAS CORRECT in that by the time Mary's ankle was deemed well enough to get back on her feet easily, the work at Longbourn was mostly beyond her ability to contribute to. In the week that Mary had kept her foot elevated, the whole first floor of Longbourn had been cleaned free of dust and grime and the floors scrubbed. As far as Mary was able to find out, they had cleared all the broken furniture from the house and there were large piles of rubbish in the old kitchen garden. The maids were currently needed at Netherfield, so they would start on cleaning the second floor in the next week or so.

Mary had not decided whether she would go with them or not. In the time she had to think while keeping off her foot, she had realized that though she wanted to be useful; she was not really trained on scrubbing and cleaning. Despite what she had thought, there was a knack to it. As nice as they had been, she realized that the maids had to take time to show her how to help them.

Finally able to walk without too much issue, Mary wanted to get out of the house. Dressing with care, Mary decided she would make her way into Meryton that morning. She knew they were running low on the ginger that was needed in the tea that helped Elizabeth, but more than that, she wanted to see the town that she had grown up near.

It had been years since they had fled Longbourn, and there was no telling how things had changed. Between her injury and trying to help with Longbourn, she had yet to visit Meryton or walk among the shops. Carefully lacing her shoe around her still bruised foot, Mary smoothed her dress and went to check on Elizabeth before she left. Maybe she could get something to tempt her appetite while in town.

Running into William in the hallway outside of the room he shared with her sister, Mary smiled in greeting. "Good morning, William. I was just going to check on Lizzie. How is she fairing today?"

Gesturing for her to follow him away from the door and down the hallway, he spoke softly. "Today has not been one of her better days. I just convinced her to try to go back to sleep."

Frowning at the news, Mary hated to hear that her sister was still unwell. Speaking softly, she replied, "Then I will not disturb her. I was planning to walk into Meryton this morning and see if there was anything there that I could get to tempt her appetite. Then, too, we are running low on ginger for the tea that Lizzie needs. What are your plans for the day?"

Continuing to speak softly, William said, "I have some letters to write to my steward at Pemberley and a few other business matters. I was going to write Georgiana as well."

Mary could not help thinking of her mother and the happiness she had found with her new husband, Mr. Hawkins. She even had a new son to dote on. Mathew was a sweet little thing with a shock of curly hair of indeterminate color. Mary was uncertain if it would stay a sandy blond or turn a darker brown. Georgiana had been visiting with Lydia and the plan had been that they would pick her up on the way down to Netherfield, but she had come down with a cold shortly before they arrived. It was quickly decided that they would let her stay with Mama and Lydia instead of coming down to Hertfordshire. There was no need to risk her getting worse by traveling. The idea of traveling in a carriage for days while ill was never a fun prospect. "The last letter I had from Lydia said they had been enjoying looking after Mathew and were planning to start a school for the children near Mr. Hawkins's estate. It sounds like she is fully recovered from her cold."

"Yes, last I heard, Georgiana was enjoying herself." Turning to watch Mary come down the stairs behind him, he frowned slightly. "You are still favoring your foot."

"Yes, I have to be careful of it still, but it is not so sore that it will keep me from going about my day," she replied, hating that she had not been able to hide the pain better. She continued following William into the family dining room that held various foods on the sideboard, as well as coffee and tea. She immediately went to the sideboard to get herself a cup of tea with a liberal splash of cream.

Getting his own cup of coffee and a pastry, William took a seat at the table. "I will make sure the carriage is available for you so that you may go into Meryton as soon as you are ready."

Mary looked at her brother-in-law, who she had grown to love. She knew he cared deeply for those around him, but sometimes that love manifested itself as heavy-handed acts of kindness. He also had the habit of saying things in a way that did not carry the meaning he intended. Should she tease him and his clumsy way of trying to look after her? It was what Elizabeth would do, but it was not her typical sort of thing. "I did say that I could walk there. Were you meaning to say something else?"

The widening of his eyes was slightly comical, but Mary did not laugh. She hated to be embarrassed herself and would never want to hurt his feelings. "Oh, that did come out rather wrong. I would just hate for you to strain your foot, as it would not do for you to hurt your foot and ankle more than it already is." With a deep breath, he tried again. "I would like to offer you the use of the carriage so that you may enjoy yourself while in town and not worry about being in pain."

It was no wonder her sister had fallen in love with her husband; he was so earnest at times. "Thank you for the consideration. Though I feel I could manage to walk to Meryton without issue, I will accept the carriage ride. That way I can buy whatever I wish without having to worry about carrying it back." Smiling, Mary took a sip of her tea, enjoying the warmth as it spread throughout her body.

# Chapter Eight

Mary smiled at Nellie, who rode across from her in the carriage. Typically, she would have brought her lady's maid, but she was without one for the moment. Her maid had married shortly before they left Derbyshire. She was now the wife of the new bookshop owner in Lambton. Mary was thrilled her maid had found love, but it was slightly inconvenient.

Currently, it wasn't a major problem since she didn't have to prepare for social events and relied on one of the maids at Netherfield for assistance if necessary. She would have to have either train or hire one, eventually, but she was not going to worry about it yet. She was glad that Nellie had been available to go into town with her since she had grown to enjoy her company.

Smoothing her skirt in a nervous fashion, Nellie said, "Thank you for having me ride in here with you. I could have just as easily ridden with the coachman on top."

"Think nothing of it. If you had ridden up top, I would have been alone." Looking out the window, she noted the autumn scenery with a smile. The leaves on the trees in their vibrant fire colored dance made her happy whenever she watched them. "I have long preferred to spend time with others rather than to be alone. What do you think of the autumn weather we have been having?"

Leaning over to look out the window, Nellie took in the view, noting the way the leaves danced in the wind. "The wind has been picking up, but so far the season has been rather mild."

"There is something in the air, a scent or a feeling that is restful to me. I enjoy the autumn weather as long as it doesn't turn too suddenly." Leaning back into the cushions of the carriage, Mary took a deep breath.

"If you are ever worried about the weather changing, you should talk to old widow Atkins. She always claims to know when a storm is coming in. She says that she can feel it in her bones." Shrugging as she settled back into the cushioned seat of the carriage, Nellie tilted her head. "I do not know how, but I haven't heard of her guessing wrong."

"How is Mrs. Atkins managing, do you know? I learned that her husband had died while we were away. She had always been so nice to me as a girl." Mary reminisced about the times the sweet woman had offered her a horehound sweet when she visited her shop.

"She is doing well enough. Her youngest son took over the bakery and he and his new wife seem to enjoy having her about the place. It's evident that they have a strong bond as a family, always showing genuine care and concern for one another." Nellie related. Seeming to calm with the conversation, Nellie's hands rested in her lap, no longer fiddling with her dress.

Mary glanced out the window again, eager to spot Meryton. Sighing, she forced herself to settle they would arrive soon enough. Looking at Nellie, she said, "I want to stop by and say hello to her. Maybe I will ask about the weather."

THERE WAS SOMETHING NOSTALGIC about walking down the streets of Meryton. It felt like everything had been the same forever and yet there were changes to be seen. There was a new color of paint on the haberdashery, and the main shop seemed to have grown somehow. Deciding to walk to the bakery first and then to the apothecary to look for the ginger that would help Elizabeth, Mary made her way down the street with Nellie in tow.

Though the weather was blustery, Mary still enjoyed herself. She was happy to watch the fallen leaves twirl as they blew down the street. It did not take long for them to get to their destination.

First, they were going to the Atkins bakery. Mary knew that they did not need to buy baked goods in town, but she wanted to check on Mrs. Atkins. The bakery was always a delightful place to the senses. The smell of yeast and sweet baked goods mixed with wood fire smell. Windows brought in plenty of light and there were always nice little embellishments here and there. Today there was a blue tablecloth that all the baked goods laid on with little flower embellishments embroidered on to the edges. The atmosphere was as inviting as it had always seemed to be, even years later.

"Welcome! How can I help you, Miss?" The kind voice of a young woman that Mary assumed was the new Mrs. Atkins came from the back of the room. She had been crouching down and doing something behind a display, so Mary had not seen her right at first.

Offering a surprised smile, Mary subtly evaluated the young woman. She appeared to be in her early twenties, and there was a gentle curve to her belly that suggested she might be in the midst of pregnancy. Mary could not recall her face and wondered if she was from Meryton or further afield. "Good morning. I was hoping to say hello to old Mrs. Atkins. It has been some time since I have been through Meryton, and I was hoping she would be here."

"Of course, she is in back, making us a pot of tea. One moment." Passing through the doorway in the back of the shop, she vanished behind a curtain that divided the space from the bustling bakery and their living quarters. Mary could hear her voice calling out, "Mother Atkins, there is someone asking for you."

Then came the well-worn voice that Mary could recognize. "I am coming, dear."

It was only a moment before both women came out of the back area. They were an interesting pair, and Mary was glad to see there was affection between them. She had heard living with one's mother-in-law could be quite difficult, but it seemed these two were managing quite well.

The older Mrs. Atkins was more weathered than Mary remembered, but there was still the smile in her eyes that had always warmed Mary's heart. "Miss Mary Bennet! I am so glad that you would be so kind as to come see an old woman like me. It has been some years since I last saw you. How are you, my girl?"

Reaching out, Mary took the woman's hands in her own and noticed the contrast between the rough, callused texture of Mrs. Atkins's work-worn hands and the delicate feel of her own skin. It hurt her heart to see how much the woman had aged. Was it the sorrow of her husband's passing that caused it? They had always been a loving couple. "I am well, Mrs. Atkins. While I was away, I heard the news that your husband had passed. I wanted to offer my condolences. He was a good man and I know he will be missed by many people."

With a nod, Mrs. Atkins pulled her hands back and took a handkerchief from her pocket to wipe at her eyes. "That he was, my girl, that he was."

"He was always so kind to me whenever I was in town. Between him sneaking me biscuits and you sneaking me horehound sweets, you both had me quite spoiled."

"You needed the spoiling. You were always so solemn and serious when you were growing up. Not that I blamed you for it. We all handle the life that comes at us in our own way." Reaching out with a motherly gesture, she smoothed back a wisp of Mary's windblown hair that had escaped her pins. "Then you became fixated on that awful book for a time. Thank goodness you started expanding your reading. What was that book called?"

Mary laughed, oddly remembering the time before Elizabeth and Jane had taken her more firmly under their wings. "Fordyce's Sermons." She had become quite fixated on the book before Elizabeth had expanded her world with other books and ideas. Now she read more than just the Bible and books of sermons. She read things by John Locke, Voltaire, Shakespeare, Woodsworth, and Coleridge. Mary grinned widely, thinking about how far she had come. "You have quite the memory, Mrs. Atkins."

"And you have quite the smile, Miss Mary. I always knew it was there." Reaching into her pocket, she took out two candies and handed both Mary and Nellie each one. "How are your sisters and mother? Are they well?"

"Mother is remarried now to an estate owner in Derbyshire named Mr. Hawkins, and I have a new little brother. Lydia is with Mother at the moment. Jane is well enough, and her family is set to arrive shortly. Kitty has recently married Theodore Fitzwilliam, the Earl of Matlock. Currently, she is in Scotland visiting one of his estates on a wedding trip. Of course, Elizabeth is now Mrs. Darcy, and she is at Netherfield even now. Her son Arthur is the most adorable little scamp that ever had his parents twisted around his little finger."

"I am happy that your mother and sisters are flourishing. It brings a warm feeling to my heart." Nodding to Mary with a smile, she added, "I hope to see your sisters while they are here."

Looking towards the shop's entrance, Mary made sure there wasn't anyone else coming in. "One reason I made the trip into town this morning is I hoped that you still made that wonderful ginger cake. I want to see if I could tempt Elizabeth with something you made."

"Poor dear, not feeling well, is she? Let us see what we have that might tempt her." Going back to the baked goods, she moved around and began bundling some things up.

Opening her reticule, Mary began to pull out her money. "How much do I owe you?"

Waving off her question with a wrinkled hand, Mrs. Hopkins beamed. "Oh, how could I charge you? It is a welcome home gift."

Somehow, Mary knew she should not be surprised that was just the kind of woman Mrs. Atkins was. She may have been a widow with limited means, but she and her husband had always found a way to be kind to others. "Thank you, Mrs. Atkins. I am sure Elizabeth will be very grateful." Mary made a note to herself to find a way to pay the family back for their kindness.

Handing the paper-wrapped package to Mary, Mrs. Atkins pat her shoulder. "I hope your sister gets to feeling better. You tell her I said hello."

"Yes, ma'am, I will do that. Have a good day." Giving a little curtsy, Mary left the shop, happy to have seen an old friend once again.

Nellie followed closely, reaching out for the package she asked. "Let me take the cake, Miss Bennet. I can easily carry it in the basket I brought."

Handing it over, Mary continued down the street. "Thank you. Nellie, do you want to stop at any of the other shops before we walk to the apothecary?"

Confused, Nellie squinted at Mary, her brow furrowed. "Pardon me?" she asked, struggling to understand.

"Did you need or want anything while we were in town? I do not mind going to one of the shops if you have need of something. We are not in a rush." Mary knew that most women in her position would never offer such a thing to a maid, but Mary embraced her own unconventional ideas. At least when it came to treating people with kindness and respect. She had seen too many hurtful actions for a lifetime. She would be kind, however, and whenever she could.

Nellie hesitated before responding, her voice filled with uncertainty. "No, I don't need anything," she said, "but I wouldn't mind admiring the displays in the shop windows as we walk to the apothecary."

"Then that is what we will do. It is a lovely day to walk along the shops." Mary looked at the people moving about the town. People were moving about shopping and running errands. Across the street, the little tea shop seemed to have a steady stream of people coming in and out. Mary enjoyed the slower pace and cozy charm of small towns, in stark contrast to the fast-paced chaos of London.

Pausing to look in the window of the dressmaker's shop, Mary wondered if the dress on the dummy in the window would look better in a less ostentatious color. The reflection in the window allowed her to see that a group of girls were crossing the street, chatting. Mary thought of turning to greet them, but then stopped when she heard them talking.

"Yes, that Bennet family is back, if you can believe it."

"But my Mama always said that Mrs. Bennet was a saint with as much as she worked to be of use to the people of Longbourn and Meryton." This voice was small and hesitant, speaking out against the first girl's obvious spite.

The first voice continued, "That may be, but Mr. Bennet was the absolute worst sort of person. I heard Mother speaking with Father about it one day. As if losing Longbourn wasn't enough, he had to find *employment* to support himself before his passing."

"Oh, my," came another voice.

The ringleader huffed and then said, "Elizabeth Bennet's marriage to a wealthy landowner may be admired, but I can't help but question how it stands in comparison to her father's lost estate. I say that leaves her in a tier below us. At least our fathers have their own estates. No matter what her husband did by buying Longbourn or owning his own properties, she is no longer the daughter of a landed gentleman."

Nellie, apparently unable to stand the girl's spouting of nonsense, confronted her. "Evaline Goulding, how dare you speak so of things that you do not understand! If this is how you are going to behave, I wonder how you were allowed to venture out of the schoolroom without supervision."

Turning around, Mary observed firsthand the girl turning her nose down at Nellie in her obvious maid's uniform. Evaline rolled her eyes. "I do not entertain remarks from *maids*."

"Then maybe you will take advice from me." Stepping forward, Mary looked over the girl before her. She was maybe twelve or thirteen. It was obvious that though Evaline spoke of the Bennet family, she did not know who they were or what they looked like. "I find it fascinating that you would disparage my family so easily, Miss Goulding. Apparently you have been at the wrong end of some misinformation and poor advice."

The girl's eyes widened ever so slightly. "Is that so?"

"If you ever want to have a season in town, you will need to realize who you speak about before you try to spread untrue and malicious gossip. I recognize your actions are most likely influenced by someone else's spite. I know from experience that it is sometimes hard to decipher who to listen to." Looking at all the girls and their various looks of shock and worry, Mary decided they could do with some good advice. "I will offer you with some of the best advice I ever received and leave you to decide for yourself your best course of action. Know that tearing people down will never make you feel the way you hope to. You will get much more happiness in your life if you exert the effort to be kind." Briskly curtsying, she turned her back on the shocked gaggle of girls and walked away with her head held high.

They walked in silence for a few moments before Nellie confessed, "I am not sure I could have been that kind."

"While it is true that they may have conducted themselves in a despicable manner, I am of the opinion that their actions were primarily influenced by the adults in their lives rather than their own maliciousness. At least I hope as much. Perhaps by being kind,

I may help them find a better path." They continued walking in comfortable silence, but Mary could not help but wonder how Mr. Goulding had turned out so very different from his little sister.

EVALINE WATCHED THE WOMAN she now realized was Miss Mary Bennet leave. So that was the woman who she suspected her brother was forming an attachment to. She was prettier than her mother would have her believe. Evaline rather liked the shades of brown and blonde that shone in her hair. It was as if her hair could not make up its mind but was fine with being different, not quite brown or blonde.

Walking along with her friends, she let them take over the conversation and continued with only the barest of inputs and agreements. She needed to think after such a confrontation and knew she would not be left alone once she got home. There were too many lessons. Even her nights were no longer her own as she now had to sleep with her hair in those little wraps to make it curl. Though her hair did not seem to stay curled past breakfast.

Her mother had always been the type to want nothing to do with her unless she was showing her off to her friends. But lately she had been spending more time with Evaline. Of course, she spent most of that time complaining about either her brother Gabriel and how he was not trying to catch a wealthy debutant or Evaline and her looks. Evaline's lack of appropriate curls was one of her chief criticisms, though there was also Evaline's apparent inability to sit and stand straight enough. She had been called graceless too often to count.

How did one exude elegance and grace, anyway? Whatever the method, Evaline's failure in her mother's eyes seemed to make her mother despair for her future. Which she proclaimed loudly and repeatedly.

Her mother would talk to her governess about all of her faults in front of her, as if she was not even there. Evaline had never noticed her freckles before and now they were a catastrophe to be quickly remedied lest they become a problem at her come out. A come out that they were already planning for, despite it being over four years away.

When her mother had invited her to come into Meryton with her, Evaline had been happy to get away from her latest round of lessons in French, the harp, and deportment. And when the opportunity presented itself to demonstrate her superiority over the other girls with the gossip she knew her mother would be sharing, Evaline had jumped at the chance.

Hadn't it been drilled into her head that she must become the leading girl of her age? That it was her responsibility to become the most eligible debutante ever seen by Meryton? She would not have the largest dowery, but she was still expected to make the best match. The only way to do so was to begin training now and start taking the lead in their small circle of society.

Sometimes Evaline hated that she had come into her mother's notice. Though she supposed she should be grateful to have her mother's attention, even if it came with a new governess and scads of lessons and rules. Evaline was a young lady now and she would simply have to adjust. If only it was not so confusing.

And yet when she had met Miss Bennet, it seemed as if she did not prescribe to her mother's rules. Was that a good thing? Her mother had told her that at twenty-two, Miss Bennet was an unmarried disgrace, but it seemed that young woman did not hold the same opinion.

As Evaline walked, she realized she was envious of Miss Bennet's confidence. It looked as though she was not afraid of anything, or at least not of anyone's comments and jibes. She spoke of things that her mother would have probably held on par with heresy. Either Miss Bennet had never had a mother demand differently of her or she had never cared. Was it wicked for Evaline to want something besides what her mother demanded of her? Probably.

"As I LIVE AND breathe, if it's not little Mary Bennet." The kindly voice of Mr. Jones's gregarious wife was the first thing Mary heard as she entered the apothecary's shop.

Smiling at the older woman, Mary greeted her. "Hello, Mrs. Jones. How are you this fine autumn day?"

Mrs. Jones's graying hair peeked out of her lace cap, curling around her face as merrily as it always had. Mrs. Jones was kind, though more bubbly than Mary could handle in large amounts. Closing the distance from where she had been across the , the woman replied, "Well enough, sweet girl, well enough. The question is, how are you? I have not seen you in an age!"

"I am well, thank you, though I am afraid I am not so little anymore."

Reaching out with a smile, Mrs. Jones squeezed Mary's hand. Eyes bright and inquisitive, she asked, "Now I heard you were staying at Netherfield with your sister, Mrs. Darcy. Did I get the right of it? Gossip can be fickle with the truth, so I never rely on it wholly."

Yes, gossip could be fickle. Mary had seen it tear down a person with wholly wrong information, but she had also seen gossip be used to rally aid for a young widow in need. Without losing her smile, Mary answered, "Well, in that, the gossip was correct. I am here with Elizabeth and her husband, Mr. Darcy. Jane should arrive with her husband, Mr. Bingley, within another sennight."

"Now I also heard that you have been helping at Longbourn. Who would have thought that it would fall back into your family's hands?" Turning, the older woman began stacking things on a shelf behind her. "I know it is not right to speak ill of the dead, but I am just right glad your father is no longer around to be a blight on that estate."

Mary could not respond without either being disrespectful to her father or Mrs. Jones, so she merely nodded her head and began to look around the shelves. There was no love lost between her and her deceased father, but it did not seem tasteful or respectful to talk so openly about him to people in town.

"Regardless, that Mr. Darcy will get things to rights. I heard tell he has a rather large estate up in Derbyshire. It will be easy enough for him to whip things into shape." Looking at Mary, she seemed to realize that she would not be sharing any more information on matters she wanted to know, so she wisely changed the subject. "Look at me talking you silly. You did not come in to chat with a doddering old lady. What have you come for?"

"I was hoping to get a good supply of ginger."

Eyes widening slightly at the request, Mrs. Jones nodded and said, "You are in luck. We have plenty on hand at the moment. I always make sure to keep it well stocked as it helps with so many ailments."

Mary knew the woman would have her suspicions. Mrs. Jones had not been the apothecary's wife for so long that she did not know why a young married woman might need ginger. "That is good to know. I would like to get powdered ginger if you have it." She was not going to confirm anything about Elizabeth's condition but was very glad to get what her sister needed.

ONCE AGAIN, WALKING DOWN the street with Nellie, Mary could not help but laugh at the events of their morning. Some people were just so driven by the need for gossip.

Looking at Mary, Nellie seemed to guess what the laugh was about. "At least you are able to laugh. Mrs. Jones is like a dog with a bone at times. Always wants news, that lady."

Nodding, Mary chuckled, saying, "Yes, though she can be discreet. If you think about it, she knows a lot about the health conditions of the folks in town. She sees who comes into the shop for what and she knows where her husband is going. Despite that, I have never heard a word about her spreading news about people's ailments and conditions. She may guess that Elizabeth is with child, but you won't hear word if it until it is spread in a different manner."

Getting a better grip on the basket she carried now that had another package, Nellie pondered out loud. "You are nice to look for the good in people. Sometimes I forget to do that."

"It is not always easy, but I keep trying." Mary looked at Nellie, wondering if she should explain how she had come to be who she was. "Once upon a time I was very judgmental and pedantic. I was always looking down on people. I did the right thing. Why did no one else? Then Elizabeth encouraged me to meet more people and pay attention to their lives. Between that and reading more widely, I realized just how hard people's lives are already. No one needs extra strife in their lives. It is better to contribute to someone's happiness than to criticize the choices they have made."

Moving around the wagon that was at the side of the street full of rolled up rugs, they made their way to where the carriage stood waiting. Mary stooped so suddenly that Nellie nearly ran into her. "Did you hear that?"

"Hear what?" Nellie tilted her head, trying to hear whatever Mary had heard.

The faintest mewl had Nellie looking towards the wagon and Mary rushing to the back of the wagon and looking in. The multicolored rugs lay in heaps. It was possible that they were being delivered to one of the shops, but that was not what drew Mary's attention. The sad, pitiable mewling that was coming from somewhere within the rugs was.

"Hey now! What are you doing to my rugs?" A gruff voice came from behind both women.

Turning to face a rather large man walking out of the nearby shop, Mary asked, "Do you by chance have an animal traveling with you? I hear something coming from the rugs."

"Wha'? I ain't got no animals, just good quality rugs for sale." Looking confused and slightly perturbed, the rugged man shook his head.

"Then why am I hearing crying coming from the rugs?"

Coming closer, the gruff gentleman examined his wares, rearing back when he too heard the small cries coming from the jumble of material. "There is something in there." Reaching out, he moved the topmost rug carefully. After a time of searching for the source of the sounds, a small furry head came into view.

A tiny calico face was blinking at them from between two of the rugs. Copper, cream, and brown splotched together on a tiny ball of fluff with two vivid blue eyes. "The poor thing must have climbed in at some point and become stuck." Carefully reaching out a hand, Mary let the kitten sniff her for a moment before scooping her up and cradling her against her own body.

"Who would have thought? I have been on the road for days. How long has it been in there?" Taking off his floppy cap, he scratched at his receding hairline. "I do not have time for an animal."

Cuddling the small kitten, Mary smiled in delight as it purred. "I have been looking for a cat since we need a mouser for Longbourn. I would be grateful if you would let me take it."

Brow scrunched in disbelief, the man said, "Won't be much of a mouser at that size, but I would be glad to let you have it."

"I am sure it will grow. Thank you, sir." Nodding to the man, Mary turned back to Nellie. "Let us return to Netherfield so that we may find this little one something to eat."

# Chapter Nine

Kɪᴇʀɴᴀɴ ʜᴏᴘᴘᴇᴅ ᴅᴏᴡɴ ꜰʀᴏᴍ the post carriage and looked around the town. It had been several years and quite a few inches since he had visited Meryton. Grabbing his luggage as it was tossed down to him, he took in a deep breath of autumn air. Hefting his tote onto his shoulder, Kiernan took off down the road that he knew would take him to Netherfield.

He knew that the Darcys were at Netherfield and soon the Bingleys would be visiting as well. School was on break for the moment, and he was glad for it. He had thought about visiting his family in Derbyshire, but he knew they were well and with Timmy there to help them, he wasn't needed. Really, what he had wanted to do was to check up on the goings on of Longbourn. There was a possibility that he could help them out with what he knew would be a large undertaking of restoring the neglected estate. He had received so much from the Darcys, he was keen to pay them back how ever he could.

Walking through the crunchy leaves as he made his way, Kiernan let his mind wander. He remembered the autumn years ago that had changed his life forever. It had not been long after he had told Miss Elizabeth he had decided to help her and her sisters out with some brotherin' that things had seemed to go sideways. His role in helping rescue Miss Elizabeth had cemented his connections with the family.

Recognizing his thirst for knowledge, Mr. Darcy had provided him with a tutor and later on, entry into Eton. His family had been tenants on Longbourn land for generations and now resided at Pemberley working on the home farm. It seemed, however, that he was becoming destined for more than simple farm work. While he did not know what that was yet, he did not mind taking the journey and finding out. It seemed like no time had passed at all before he was being greeted at Netherfield.

He was just putting down his pack when Darcy came to greet him in the hall. "Kiernan, I was not expecting you! I thought you would visit your family when your classes let out." Reaching out, Darcy gave him one of those half hugs as men seemed to be so fond of.

Good-naturedly accepting the ruffling of his hair and the accompanied hard clap on the back, Kiernan replied, "They are all well enough without me. I heard that new lad Timmy is working out well helping on the home farm. Anyway, I was eager to see about Longbourn. I am sure I can be of some sort of use while here. I will need to go back to Eton in a few weeks, but until then, I am here to help."

Darcy shook his head, but smiled warmly at him. "You are always welcome at any of my homes, Kiernan. Though you know you do not have to keep helping out. You do not have to work for your keep, or anything for that matter."

Waving his arguments off, Kiernan said, "I like being of use. I get antsy if I have to stay idle for too long. How are my sisters?" Though he was not actually related to any of the Bennet ladies, he had promised to be brotherly to them all and over time he had started calling them his sisters. He loved them all as if they were his blood anyway.

"Lydia and Georgiana are back in Derbyshire with Mrs. Hawkins. Only Elizabeth and Mary are here right now, though Jane will be arriving with Bingley and their daughter soon enough." Reaching out, Darcy grabbed the pack by Kiernan's feet and called over to one of the footmen and handing him the pack asked him to see to it that Kiernan was prepared a room in the family wing.

Kiernan thought of protesting his placement in one of the family rooms but knew that he would get nowhere with Darcy on the matter. Though the gentleman was kind and caring despite his anxiety around strangers and at gatherings, he was also rather stubborn. Letting it slide, Kiernan asked, "How is little Artie doing?"

Darcy's grin, if possible, grew larger. "He has everyone wrapped around his little finger and his vocabulary grows by the day."

Barking with laughter, Kiernan had to wait to regain his breath before responding. "Well, that has to be expected. Look at who his parents are."

"OH, HOW DARLING! Is it a boy or a girl?" Elizabeth exclaimed, her eyes wide with adoration as she watched the striking kitten curiously explore a footstool.

They both sat on the floor with the kitten running between them. "With her cute appearance and affectionate personality, she is simply irresistible," Mary agreed.

Pulling out a feather, Elizabeth attempted to get the kitten to play. "What will you name her?"

Biting her lip in thought, Mary said, "I was thinking of naming her Cleopatra."

"Why Cleopatra of all things?" Handing the feather off to Mary, Elizabeth laughed at the kitten's apparent confusion.

"We found her in a stack of rugs. It made me think of the story of how Cleopatra snuck herself to Caesar in a rug." Mary flicked the feather out of the kitten's reach, entertaining it with a chase. "Then too, she has dark markings around her eyes, like you see in the Egyptian paintings."

"Then I think Cleopatra is perfect."

Mary watched as her sister played with the kitten, happy to see her so well and joyous. Elizabeth was finally getting over much of her morning sickness, and while it was by no means gone, it had receded enough that Mary no longer worried so much about her health.

In fact, there were actually several things that Mary was happy about. As she reflected on her little excursion, she was pleased to note that her ankle had performed admirably, giving her confidence that she was mostly recovered from her unexpected mishap of falling through the floor. And while it would be quite some time before Cleopatra became a mouser, Mary had found a cat for Longbourn. Though she hoped there would not be a rodent problem at her former home for very long. From what she had heard from William, the estate was coming together nicely. It was not livable at that point, but everything was going in the right direction. There had been no unexpected problems cropping up, well besides the rot in the floorboards she had discovered. Soon enough, Longbourn would be a fresh slate ready for new possibilities and happier memories.

Yes, things were definitely looking up.

COMING DOWN FROM HIS horse with a thud, Gabriel looked around the yard by Longbourn's stable with a critical eye. They would have to do something with all the discarded ruins of what once was the insides of Longbourn. It was unseemly to have such heaps of trash surrounding a manor house.

The sound of a horse and rider approaching had Gabriel looking up and shielding his eyes from the sun to see who was coming his way. It appeared to be a young man on a rather energetic steed. Despite his stylishly cut brown hair and matching brown eyes, he was dressed in practical work attire. While his clothes implied that he was a worker, his horse implied that he had money. Its sleek lines and powerful build were easily notable. He looked somewhat familiar, but Gabriel could not place his name.

Calling out, Gabriel questioned the new arrival. "Hello. Can I help you?"

Bouncing down from his horse with the boundless energy of youth, the stranger turned around and smiled. "Actually, I have come to see if I could help you." Giving a sharp bow with the horse's reins carefully in hand, he explained, "I am Kiernan Anderson, and you could say I am good friends with the Darcys. Since I am on break from school and came to visit, I hoped I could do something useful while I was here. I am not formed to be idle and was looking to get my hands dirty, so I have come to offer my services."

Gabriel's memory was jogged by the younger man's introduction. Kiernan was the little boy that had helped Darcy rescue Mrs. Darcy all those years ago. That would certainly develop a close friendship if anything did. It seemed that he was a little boy no longer. He looked to be around fourteen and was probably as tall as Miss Mary. He was going to be a rather large man soon enough.

Gabriel could well remember the age where he felt he would burst if he did not have some sort of activity to engage in. "You are more than welcome to come  and help me. I was trying to decide what to do with all this debris when you arrived."

"While the Bennet ladies are good to be rid of him, it looks like Mr. Bennet left quite the mess to take care of in his absence." Kicking at the horribly broken remains of a table, or possibly a chair, Kiernan shook his head. "You might burn it all, but you would need to keep a good watch. With it being autumn and all the leaves on the ground, there is the risk of an uncontrollable fire. I can understand why you want to be rid of it, though. An early snow would make it impossible to work with all this before spring. Have you thought of reaching out to people, like the blacksmith or one of the carpenters? Perhaps they might have use of some of it?"

"I had not considered that anyone else might have use of it." Looking at the young man with new understanding, Gabriel realized he was more than he might have originally assumed. "I had been thinking of the possibility of burning it all. It has been some time since we have had a snow this early, but it would be just the sort of thing to make the situation even more difficult. At least the windows are boarded over until the glacier comes tomorrow."

Looking up at the clouds, Kiernan narrowed his eyes before turning his attention to the manor's boarded-up windows. "Have you checked the tenant houses over yet? I would be curious to know how my childhood home fared."

With a slight grimace, Gabriel shook his head. "Only a cursory glance. For the most part, I have been working on the manor. There was unexpected damage on the second floor that necessitated more attention than anticipated. The broken windows letting in the weather had caused damage to the stability of the flooring."

"I can imagine that broken windows could have caused problems with rot and the like. I hope no one was injured."

Looking down, Gabriel felt his face flush with shame as he rubbed at the back of his neck. "Miss Mary experienced a mishap where she ended up partially falling through the second floor. It resulted in her leg being visible through the ceiling of the first floor." Clearing his throat, Gabriel forced himself to continue. "She actually became stuck, and it took some work to free her. She escaped with minor injuries, but it was certainly a harrowing moment."

"I can imagine," Kiernan replied, his tone oddly full of amusement despite the topic of conversation. "I am glad that she is well. She certainly seemed fine when I greeted her yesterday."

"That is good. I have not seen her since the accident and hoped that she had recovered." Deciding that he would ask a few of the men in town if they had any use for the ruined furniture pieces before he set about burning things, Gabriel made a snap decision. "Would you be interested in riding to a few of the tenant homes with me? I would like to survey what needs to be corrected before anyone can resume living in them. I have a feeling you might be able to direct me to them better than my own wanderings."

"I would be happy to go with you. My family home is probably one of the closest. I can easily show you the way." Swinging back up on to his horse in a single fluid motion, Kiernan was ready to go.

Gabriel mounted his own horse and allowed Kiernan to take the lead. For a while, he pondered things in silence. Thinking about the possibility of needing to redesign a tenant cottage or two if they had become too damaged. Though his skill was not anything special, he enjoyed studying architectural design, and he hoped that he would have the ability to make a comfortably livable home.

Quickly, though, his mind seemed to wander to Miss Mary. He was glad to hear that she had recovered sufficiently from her accident. The nagging feeling of regret gnawed at him, knowing he had missed his chance to prevent it. The incident had reinforced just how much he loved her. He had admitted to himself that he had feelings for her for some time. Strong feelings. For a while now he had been putting off any action, and though it ate at him, he knew it was for her own good to wait until he could provide what she deserved.

They had been dancing around each other for the longest time. Would he ever reach a point where he could offer Mary a home and a life worthy of her? How long would that take?

It was not long before Gabriel realized they had arrived, and he was forced to push his mind back to the work at hand. Dismounting, Kiernan looped his reigns loosely over a nearby branch and approached the building. It was big for a tenant home, with a second story and what must have been a pretty little garden. Going into the garden, he knelt down and ran his fingers over some of the herbs that were still growing and had gone rather wild.

Getting off his own horse, he looked the home over. It was obvious to Gabriel that the house had been loved before it had been abandoned. They had taken the time to board up the windows to prevent the sort of problem like Longbourn had. "It seems that your family took good care of your home. It must have been hard to leave it."

"Yes, it was. Our family had lived on Longbourn land for nearly as many generations as the Bennets. But we understood that without the Bennet ladies overseeing things, it would become unlivable." Breaking off a piece of what seemed like mint, Kiernan rubbed it between his fingers and sighed. "Darcy offered my family a larger house at the Home Farm at Pemberley. They took the opportunity with the understanding that if they chose to come back here, the Darcys would make the way for them. I think my parents have decided to stay at Pemberley, but I have an older brother who is considering coming back to Longbourn at some point."

Unsure of what to say to the young man, Gabriel offered a platitude. "That is good, I suppose." Then, looking at him more closely, he asked, "Do you not want to come back to Longbourn?"

"No, with the Darcys sending me to Eton and soon enough to Cambridge, I have a different path in front of me than my family had." Dropping the mint, he turned to face Gabriel more fully, a small grin on his face. "I have also been growing a nest egg to enable me to do interesting things with my future." Walking back to his horse, he gave him a rub behind the ears and wrapped the reins around a nearby branch. "Did you want to go in?"

"I think that will be a good idea. We can check out if there has been any damage that needs to be corrected." Meanwhile, his mind was wondering how a tenant child could manage to grow any kind of nest egg by the tender age of fourteen.

They had made their way inside and were examining the home. They soon realized that besides the rodent issue, something had made a home in one of the two chimneys. That would have to be dealt with carefully, as they did not want to risk injury or rabies from a badger or whatever was in there. It also looked as if the kitchen door had been gnawed through and would need to be replaced. Beyond those problems, the house should not require much more than a thorough cleaning.

Gabriel's mind was so focused on whether he should ask Jeremy and Isaac to tackle this house next or to work on the patching of the holes in the walls that he was completely taken off guard by Kiernan's comment.

"So, when are you going to make Miss Mary happy and ask her to marry you?" Kiernan looked at him with a grin.

Stepping back from the door he had been examining, Gabriel had to force his mouth shut to not gape before responding to Kiernan. "What? What did you just ask?" The boy couldn't have just asked what he thought he did.

Shaking his head at the question, Kiernan gave a little laugh. "Do not try to deny it. Between the color you are changing, the way you called her Mary before and not Miss Bennet and the information I get in letters from the Bennet ladies. I know it is not a matter of if you like or love her, it is a matter of when you will act on your inclination."

Grasping at the first thing that came to mind, Gabriel blurted, "First off, I let her fall through the floor. I did not know that the floor was so unstable. I did not sufficiently warn her." There was no way he was having a conversation about how much he loved Mary. It just was just not happening. More than that, how could a boy of what was he fourteen... fifteen... know?

"Love allows for a lot in my experience. Darcy allowed Miss Elizabeth to be tossed off a cliff by a childhood friend of his that had gone bad. Love is not constrained by the bad things that happen. If it is actually love, you overcome the things like falling down the cliff and grow closer together." Laughing, Kiernan looked at Gabriel. It was not long before his gaze became serious, however. "I am sure that Miss Mary can forgive you for letting her get her foot stuck, but first you must forgive yourself. Besides, she is more likely to be upset about your hesitation. If I have learned anything, it is that women and girls, my sisters included, do not look at things the way men do."

What in the world gave this boy such insight? And falling off a cliff? He knew that Mrs. Darcy had needed rescuing, but it was obvious that he did not have all of the story. Fighting against embarrassment, Gabriel considered confiding in the young man. Even after only an hour of conversation, he realized he could become friends with Kiernan despite their age difference and class divide. It seemed as if the young man had an inside angle that might help him in his attachment to Mary. "Yes, I have feelings for Mary that apparently, I cannot deny, but what good are feelings when I can do nothing about it? I am a second son with no estate or even a place to live with her available. I would never take her to my family's home. My family would never treat her as she should be treated."

"Do you think you would not be instantly invited to stay at Netherfield or with any of her sisters?" Kiernan gaped at Gabriel as if he was stupid for using the excuse that he was. "Even her mother lives on a prosperous estate that I am sure you could make yourself of use at."

"But what woman wants to marry without good provision? My mother complains all the time that she should have married better, as what my father has is beneath her." Of course, his mother rarely spoke of it directly to his father, but he had often heard her complaining of it to her sister when she came to visit. "I could not bear it if eventually Mary felt that way."

Walking away from Gabriel for a moment, Kiernan paced and then turned back to confront him. "Do you think they only married because of where they might live and the clothes they might have? If so, then you are fooling yourself. Jane, Elizbeth, and Catherine married for love and nothing else. If Bingley, Darcy, or Colonel Fitzwilliam had been anything else—book seller, steward, or common soldier—it would have changed nothing." Looking at Gabriel discerningly, Kiernan seemed to judge him for a moment before continuing. "I will guess that Mary is more hurt by your hesitation than your lack of a grand home or jewelry that you have to offer her. The Bennet ladies are not like others of their station: they escaped a hell at Longbourn despite the nice things and position it offered. Now free, they will accept nothing but love and respect."

It took a moment for Gabriel to absorb all that he had been told. He knew that the Bennet sisters all married for love, but would they really have married to their disadvantage? Was Mary hurt by his inaction? Gazing at the younger man, he recognized that this had not been a conversation that had taken place by accident. "Thank you for talking to me about this. I have a great deal to ponder and a few beliefs that need reevaluating. It seems that I may expect to be happy much sooner than I had ever hoped."

"I suggest you take care of matters soon. I dislike seeing my sisters in pain." Kiernan glared at him momentarily, but his features soon softened as he changed the subject. "What do you suppose we speak with the blacksmith and carpenter to see if they would be interested in anything in the piles of rubbish?"

Gabriel readily agreed and soon they were both back on their horses, trotting towards Meryton. He was glad his horse knew what it was about because there was so much whirling through his mind that it was very possible that he would have become unseated easily. It had been a while since he realized Mary was the woman he wanted to love forever. There had never been any coyness between them. For some time now, they had both acknowledged that there were feelings left unsaid. Was what Kiernan was implying true? Was Mary in pain because of his hesitation to move things forward? If so, he was a cad for allowing her to suffer for his own misplaced pride.

He went about the rest of the day quieter than was his wont. Things were accomplished around Longbourn. The blacksmith and carpenter came to see what they had and were surprisingly interested in hauling quite a bit off. Kiernan allowed him to think as they burned the remainder of the rubbish and take care of other things around the manor. His mind was focused inward, no matter what he was doing on the outside. He had to make things right with Mary. But how would he go about it?

# Chapter Ten

A CHUBBY LITTLE BODY slamming into his legs had Kiernan looking down at a gleeful little face. "K'nan! Are back to play?"

Leaning down, Kiernan scooped the almost two-year-old up and tossed him up and caught him. "Of course, I came back to play with you. Why else would I visit?"

Looking ponderous for a moment, his little face deep in thought, his little brows narrowed cutely. "Play wit Crumb?"

Looking at the toddler with an astounding amount of clarity for one so small, he nodded. "Yes, I could have come to visit with Crumpet, but I will tell you a secret."

Head tilted and a curl falling over his eye, Artie asked, "Wat s'cret?"

Lowering his voice, Kiernan acted like he was about to reveal state secrets, making little Artie giggle with glee and fight to act serious. "I think you are more fun to play with than Crumpet. But do not tell him. I do not want to hurt his feelings."

Nodding solemnly, Artie answered. "No, not hurt feelings, not nice." Then, getting a mischievous look on his face, he continued. "We can give c'rot latter, good Crumb."

Raising his brows at the look on Artie's face, Kiernan tried not to snicker at his attempt at subterfuge. "Yes, I am sure we can give Crumpet some carrots while I am here. As long as your parents say it is fine."

The little lip that jutted out on Artie as he looked at Kiernan had him struggling not to laugh at the boy's antics. They were going to have trouble with this kid. Highly intelligent, like both his parents and with Miss Elizabeth's zest for life. Darcy was right. He would have everyone wrapped around his little finger.

Entering the room to greet Kiernan, Mary saw the interaction he was having with Artie and could not help but snicker. Kiernan had only been back with them for a little over a day and a half, but it was almost as if he had never left. Then, thinking, she turned around and began looking for his nurse. How had he found Kiernan by himself? Where was his nurse? "Artie where is nurse Sarah?"

Artie's chubby little face became all wide eyes and innocence. "Um? Nurse Sarawh?"

Mary struggled not to laugh as Artie pretended not to understand what they were asking, as if he did not know who she was. "She is probably searching for you." Turning her gaze to Kiernan, she smiled and gave him a nod in greeting, uncertain if a boy as old as he would be willing to accept a hug from her now that he was so big and tall. "I swear we will either need to get another nurse or pay her extra not to quit for as much as she has to chase after him. I am glad you are back, Kiernan."

Kiernan looked at the young charge in his arms. "Did you sneak away from your nurse? Was that very nice of you to do?"

Sticking his lip out in shame, Artie hung his little head. Then ruined the whole effect by trying to peek up at Kiernan from under his wild mess of curls.

"Oh, Miss Bennet, have you seen young Master Arthur? He was asleep, and I only went to use the necessity, but when I returned, he had vanished." The young nursemaid's color was pale, and she was ringing her hands in a frantic manner.

Mary knew that the young woman truly had affection for her young charge and was constantly run ragged by the little man. "We have him, nurse Sarah. It seems that he somehow learned of Kiernan's presence and snuck out to find him."

"I am sorry to be the cause of your panic, nurse Sarah. I should have realized that he had snuck off." Putting little Artie on the ground, he knelt on the floor next to him. "Artie, look how scared your nurse is. Do gentlemen scare ladies like that?"

"No." Artie's small voice came out clearly, though obviously upset. Looking over at his nurse, he saw the fright in her eyes and how she was clutching at her chest. Then, launching himself as he often did, he flung himself at her. Clutching at her skirts, he looked up at her fretfully, his little eyebrow drawn together in a small tight line. "I sorry, K'nan came and I said ello. I should not leave wit out nurse Sarawh."

Reaching down, she scooped up her young charge and gave him a hug, holding him tight to her chest. "You gave me such a fright, Master Arthur. Next time, ask me if we can visit one of your friends."

Reaching up, Artie patted her cheek soothingly. "I not again. I sorry, nurse Sarawh"

"You are going to be quite the charmer in the future, but for now, we are going back to the nursery." Looking to Mary and Kiernan, she gave a little bob of a curtsy. "I am sorry to have let him get away from me."

"Think nothing of it, Sarah. I am sorry he can be such a handful. He definitely takes after Mrs. Darcy. My mother could tell you stories all day long." Mary shook her head as she watched the two of them leave. Turning back to Kiernan, she looked him over more closely this time. He had grown even since the last she had seen him at Catherine's wedding. At this rate, he would be taller than William in no time. "So, what are your plans while you are here?"

Shrugging, he said, "Nothing grand. I would like to help at Longbourn as much as I can. I am sure there is plenty that s to be done."

Studying the mean of the young man who meant so much to her family, Mary asked, "Are you sure that you want to do hard work while you are supposed to be taking a break from school?" What almost fifteen-year-old boy wanted to do hard labor when he could visit his family. Granted, his mother and father would probably put him to work on the home farm too, so there was that.

"I am more used to hard work than sitting and learning all the time. It is actually something I miss sometimes." Despite his recent rapid growth, his wide grin was the same that Mary remembered from years ago when she helped teach him to read and write. "Moreover, I prefer taking action to address a situation that needs improvement rather than passively observing it. In fact, I have even counseled men that I know that inaction is just as foolish as acting wrongly or with spite."

Mary felt her lips purse as she tried to digest what Kiernan had just said. Just who had he been speaking to, and about what? It felt as if he was speaking of something more than the reconstruction of Longbourn, but she was not quite able to grasp what. Giving up her line of thought, Mary changed the subject. "Do you have anything to keep you active at school?"

"It is not the same thing, but I have a few friends and we are learning to fence." Rubbing at the edge of his nose, a slight blush shading his cheeks. "I am becoming rather fond of it."

Mary was happy that he had seemed to find his place. Though she often worried that the rich boys would find a way to take advantage of him. "I am glad. You would tell us if the boys at school were too much, wouldn't you? I have heard some horror stories of how the boys there sometimes treat those they feel are outsiders."

Reaching out, he gave her a half hug, suggesting that he knew his sisters often worried about him. "I do well enough. I have made my own circle of friends. None of us are from the top circle, but we get along well enough." Letting go, he stepped back and smiled.

Elizabeth was still struggling with feeling unwell most mornings. Not nearly as bad, but still not well. She had, however, been doing much better in the afternoons. So it was that she had been downstairs with her whole family and Kiernan, enjoying a cozy autumn day when there was a commotion in the hall. She was happy to discover that Jane and Bingley had arrived early. Soon everyone was being greeted with a flurry of warm embraces.

After she directed the staff to make up the room for Jane and Bingley, Elizabeth cooed over their small daughter. She took so strongly after her mother that she was quite the little beauty. "Oh, Jane, she has grown so in only a few months!"

"Artie is no different. He already seems to be a complete little man." Came Jane's reply.

While Artie and little Eleanor Francine had met before, it had been before his vocabulary and rapid desire for communication had flourished. Elizabeth gathered her son close and brought him over to Eleanor. "Artie, this is your little cousin Eleanor Francine. She is younger than you, but I think you may become good friends."

Artie examined his little cousin carefully for a moment before carefully leaning in to give her a hug. "Ello Ellie," leaning back he asked, "I have bocks, you want to play?"

Elizabeth noticed the adults all exchanging smiles. Locking eyes with Jane, Elizabeth grinned at the new nickname for her niece. Ellie was the very essence of a beautiful baby. The vivid blue of her eyes and the pale complexion she inherited from her mother were strikingly beautiful. If not for her strawberry blond hair, one would think she was a copy of her mother entirely with no input from her father at all.

As all the adults followed the children into the sitting room to watch the children play, Elizabeth moved to her husband's side. When William made it to their favorite settee, he pulled her onto his lap with a grin. Seeing her expression, he said, "What? There may not be enough seats for everyone."

"Wills, there are plenty of seats for everyone." Giggling, she lay her head on his shoulder, not wanting to move in the slightest despite what she said.

They whispered back and forth, watching the children play and their family chat. Elizabeth enjoyed the comfort of her husband's hold while watching it all. Ellie had certainly inherited her mother's physical beauty, but she had inherited her father's amiable personality. Always laughing and happy, she seemed to accept everything and everyone that went on around her with a smile or a laugh. Ellie and Artie were swiftly becoming the best of friends, bonding in a way that made all the adults glad.

IT HAD BEEN SUCH an adjustment for Jane to spend so much time away from her sisters once she married. She had spent almost all of her life with them as companions and helpmates, so it was nice to be able to be with them again. Yes, they had gathered not that long ago for Kitty's wedding, but she relished any opportunity she had to be with her sisters once more.

Elizabeth, though happy and outgoing, was still pale. It had taken Jane all of a few seconds to realize what her sister's problem was when she watched the way Elizabeth nibbled at the dry toast that had been brought with her ginger tea. "Are you hoping for a girl this time, Lizzie?"

Shaking her head ruefully, Elizabeth said, "I should have known you would guess straight away. Yes, I would love to have a girl and so would William, but we shall see. This pregnancy has been rather more difficult than the last, but I am managing. Mary has made sure that I have a constant supply of the ginger tea that helps so much."

"Yes, whether or not you had said you were pregnant, there was no missing the signs. I was not about to let you suffer without a good supply of ginger. If I hadn't seen to it, then William certainly would have taken care of it. Your husband is devoted to you, Lizzie," Mary commented, and though her tone was cheerful, it did not quite match the expression that flitted across her face.

Studying Mary closer, Jane noted a sliver of disquiet in her countenance. Jane was not the oldest of five sisters for nothing. She could read them all nearly as well as she could herself. That half quirk of her lips meant Mary was unhappy about something, though she seemed to fight it. Glancing at Elizabeth, she raised her eyebrows ever so slightly. When Elizabeth pursed her lips in reply, Jane knew she would have to have a conversation with her middle sister. It would not do for her to fall into the doldrums if they could help it.

When Elizabeth left the room on the pretense that she had to see to something about dinner, Jane decided it was as good a time as any. "I hear that you were working with Mr. Goulding to help bring Longbourn back in shape." Jane looked steadily at her younger sister for a moment before saying, "That man is smitten with you, Mary." Jane set a cup of tea in front of Mary and then took to her chair across from her.

"That may be, but he certainly has done nothing about it as of yet. We have known each other for years and nothing." Mary ended her comment in a frustrated huff.

Observing her sister, Jane tilted her head. It was simple for her to note that her Mary was not her usual self, and Jane wondered if it was possible that she could help prod her to action rather than mopery. Reaching out, she took up her tea and stirred it idly with her spoon. "What age do gentleman normally start turning their minds to marriage?"

"I don't know, perhaps twenty-five or slightly older. I believe Darcy was twenty-eight years old when he married Elizabeth. Bingley was a little younger when he married you, I think." Mary paused for a moment with her eyes narrowed with obvious confusion. "Why do you ask?"

Jane maintained her serene countenance, happy to lead her sister to some new understandings. "How old is your Mr. Goulding?"

Twisting her lips in thought, Mary wondered aloud, "I know he is less than a year older than me, so I presume twenty-three?"

Nodding, Jane continued, "The reason most men wait until they are older is because it takes them that long to get set up enough to provide a home for their future wife and children. Mr. Goulding may be all that is charming, and he may be in love, but he has no home to offer you." Putting her spoon down on the saucer, Jane took a sip of her tea, savoring the warm flavor. Tea always seemed to imbue her with contentment. Jane was a woman of simple needs and desires, and her ultimate desire was for the happiness of her family and those around her. Beyond their happiness, she was content with a pleasant home and a warm cup of tea on a cool day. She had her cup of tea, and now she only needed to wait for her sister to reach out for her own happiness.

Huffing in frustration, Mary let her head fall back against her chair. "That thought is both sweet and alarming. I do not want to wait until I am twenty-four or twenty-five to marry. Even at twenty-two, people think I am a spinster."

"Then do something about it. You are not one of the helpless debutantes that the word insists most woman be." Jane looked into the eyes of her little sister and displayed the unflinching strength she had developed over time. She may be the sister most remarked upon for her serenity, but she was not weak or easily swayed. "You are a Bennet; we have all done amazing things merely trying to survive our childhood. Use some of that strength now and allow him to see that he does not have to take everything on his shoulders. If he is too afraid to step up to the challenge, move on." Shrugging in an offhanded manner, Jane continued, "You are not tied to him in any important way. You can be remarkable on your own if you must. I have faith in you."

Mary looked up at her older sister, her eyes contemplative. Jane knew there was certainly much that she was going to have to think about, but she was confident Mary would find her way.

# Chapter Eleven

THE NEXT MORNING, KIERNAN was happy to spend time playing with Artie and Ellie in the garden behind the house, their nurses looking on from a suitable distance. The children were not being raised as most children of high-class families would have been. They were allowed to play and romp and get dirty. It had been interesting to learn from the boys he met at school about how differently they were raised. He was glad that neither the Darcy nor the Bingley families believed that children should be kept indoors and trained up to be little porcelain copies of their fathers and mothers without a thought to themselves.

"Look, K'nan!" Artie waved at his older friend in gleeful ignorance of the mud flinging off his hands as he did so. "Mud House!"

Kiernan approached the two children carefully. With the discovery of a muddy patch between two rosebushes, the cousins had promptly attempted an endeavor to build some form of structure with the sticky, clumpy substance. Mud clung to both their hands and up their arms, while some had even made its way on to Artie's face.

"Don't you two look like you are having fun! Are you building a house?"

Nodding gleefully, Artie answered, "Yes, mud house."

"Mud house, I stand corrected." Grinning ruefully at the pair, he knew that they would both be in for a bath later, but for the moment he wouldn't worry. He was glad they were enjoying themselves. "Who is going to live in your mud house?"

While Ellie, who was still not very talkative at all, played by patting the substance into a form that she liked, Artie seemed to ponder the question. Tilting his head, his mud-smudged face lit up with glee as he said, "Crumb House."

Laughing out loud, Kiernan smiled. He could see the cunning in Artie's eyes. The lad was making a joke. "You expect that great big horse to fit in there? I think you have some proportion problems if you think he is going to fit."

"Not Crumb, little Crumb." Gesturing with his muddy hands, Artie implied a small toy size horse. Then pointing to Kiernan, he said, "You make little Crumb."

"You want me to make you something to be Crumpet?"

"Yes, little Crumb. I make house. Ellie help." With the attitude of a much older person issuing orders, Artie dismissed Kiernan to apparently make a toy horse to go with their mud house. Ellie, clearly happy to be playing and helping her older cousin, looked up and smiled at Kiernan. She babbled a few indecipherable phrases before once again concentrating on squelching the gooey substance through her fingers.

Standing up from his squat next to them, Kiernan cast about, looking for a few sticks or something with which he could build a small horse. There had to be something he could use.

EVALINE WAS NOT HAPPY. Not happy in the least. She would have kicked at a pebble to vent her frustration, but she knew it was not a ladylike endeavor. So she refrained from kicking anything, though that did not help her feel better, only angrier.

Ignored for the majority of her life, Evaline had recently had her loving nurse taken away, only to be replaced by a strict and overbearing governess who found nothing she did satisfactory. All she heard now was, "Young ladies do not do this, young ladies do not do that." For the life of her, she could not fathom what young ladies might actually do besides die of boredom and frustration.

She had jumped at the chance to accompany her brother to Netherfield, not because she wished to see the ladies of the house, but because she just had to get away from her governess. Any more of her strict control and Evaline might just scream. Or not—who knows what punishment that kind of behavior might merit? Only that morning, her governess had threatened to make her walk with the book on her head again for slouching as she read. When her brother had asked her to join him, she had been eager to escape for a time.

While her brother spoke with the fancy Mr. Darcy, she decided to explore a little. The moment she stepped outside, she felt a surge of liberation and fully embraced the idea of newfound freedom. She had told Gabriel that she would speak with the Bennet sisters, and she might...eventually. Who knew? Perhaps they were outside. Her mother had never been shy about her disapproval of the now Mrs. Darcy, always complaining that Mrs. Darcy had grown up to be a hoyden, often traipsing around and getting *dirty*.

Coming around a bend in the path as she walked through the garden, she spotted two young children playing in the mud. Upon closer inspection, she realized they were not even children but babies. Who let their babies alone long enough to play in the mud? Looking around, she tried to see if there was a nurse or someone about that should have been taking the children in hand. She certainly would never have been allowed to play that way.

Spotting no one but an older boy who was looking the other way, Evaline gave a little huff. Just what should she do? Her thought process stopped when she saw the smaller of the two babies get up and toddle towards her.

The little child was coated in mud and, though she had the most angelic smile, Evaline shook her head in revulsion. A string of baby jabber did not warm Evaline up to the small thing either. As the youngest child of her family, who had never been exposed to young children, she was completely out of sorts with the situation. When the little girl tried to hand her a blob of mud, it was simply the last straw. Shoving the small figure away with more force than was strictly required, Evaline was appalled to watch her tumble backwards into a rosebush.

Though not screaming or sobbing, the small face with shockingly blue eyes looked at her with such hurt and confusion that Evaline was cut to the quick. When tears welled up and fell down her mud-streaked cheeks, it made Evaline want to cry herself. Evaline was trying to decide what she could or should do when a small tornado of fury popped out of nowhere and made her wish she had never agreed to come to Netherfield.

"No. No! Bad you not hurt Ellie! No!" Artie stood his ground in front of his crying cousin. Arms outstretched, he blocked the stranger from causing her more harm. He did not understand why someone would hurt his little Ellie, but he was going to stop it if he could. Though looking at the bigger girl, he realized it would not be easy to stop her if she tried again. Looking around frantically, he screamed, "K'Nan!" Then looking at the girl again, he scolded, "No hurt Ellie!"

Rushing to Artie as he heard the tyke shout, Kiernan tried to take in the situation with a swift glance. Poor little Ellie was in a rosebush, big tears silently running down her cheeks. Artie's chubby face was red with anger and a girl he did not recognize looked as though she was appalled by the entire situation. He looked askance at the girl as he passed her to scoop up little Ellie.

Artie looked up at Kiernan. His little face was as fierce as an almost two-year-old could be. He pointed at the intruder, his finger shaking, and explained, "K'nan! Bad girl hurt Ellie."

"I can see that, little man. Thank you for trying to protect her." Looking over, he saw the nurses rushing their way. He rubbed Ellie's back, trying to soothe her as she burrowed into his chest looking for comfort.

Though the stranger did seem to look at Ellie with concern, any possibility of such emotion was ruined by her words. "I do not know who you are, but the child fell all on her own." With her nose in the air, the unknown girl flipped her brown hair over her shoulder.

Ellie peeked out at the girl from under her muddy strawberry locks. Her lower lip trembled momentarily before she offered one of the few words she knew. "No."

"Bad girl lies, K'nan. Lies bad!" Artie shook his finger at her again, then looked up at Kiernan with a thoughtful look that suggested his young mind was busy plotting something mischievous. "I kick her maybe?"

Gently placing a restraining hand on Artie's small shoulder, Kiernan forced himself not to laugh at the lad's vengeful intentions. "No, Arthur Theodore, you will not kick her. No matter what she may have done, you are a gentleman, and gentlemen do not ever hurt ladies or girls, no matter how unmannerly they behave." Handing Ellie to her worried nurse, he returned his attention to the stranger.

Eyes growing round under his scrutiny, the girl glanced around nervously. "I do not know who these filthy children are, but I will have you know that I am the daughter of one of the most prominent landowners in the area. Who do you think people will believe—me or these two filthy brats?"

Kiernan's eyes narrowed at the girl's words. Leaning down, he scooped up Artie before the tyke did something rash. "Why don't we go inside so that you may meet the parents of 'these filthy children' and we can see whom they believe?" Without waiting for a response, he marched toward the house, and knowing that Mr. Darcy would be in his study, Kiernan made his way there directly.

***

Mary sat in her sitting room with a book in her lap. She was trying to read one of her old favorites, but she could not find the concentration to focus on any of the words on the page. The sea of fuzzy words did nothing to settle her thoughts or her unease.

More so than her other sisters, she was always one for following the rules. Showing respect for the proper way of things meant something to her. She had a sort of need, or maybe compulsion for the order that it provided. But now this need for order was causing her a problem. Rules of society dictated that a woman never approached the gentleman about their attachment. Instead, they waited for him to make the first move. Mary had been waiting, and waiting, and she felt she had been more than patient, yet she had nothing to show for it.

Could she possibly approach Mr. Goulding and let him know how she felt about the matter? Ever since she spoke with Jane, the unusual thought did not seem so implausible anymore. However, it did bring up another issue—how did she feel about the possibility of ending their friendship? Mary had often shied away from looking the issue in the face, as it made her too sad. Mary forced herself to examine her emotions and admit that yes, she loved Mr. Goulding. She wanted to have a future with him. She wanted to find a way to make it work, but was continuing to wait around for him to make a move, any move, something she was willing to do?

Mary focused on what she wanted. She wanted a life with the man she loved. She wanted a chance to have children. Mary was not stupid. She knew he could not offer her the estates and fancy things that her sister's husbands had at their disposal, but to her, none of that mattered. She was not fond of London or society at large. Mary liked helping people. She would love the opportunity to teach children wherever they were.

Could she wait for him on whatever his timetable was? Did she deserve to have to wait? If she confronted Mr. Goulding, what would she say? Though Jane had said she was strong, Mary was uncertain if that strength meant she had the audacity needed to disregard societal expectations. Or did it? Could she demand he propose to her, or was it beyond what she was capable of? If he decided that he did not want a life with her, what did she want to do?

Now that was a question. If she could not have Mr. Goulding and his love, she did not think she could just marry someone else. She was incapable of marrying one man while loving another. It was in her mind a betrayal to herself as well as whoever she married. No, if she did not marry Mr. Goulding, she would ask to manage Longbourn. She had joked about it before with her sisters, but she was uncertain if they ever realized that she had been half serious.

Jane was right about her strength and if forced, she would have the fortitude to do what she must to find her way to happiness. She would not allow Gabriel's stubborn refusal to act to curtail her joy any longer. She began to formulate a plan in small stages. It would not be easy, but it was necessary. She would need a tremendous amount of courage, but she felt that it was going to be her best chance at happiness.

# Chapter Twelve

Looking up from his conversation with Mr. Goulding at his desk, his smile for his son and Kiernan never wavered despite the fact that his son was covered in mud and Kiernan appeared rather perturbed. Putting down his writing implement he asked, "What can I help you with Kiernan?" Watching his son fume but remain quiet, Darcy managed not to laugh, but only just. Though Artie seemed to have an equal sharing of his parents' qualities when it came to the expression on his face, at that moment, it was all his Elizabeth.

With an amount of eye contact that communicated volumes, Kiernan spoke up with a civil tone despite any misgivings he may have had. "Well, Mr. Darcy, this young *lady* is in a disagreement about a few things with Artie."

Noticing his sister, Mr. Goulding turned in his chair to face her, "Evaline? What is going on? I thought you were going to visit with the ladies?" Looking her over, he observed that though she seemed uninjured, she did not seem happy about the current situation at all.

Glancing momentarily at the dirty face of Artie who stared at her in contempt she looked back to her brother and after straitening her shoulders began her story. "I was outside in the garden when two dirty children started crying some nonsense. I do not know what is going on."

Taking a moment to study his son, Darcy saw that all was not well. Only a child as precocious as his own could pull off such a look of wrath despite a thorough coating of mud. Artie's glare seemed capable of piercing through the strongest armor. "Artie, do you have something to say?" Darcy already knew that there was going to be quite the story. His son's expressive green eyes held a world of anger.

Looking first at Evaline and then his father Artie began his impassioned declaration, "Bad girl is liar! Ellie was nice. Bad girl, not nice, she push Ellie. Ellie fell an' cry. Bad girl lie." Shaking his tiny, pointed finger at the culprit, he growled in anger. Then pausing, he seemed to consider something and then added, "I not kick bad girl 'cause, she girl, kicking girls wrong, K'nan said. But bad girl still lies!"

Placing his hand in front of his mouth, Darcy covered the grin that he could not help. The earnest confession of his son not kicking the girl was too much, but he knew he had to remain stoic for the moment. "Mighty charges indeed." Looking to Kiernan, he asked, "What did you observe?"

"While I had my back turned for a moment, I did not see the initial confrontation. I did, however, turn to see Ellie stuck in a rose bush crying and little Artie here standing protectively in front of her telling the young lady that she was bad and she should not hurt Ellie. He was quite adamant in his protection of his cousin." Looking down at the muddy tyke in his arms, he ruffled his hair. "You would be proud."

"Evaline, how could you?" Mr. Goulding could not look more disappointed if he tried to. Then turning to Darcy, his face contrite, he apologized. "I am so sorry, Mr. Darcy. I do not know what came over my sister. I had thought giving the chance to spend time with Mrs. Darcy, Mrs. Bingley, and Miss Bennet would help her, but I never would have brought her here if I had thought she would behave thusly."

Eyes wide and pleading, her lips stretched in a wordless oh for some moments. Evaline managed to ground out, "Brother, you would apologize for my behavior over what that little boy said? He cannot even speak in proper sentences."

"Yes, I would take his word over yours. Go stand in the hall, Evaline, you will come with me to Longbourn after you apologize to Mrs. Bingley and Mrs. Darcy for your behavior towards their children."

With an inarticulate sound that was akin to an outraged cat being bathed, Evaline turned and stalked out of the room. Her head held high, though if one were to look closely, they could see tears in her eyes. She disappeared through the door, not quite slamming it behind her.

Coming out from behind his desk, Darcy gestured to Kiernan with his chin, signaling that he should set his son down, mud and all. Then, with his son standing before him, he knelt so that he could look him in the eye. "Kiernan is right. We do not kick girls and

I am glad that you did not hurt Evaline, no matter what she may have done." Pausing, he made sure that his son seemed to absorb the information. Artie nodded his little head as if aware of the serious nature of their discussion. "I am proud of you, Artie. You did what you could to protect your little cousin. Well done, my boy."

"Tan'k you Papa. I check Ellie now?"

"I believe that you will need to bathe first as you are rather muddy, but then yes, you may check on your cousin." Looking up at Kiernan, Darcy asked, "She was not hurt too badly, was she?"

"No, I think she was mostly just shocked that she had been treated differently than she was used to. She might have a scrape or two from the rosebush, though her nurse bundled her away quickly, so I am not sure." Kiernan looked down at his own muddy clothes. "I am sure her nurse probably intended to give her a bath as well. She was just as muddy as we have turned out to be."

Tapping his son on his muddy nose, Darcy asked, "Artie what were you doing that you got so dirty?"

Artie beamed proudly, saying, "Mud house for Crumb."

Smiling, Darcy looked up at Kiernan, glad that the boy was so tolerant of his son's various entertainments. Kiernan was getting to the age where boys could start to turn off their original course. By fifteen, Wickham had already begun laying wagers on one thing or another and cheating where he could. Yet Kiernan was ever the same, ever good and loyal to those he counted as friends and family. He was what his father had wanted to foster in Wickham, what never was but could have been. "Of course, and what were you doing, Kiernan?"

Grinning with all seriousness that Artie would expect of him, he answered, "Oh, I had been tasked with building a Crumb. They needed a horse to go with the house."

"Little Crumb." Artie showed with his hands how big the little crumb was going to be before things had gone wrong.

"An important endeavor indeed." With one last ruffle of his son's hair, Darcy nodded to Kiernan, who scooped up Artie. He would spare his valet a fit of the vapors by saving his clothes from the mud if he could. "Go get and clean. The both of you. Mrs. Nichols will have my hide if she sees either of you tracking mud all around the house."

"Come along scamp, let's go get you clean and then I will get clean as well." Swinging Artie around a bit before they left the room, Kiernan gave the boy a conspiratorial grin. "Do you think you have any clothes I could borrow? You are the one who got me dirty, after all."

"No, you not fit my clothes, you too big!" Giggles followed Artie and Kiernan out of the room as they went.

After the door closed behind them, Mr. Goulding began, "I am so sorry about Evaline."

Waving his comment off, Darcy settled more comfortably in his chair. "I am sure Eleanor is fine. I would say think nothing of it, but I know you will, regardless. We none of us are responsible for the actions of others. I can tell that you are trying to help her along a better path."

Shaking his head in apparent discouragement, Mr. Goulding sighed. "I was away at school for so much of her life. I am just trying to get to know her, and I am finding I am not fond of who it is that she has been trained to become."

Trying to help his young friend. Darcy pondered what to say for a moment. He had become better at expressing himself, but he still had to think about things at times so that he was not offending people. "I understand what you mean. It is worth noting that sometimes we can become the people we are despite the influences of our parents and the people who raise us. She is still young enough to forge her own path. I do not think her personality is a set thing, be patient with her." Darcy looked at the plans on the table. "I think that the plans we have in place for the first few tenant homes will work and the glaciers have finished the windows. So we can be confident that there will be no more damage to the floors moving forward. What were you planning on working on today?"

JANE SAT, LOOKING AT the little girl before her. Around twelve maybe, she had brown hair that appeared to have fallen out of curls. Though she was apologizing, it was in a very unapologizing way. There was no regret and possibly only the slightest amount of remorse. "I have already checked on Eleanor, and she seems fine, all things considering." Giving the sulky girl a smile that was rather wide and genuine, Jane tilted her head "I thank you for your apology,

Evaline. Maybe in the future you can find another way to protect your nice dress. Eleanor was really rather muddy and though the mud will wash out, I can understand your hesitation with the dirt."

Evaline's eyes widened, apparently shocked that the beautiful woman in front of her had guessed the issue with little difficulty. "I am not fond of mud, and neither is my mother."

Jane's eyes widened in even greater understanding. The poor girl had one of those mothers who might very well punish her for even the smallest hair out of place, or a speck of mud on an outfit. She watched as Evaline gave a precise curtsy and walked out of the room and into the hallway.

Mr. Goulding stepped forward, his apprehension still evident in the hard lines on his face. "Thank you for speaking with my sister. I had thought that you and your sisters might be positive influences on her. I never would have brought her with me if I had thought she would act in such a manner."

Smiling at the man she hoped would one day be her brother-in-law, Jane said, "Do not worry too much about it. Despite everything, I am more than willing to have her visit again. She is at a very hard age, and I am sure that with time, my sisters and I could help her find her way."

"That is very kind of you. For today I will take her with me to Longbourn. I want to check on how some of the plaster is drying and if the new door for one of the tenant cottages has been delivered."

Looking out the nearby window, Jane frowned at the visible gathering of clouds in the sky. "Do be careful to keep an eye on the weather. I would hate for you two to be caught in a downpour. Autumn weather here can be very intemperate."

"I am sure we will be fine, Mrs. Bingley. The weather has cooperated thus far." With a bow, Mr. Goulding excused himself and left the room.

Jane frowned as he left. Just because the weather had cooperated thus far did not mean that it would continue to do so. Rolling her eyes, as she only did when she was alone or with her sisters, Jane rang for more tea. She just did not understand how men thought sometimes.

MARY MADE HER WAY to the stables just in time to see Mr. Goulding and his sister leave. She had heard from one of the maids that there had been a bit of a kerfuffle between Evaline and the children. Though she did not know the specifics, she had hoped to take advantage of Mr. Goulding's presence to speak with him about what was in her heart. She could wait until the next day, but she was afraid her courage would falter. Mary continued to ponder, a frown forming on her face.

"Did you need something, Miss Mary?" Kiernan's voice came from further down in one of the stalls.

Whirling, Mary put her hand over her pounding heart. She had thought she was alone in her contemplation. "Oh, Kiernan, I did not see you there. I was hoping to catch Mr. Goulding before he left."

Looking after the swiftly retreating figure of the two riders, Mary continued in a much harder tone of voice. "I had wanted to have a much overdue conversation with the gentleman."

"I could saddle one of the horses for you if you wanted to follow him. It would not take you long to catch up. Besides, they are only going to Longbourn. It is not far, and you know the way." Kiernan smiled mischievously and wagged his eyebrows. "I am sure that you are eager to have this conversation with him as soon as possible."

Mary hesitated a moment, considering the implications of following after Mr. Goulding. It was not the most proper idea she had ever had, but then again, being proper had not brought her the one thing she desired most. It was not completely out of the bounds either. Mary was sure there would be workers at Longbourn who could act as chaperones, and then there was also  Evaline. Squaring her shoulders, Mary nodded her head confidently. She knew that if she wanted to confront the man she loved, she had to summon the courage to follow after him. "Maybe that is a good idea. I am certain he would prefer our conversation to be private." Mary knew the way she responded fully implied it may very well become an argument or a lesson in patience, depending on how things progressed.

Helping Mary up into the side saddle that he had affixed to her horse, Kiernan gave the placid mare a pat before looking up at her. "I am planning on going over soon enough, so if you need me to, I can have a conversation with him as well." Then, as she nudged her horse into action, he added, "Be careful on your ride, Miss Mary."

Mary had become a competent horsewoman in the time since Elizabeth had married and they had moved to Pemberley. William's property was so much larger than Longbourn that she could not properly visit the tenants without the ability to ride. She was not going to win any races, especially side saddle, but she was perfectly capable of making her way to Longbourn. Normally she would take a groom with her if she went about, but she had been in such a rush that she did not think of it. But it was no matter. There would be any number of grooms at Longbourn doing various things, in addition to Mr. Goulding and Evaline.

In no time at all, she had arrived at Longbourn and was happy to see that it was a small hive of activity already looking much better than the last time she had seen it. The piles of trash were gone and there were no longer any broken windows marring its once proud frame. Her review of her childhood home came up short, however, when she heard Mr. Goulding's angry voice.

"How could you? Eleanor is barely more than a baby, all of fourteen months. What could she have done that would make you shove her down?" Mr. Goulding shook his head, disappointment and anger evident in every line of his face and body.

Shaking her head so much that her hair swirled around her head in a curtain, Evaline cried. "I don't know. She was all muddy. I..." Trailing off, she looked up, her eyes glistening, her small shoulders trembling with repressed emotion.

"You what, Evaline? Shoved a toddler into a rosebush because she was muddy?" Running his hand through his hair in frustration, Mr.

Goulding sighed. "I know we have never been close. I was away at school for most of your life, but I am just now realizing how much I do not know you. My own sister... And to have you act in such a way that I am ashamed. I like and respect that family a great deal, and you embarrassed me by your actions."

"You do not understand! No one understands." Her last words were soft and barely audible. With one last hurt look, she dashed away, running through the garden and into what had once been the little wilderness the Bennet ladies had cultivated so long ago.

Having quietly dismounted from her horse during the argument, Mary walked over to Mr. Goulding. When he had not noticed her approach, she spoke up, "You were rather harsh on your little sister."

"Miss M... Miss Bennet, I did not know you were there."

Tilting her head, Mary smiled blandly. "Yes, well, I did not feel it was right to make myself known during your fight."

Eyebrows raised in confusion, he said, "I am surprised that you would be so kind to her. She pushed your niece into a rosebush."

"It appeared to me that she was struggling and was remorseful. I am not saying that her actions were acceptable by any means, but she appears to be having a difficult time and may need support, not castigation." Mary squared off against Mr. Goulding as her own frustration with him fed into their dispute.

After a moment of hesitation, Mr. Goulding made a face, his voice lacking its previous vigor as he asked, "What makes you say that?"

"I grew up with four sisters and I know more of what her heart must be struggling with. When I was her age, I came upon Fordyce's sermons. I would have done much better if someone had questioned why I had become so obsessed than merely rolling their eyes and avoiding me. Instead, it took several years for someone to realize my insecurities and get me to come out of my shell." Looking at the broken home reflected so much of her broken childhood, Mary shrugged. "Not that I blame anyone, of course. Life then was difficult for us all."

Nosing the tip of his boot in the dirt at his feet, Mr. Goulding seemed to think before he responded. "I will take it into consideration. As it is, I barely know my sister and I am finding that I am not fond of what I am discovering about her." Then, narrowing his eyes at her, his eyebrows drawn together in question, he asked, "Why are you here, Miss Bennet? The maids are not working today, and there are not any tasks for you to do. I was only going to check on the plasterwork that was drying and see that the woodwork had been delivered as it should have been."

Catching a loose strand of hair blowing in her face, Mary tucked it behind her ear in frustration. She hated it when her hair came loose and got in her face. "We need to talk, and you left Netherfield too quickly for me to speak with you before you rode off."

Eyes widening slightly, Mr. Goulding swallowed convulsively before speaking, "Speak with me? What about?"

Eye narrowing at the sign of nervousness in the man before her, Mary plunged forward, earnestly desiring to learn the truth. "What are your intentions with regard to our relationship, Mr. Goulding?"

EVALINE SAT ON A bench under an overgrown arbor, weeping for all that she was worth. Why were things so difficult? Her mother found her lacking, her father ignored her existence, and now her brother was disappointed in her.

Gabriel was right. He did not know her much at all and they had never spent much time together, but she had half hoped that he would become an ally of sorts. After all, mother and father did not care for him just as much as they did not care for her.

Of course, there was also her other brother Jude, but he had tormented her whenever he could. When she was younger, he would push her into the mud and then tell mother that he saw her playing in the mud. How many times had she gone without dinner as punishment for something he did? Now all she received from him was petty sniping at her looks and deportment.

Why had she pushed the little girl? She had been so happy despite being covered in mud, but that had changed so fast. Her angelic features had quickly turned into something sad and pitiable. It was as if she did not understand, could not comprehend her goodness being rejected. Or possibly, the very concept of mistreatment was foreign to her.

And that little boy! He was astounding. Evaline knew she had never really been around children of his size, but did they all speak that much? He had moved so quickly to protect his little cousin. He showed such passion and determination to do what was right at such a young age.

Would anyone ever want to protect her in such a manner? If Jude had seen her pushed into a rosebush, he would not have tried to help or protect her. He would have laughed. Her mother would have berated her for soiling her dress. Her father would not have noticed. What would Gabriel have done? She could not know. At one time she would have hoped that he would come to her rescue, but now, with his disappointment in her evident she was uncertain.

Getting up, she continued along the overgrown path, heart sore and confused. She knew that someone might come looking for her, but until then, she wanted to walk. Something made her crave movement. If no one was watching, no one would complain about having the proper posture or keeping her eyes demurely cast to the ground. The little wilderness she had found was pretty, even if all the leaves had mostly fallen. It could not hurt to explore it for a while. Her brother had said he had work to do, anyway.

# Chapter Thirteen

Gabriel stared at the woman before him. It was easy to see that she was rather put out with him. Her lips were compressed into a hard line, and her eyebrows were raised as if to encourage a prompt response by communicating her evident impatience. God, how he loved her. Looking at her, even with her angry at him, struck home how much he cared for Mary. Apparently, Gabriel had watched her anger for far too long without the inclination to respond because her eyes went from questioning to hardened.

"I have, up until this point, been operating under the idea that you had feelings for me. I had hoped that given time, our shared emotional attachment, or if I may be impertinent to say our love, would lead us to the happy state of marriage. I had assumed that was something that we were both hoping for, and yet I have waited, and nothing has proceeded according to my assumptions." Hazel eyes snapping in growing frustration, Mary forged forward. "Now I know this is probably my fault. Assuming things is never wise, I know. It is much better to have a full understanding of the matter. So,

I will ask again, what are your intentions in regard to our relationship, Mr. Goulding?"

Forcing himself to respond instead of simply watching a side of Mary that he rarely got to see, Gabriel responded the only way he could. "You know I care for you."

"So you care for me?" Rearing back as if he had slapped her, Mary all but growled. "I thought as much, but that still does not leave me with the answer that I want. No, more than that, it is an answer that I need."

Despite the cool temperatures and the autumn wind, Gabriel began to sweat. Kiernan had been right; Mary was hurt by his hesitation, and this was the result.

"Is it my looks that make you hesitate, or something more material? I know that of my sisters I am the least handsome, but I long ago decided that if a man truly loved me, something as fleeting as beauty would not keep him from declaring himself." Hand clutching her throat, Mary shook her head. "I thought you were the sort of man who could love me for the person I am and not be distracted by my less than stellar attributes."

Shocked to the core by her statement, Gabriel finally found it within himself to reply in an ardent fashion. "Less than stellar attributes? What have I ever done or said to leave you to believe that I did not find you attractive? I know your sisters are spoken of for their beauty, and I suppose they are pretty enough, but different people have different tastes. My tastes lean towards a woman with ever changing hazel eyes that snap gloriously when angry. Of all your sisters, no, of all the ladies I know, you have the most fascinating hair I have ever seen. It is not blonde, but neither is it simply brown. It is something in between and everything at once. Gold and bronze and glorious." Reaching out, he caught one of the strands of hair that had come loose and was flying about her face in the most distracting fashion. Then, taking care, he tucked it behind her ear, letting his thumb brush lingeringly over the crest of her cheek before he brought his hand back into his own space.

Mary's eyes widened into something akin to surprise. Then, swallowing, she gave a wobbly smile. It was not exactly confident, but it was an improvement on her earlier scowl. "That is not something you had ever told me before."

"It is not something, strictly speaking, I should tell you. Society demands that two single people have very little contact and time to actually speak with one another. Comments like that are meant for once people were engaged at the very least." Sighing, Gabriel took a moment to look around the abandoned yard. "Strictly speaking, we should not be here alone and speaking as we are."

"But I thought surely there would be workers here." Looking around, Mary saw that indeed they were alone. Narrowing her eyes, she looked back at Gabriel, a blush spreading across her cheeks. "Well, at least your sister is here to chaperone."

Grinning at Mary's growing embarrassment, Gabriel said, "Well, the workers had to go into Meryton to gather more supplies this morning. As for my sister acting as chaperone, do you mean my sister that ran off and left us alone?"

Seeing the grin, Mary tilted her head and narrowed her eyes. "No matter how we found ourselves in this situation, I will not lose the opportunity to speak with you as I must." Taking a breath to begin another argument, Mary became distracted when something cold struck her face. Absentmindedly touching her cheek, she looked at the sky, her eyes widening in dismay.

The wind had been picking up steadily for some time, but their argument had distracted them both from the implication of such an action. Now looking up, they both took in the churning sky and the foreboding feel in the air. Between one breath and the next, the wind brought with it sleet, pelting them both with hard pellets of ice and a biting cold.

"We have to get to shelter." Reaching out, Gabriel grabbed his horse's bridle and moved towards his sister's placid mount, who had been munching on random plants in the yard. Rushing to the stable, he called to Mary, his voice wiped around in the ever-increasing wind. "Get in the house. I will get your horse next."

Mary, who had already been leading her horse to the stable, rolled her eyes and shouted back at him, "I am perfectly capable of leading my horse to the stable."

Gabriel rushed the horses to the stalls and was glad to see that the area was well stocked, and there would be enough room for the three horses. The mare saw the hay and instantly began placidly munching again. Fox, his gelding, seemed to sense the change in the air and threw his head unhappily stomping in the stall where he had been placed. Gabriel cursed his inattention. He could sense the drop in temperature, a sure sign that snow was lurking within the dark clouds.

Mary came in to the stable and escorted her mare into the last stall, but then instead of moving into the house like Gabriel expected, she ran off. Boggled at her sudden action, he left the horses and ran after her. "What are you doing? Get in the house!"

Not even bothering to turn and speak to him, she shouted over the howling wind. "Have you forgotten your sister is out in this? She is most likely upset and scared. We must find her before it becomes too difficult to see."

Grabbing her by the shoulders, Gabriel forced Mary to face him. "I will find her. Go back to the house!"

"No!" If she had the time, Gabriel knew the mutiny on her face would have shown itself in a stomp of her foot, but Mary wrenched herself free and forged on. "I know Longbourn land better than you do. Even overgrown and in a snowstorm, I have a better chance of finding her and making it back to the house safely."

Snow was blowing around them, quickly coating the landscape in white. Gabriel could see Mary shiver. None of them were in winter clothes and the dramatic drop in temperature was quickly becoming a problem. Realizing that it would not do to fight the issue, Gabriel merely nodded his head and gestured her forward. "Fine, lead the way."

Rushing on, Mary called back to him, "She went into the little wilderness."

"This looks like more than a little wilderness. This is a wilderness, wilderness." They were having to shout now in order to be heard over the storm.

He could imagine her huff of frustration by the movement of her shoulders, but he could certainly not hear it. Mary took the time to look at him for a brief moment before saying, "It was less of a wilderness before it was left on its own for a couple of years."

Were they really have one of their first real arguments in the midst of a snowstorm while searching for his missing little sister? "Do you know where Evaline might have gone to take cover?" Mary had been right. Though it was not impossible to see, it was quickly getting to the point to where he was having difficulty recognizing their surroundings. Of course, he had never visited Mary at Longbourn. He had been to Darcy House in London and to Pemberley as well as the Bingley estate, but never Longbourn.

Arms wrapped around herself and her shawl up around her head, Mary called back over her shoulder. "There is a bench up ahead under what was an arbor, but after that, the path veers off with little shelter before the great oak at the extremity of what we called our little wilderness. The closest buildings to Longbourn are part of the old Anderson farm, and that is over a mile away. She won't have made it that far in such a short period of time."

Casting his gaze around despite the swirling snow, Gabriel searched for his sister's form with ever-increasing anxiety. It did not help that she had been wearing a pale cream dress with blue ribbons. She would blend in with the weather. Once they reached the bench, he paused and, taking a great breath, shouted for his sister. His only answer was the howl of the wind.

EVALINE COULD NOT UNDERSTAND what had happened. The weather and been breezy but that had swiftly changed. A breeze had grown into wind and then sleet and snow. Now she was huddled at the base of a tree, wondering how long it would take her to freeze to death. Sneezing uncontrollably, she franticly rummaged through her pockets with numb fingers. She celebrated the minor victory of finding her handkerchief. With her luck in this weather, her snot was going to freeze running down her face.

She had ducked down by the tree, hoping to get out of the wind, but she was finding it ineffective. Evaline knew she had to make her way back, but she did not know which way to go. With everything covered in a layer of snow, things were beginning to look the same wherever she looked. She had considered forging ahead despite that, but what if she ended up going farther away from the house?

No, she would stay where she was and then maybe someone could find her. The question was, however, did anyone want to find her? Was her brother looking? It would, of course, make sense that she froze to death on the worst day of her life. It was only fitting. Curling into as small of a ball as she could muster, Evaline tried not to cry. The freezing temperature made tears on her face only slightly more bearable than the idea of frozen snot.

IT WAS GETTING HARDER to trudge along as the feeling in his feet was slowly fading. Gabriel knew that could not be good. He had to find his sister and get her and Mary back to Longbourn. While he was wearing fairly sturdy work boots, he did not know what either of the girls were wearing. He only knew that whatever it was had not seemed sturdy at all.

Suddenly, Mary tripped and started to fall. Grabbing her by the arm, he pulled her into his side, intending to share his warmth and keep her steady. He hoped that by working together, they would be less likely to succumb to the environment. They had ceased arguing and instead were saving their breath to scream for Evaline.

"Evaline!" Once again Mary shouted, then shaking her head. He felt her shudder and cry, "I am afraid she will fall asleep in the cold and not hear us. We have to find her, Gabriel. We must!"

It was the first time his name had crossed her lips in his hearing, and despite the biting cold, he felt a flash of joy. It meant a lot to him that, despite everything, she wanted to help him find his sister. She always cared for people and helped however she could. She was the best person he knew and here she was risking everything to help him for no other reason than it needed to be done and she could do it. He would find a way to explain it to her, to make everything up to her, but first he had to find his sister and get them both back to the safety of Longbourn.

"Are we close to the oak tree you spoke of?" Nearly frantic, Gabriel looked in all directions but saw nothing that could have told him where his sister went.

"Yes, we are not far. There is a fence just past it. I do not think she would have gone past the fence. If we hit the fence, we must have passed her up in the snow." Mary spoke into his shoulder as Gabriel tried to protect her from the wind and snow as much as he could.

Gabriel once again called out, afraid that his voice would soon grow hoarse. "Evaline! We are coming! Evaline!"

He continued to march on with Mary at his side. He could see the shadow of the oak through the snow now, and he worried they had passed his sister somehow. Suddenly, Mary halted and grabbed at his sleeve. Worried, he looked at her.

"I think I heard something," Stepping away from him Mary screamed once more, "Evaline! Let us know where you are!"

"Here," a small voice called out above the storm, "I am here!"

Gabriel searched franticly in the ever-growing wall of white but could not see her. Her voice had been so buffeted by the snow that he could not tell exactly where it had come from. When Mary began moving at a hurried pace, he followed her, hoping desperately that she knew where she was going and that his sister would be at the end of their rush into the wall of white.

Soon enough, he saw movement in front of him and he knew it was his sister. "Evaline!" Gabriel did not know what else to say to his little sister. It was clear that he had come or was coming close to losing her. They still had to make their way back to the manor.

It seemed like forever before her weight was ramming into him. As he wrapped his arms around her, he felt a sense of relief wash over him, as if he could finally exhale after holding his breath for ages. Looking down, all he saw was her snow-covered hair, but he could feel her trembling.

Taking off her shawl, Mary wrapped it around Evaline's slight form. "Oh, you poor dear, we must get you inside and dry."

Pulling her head back, Evaline's tear-stained face looked at Mary in desperation. "I couldn't tell which way to go."

"And that is why I came to find you. I know the way." Looking up at Gabriel, her eyes filled with worry, Mary said, "We must hurry. Can you carry her?"

Scooping up his sister, he pressed her against his chest, feeling a sense of discomfort as he noticed the sound of her teeth chattering while she nuzzled her face into the curve of his neck. "Yes, but like Evaline, I am lost. You were right to say you needed to help. Will you lead the way?"

Sparing a moment to grin at him despite the urgent conditions, Mary nodded. "I will not give in to saying I told you so."

The storm's fury continued to amplify as they made their way, both stumbling on unseen obstacles. Though it was the same path that they had traversed on the way out to find Evaline, it became more arduous with every step. Gabriel watched Mary forge ahead of him. Only she seemed to know the way while he was lost in a white-coated wilderness.

# Chapter Fourteen

Mary cast about for landmarks. Never in her memory had a storm come up this quickly at Longbourn. Though, to be fair, she was not paying attention to the weather as she fought with Gabriel. There she spotted the low hedge around what was once had been Jane's herb garden. They were going in the right direction, at least.

She did not bother to speak. She knew it would waste energy that she did not have. Even now, she could feel the tremble running along her muscles at the exertion of slogging through the rough terrain. In the span of what must be less than an hour, there were already several inches of snow, possibly as much as six. Her slight half boots were certainly not up to the task as snow kept sloshing over the sides and creeping down her ankle.

After an eternity, Mary finally saw the edge of the house. Her heart leapt within her. Finally! Shelter was near. They had to rush and get dry and warm, or they would all be horribly sick. They might be sick anyway, but staying out any longer would be worse. Calling back to the silent bulwark of support that was Mr. Goulding, Mary said, "We are almost there! Can you see the house?"

As if spurred on by the sight, Mr. Goulding nodded and picked up his pace and passed Mary up. She had to admit that it was easier to follow him because she could step in his footprints and not have to fight with the snow as much. After such a struggle, it was almost a letdown to finally make it through the kitchen door.

They all collapsed on the floor, gasping for breath. Mary lay there for a moment, simply happy to be out of the wind and snow. It was only a minute though because very quickly she started hearing Evaline's teeth chattering. That would not do. They could not lay in their wet clothes without doing something about it or things would go downhill fast.

Rolling up, she crawled over to where Evaline lay next to her brother. Her eyes were closed, and her face flushed, and her lips were nearly blue. She had to get her out of her wet things and into something warm, but what was there for her to wear? They needed a fire and something hot to drink as well. Shoving at Gabriel, she got his attention and when his eyes opened and he focused in on her, she said, "We need to get warm. I am going to look for things to change into, but we need a fire. Can you build a fire?"

When he nodded his head and sat up, he gently handed his sister over to her. "We have plenty of wood to burn in the kitchen stove. I will bring some in from the stables." Getting up, he went in the direction of the stables, following the line of the building, in search of whatever they had to burn.

Mary held Evaline to her for a moment before holding her out from herself. She hated to do it, but she needed to get her up and moving. "Evaline, honey, I need you to wake up. We have to look for something to change into and blankets." Standing awkwardly, Mary pulled the girl to her feet and then, when she did not respond, she shook her slightly.

"I'm sorry. I should not have pushed her." Evaline's words were sloppy and confused, but at least she was blinking owlishly at Mary.

"I know, honey, I know I forgive you and we can talk about that later if you like, but we have to find dry clothes." Wrapping her arm around Evaline, Mary forced her to walk with her. Walking down the hallway away from the kitchen, Mary found the linen cupboard.

She knew that her father may very well have torn all the linen to shreds, but she was hoping he had overlooked the sheets and blankets that were there. It was safe to say the man never would have contemplated where his clean sheets came from or how they were replenished.

Opening the cupboard, she was glad to see that there were some sheets and blankets. They smelled vaguely musty, but it would have to do. Debating whether she should bring the blankets into the kitchen now or later. In the end, she decided that if she brought the blankets back to the kitchen, they might warm up near the fire that Gabriel was going to be making in the kitchen stove. Handing Evaline some blankets to carry, Mary hoped if she could get the girl moving and interacting, she could stave off the possibility of hypothermia.

Evaline took the blankets and moved as directed but was not talkative, which worried Mary. Going back into the kitchen with the blankets and Evaline, she was happy to see Gabriel bringing in the wood that they would need. "I found some blankets and hopefully I can find something for us to change into."

Putting down what appeared to be a second or third load of wood down next to the stove, he fed the fire that was starting to blaze merrily. "It will take a while for this room to warm. The temperature has dropped so dramatically."

Studying the stacked wood, Mary asked worriedly. "Is there enough wood, do you think?" Moving over, she took the blankets from Evaline and staked them with her own on the kitchen table.

Looking at his sister in concern, he commented, "Yes, either Isaac or Jeremy must have stocked wood to prepare for winter. The horses seem well enough with hay and water. Your stable is surprisingly insulated. I put blankets on the horses, so they should manage well enough for now."

Looking into Evaline's slightly glazed eyes, Mary smiled kindly. "I am going to look for clothes that I think were put in one of the chests." Moving to brush her damp hair back from her face, she said, "Evaline, why don't you stay with your brother here by the fire, sweet girl? Maybe your brother can help you dry your hair with one of the towels I brought."

Mary made eye contact with Gabriel, and they seemed to communicate over their mutual concern for the quiet girl. Turning to leave, she squeezed the girl's trembling shoulder. She was glad that she was at least still shivering. It would be very bad if she had suddenly stopped shaking.

Hurrying away, she made her way through the silent and cold home. Ignoring her own clacking teeth as she looked for the clothes that they would need to change into. She knew that they had not taken everything with them when they left Longbourn. There simply had not been room. If she remembered correctly, there should be several trunks of clothes that had been stored in the attic.

In no time at all, she had made her way to the much colder attic and was opening the trunks with uncooperative fingers. It had only taken a few tries before she found a trunk with dresses that they had all outgrown. Grabbing a dress or two that might fit Evaline, she moved on until she found a trunk that must have contained some of Grandmother Catherine's clothes. Though the dresses were many years out of style, they were dry. The next chest must have contained some long-deceased male relatives' clothes. They were horribly out of date, but would be the best option for Gabriel.

Moving down the stairs with her arms full of clothes and a few knitted blankets that she had also found she peeked in a few of the rooms on the second floor and noticed that there were a few quilts that they could bring down to the kitchen, but she did not have the room for it in her arms full of clothes. Maybe later she would come back after they were all warm and dry.

When she returned, she found Gabriel attempting to dry his own hair. His sister was sitting on the floor next to the stove, her hair mostly dry. At least she looked up at her and smiled faintly when Mary walked in. That was progress.

"I found us clothes. I am uncertain of their style or smell after being stored for so long, but it is something that is dry, and we all need that." Putting the clothes in a pile on the table and the blankets stacked in a pile on the counter next to the stove, Mary moved to the cabinet and lit another candle. Gabriel had lit several candles, but the storm was blocking out all the light that normally came into the kitchen. "Evaline, why don't you and I move into the pantry so that we can change. We can take a few candles with us so that it is not so dark in there."

"All right." Evaline's voice was low and rough, but at least she had responded.

Sorting through the clothes, she picked out what they would need to bring with them. She startled when Gabriel came up next to her and took up the clothes that she had brought down for him. "Why don't you and Evaline stay here by the fire where it's warm? I can get dressed in the pantry. "

Blushing, Mary nodded her head. She did not have time to fully process how untoward the entire situation was, but hearing Gabriel speak of changing had definitely hit a cord. Already she had spotted that his shoes were next to her in front of the fire. Had she ever seen a man's stocking feet? Not that she could recall. It was surprising that she had yet to catch fire from the mortification that she felt in the situation. She would just endeavor to act as normally as possible. "I think that is a good enough idea. Evaline needs to stay warm. Our next thing to worry about is going to be getting something warm into her. Did you check to see if the pump was working?"

"I had not thought to check. I know it was working when you all cleaned. But the drop in temperature could cause things to freeze. I will work on that next." Leaving with an arm full of clothes and a candle, he shut the door behind him.

Mary wondered with as cold as she was if her tendance to blush outrageously could be discerned. Gathering the clothes that she had brought down for Evaline, she knelt in front of the girl. "Let us get you out of those wet things. I brought two dresses as well as an assortment of under things down. I am uncertain which will fit you, but we will manage somehow, I am sure."

Evaline looked to the pantry where her brother was changing and frowned. "This is rather irregular." Her voice was still a rough whisper.

"Yes, I know. I do not like it either, but unless you would like to go upstairs, I see no other way. We can change in one of the bedrooms, but it is much colder up there, and the floor is rather unpredictable." Seeing Evaline's confusion, Mary explained, "I fell through the floor a few weeks ago when I was trying to check on my old bedroom."

Eyes as round as saucers at the information, Evaline shrugged and then rolled her eyes. "I would rather not fall through the floor on top of everything else." Sneezing, she added hoarsely, "We can change here by the fire."

"Yes, we will just have to be quick and try to preserve our maidenly sensibilities." Looking around the room, Mary noticed a chair had been brought in at some point. It was not a kitchen chair and seemed to be imposing and heavy, but it gave her an idea. "What say you to locking your brother in the pantry by pushing the chair in front of the door?"

A smile crept across Evaline's face. Obviously, the idea of locking her brother into a small room had its appeal. "I would find that ... comforting."

Mary laughed, glad that Evaline seemed to be perking back up. She would only improve with dry clothes and warmth. "Do you want to help me move the chair?"

They made quick work of moving the chair in front of the door so that Gabriel could not come out and surprise them in a state of undress. If they laughed at the idea while they did, it was only fair. After all, he was a man, and both ladies had cause to be annoyed by him. Never had two ladies rushed to get dressed in such a swift fashion. What Evaline had said was correct: it was very irregular and neither of them felt comfortable dressing in a kitchen, but needs must.

"How do I look?" Mary looked down at her apparel with a frown. The dress she wore was probably from after her grandmother lost her husband and she had entered a prolonged mourning. It was a dowdy dress, especially compared to today's styles, that reminded her of how she had dressed when she was not much older than Evaline. For a time, she had eschewed girlish fripperies as vain and wore only somber colors. In reality, she was uncomfortable with her appearance when compared with her sisters and felt that she would never look as pretty as her sisters anyway, so why try?

Biting her lip, Evaline seemed to debate about what to say. "I do not think it is your color, but at least you are warm." She offered an obliging smile, possibly in consolation, then snuggled into the blanket she had wrapped around her shoulders.

Grabbing her own blanket, Mary shrugged before saying, "Very true. You sound like my sister Kitty. She was always the one with an eye for color." Mary began arranging their clothes near the stove, hoping that they would dry soon enough.

"Hello? Miss Mary, is it all right for me to come out now?" Gabriel's voice sounded hollow as he called from inside the locked pantry.

"One moment." Lowering her voice, Mary whispered, "I suppose we should move the chair and let him out."

Evaline sighed, "I suppose we must." This was followed by a peal of laughter from both ladies as they hurried to move the chair. Leaning against Mary, Evaline called out, "You can come out now, Gabriel!"

EVALINE SAW HER BROTHER'S odd apparel and only started laughing harder. The outfit fit him, but it was from some time long past that had a style of fashion that was well forgotten. Catching her breath, Evaline continued to lean into Miss Bennet's warm side. The day had been a tumult of emotions, and she was worn and tired.

While her head ached strangely, and she was becoming rather snuffy, she was also happier than she had been in an age. Somehow, in a way that she had never expected, she found Miss Bennet's presence soothing. She was kind and laughed with her. It was an experience that Evaline had never known.

Tilting his head, her brother asked, "What is so funny?"

Looking up at Miss Bennet in bewilderment for a moment, Evaline struggled with what she could possibly say. She was glad when Miss Bennet answered instead of her. "We could not tell you if we tried. I see the clothes fit. Though, like mine, they are from a generation ago and are quite out of date."

"I thought I looked rather dashing." Her brother puffed out his chest and struck a heroic pose that only made Evaline burst out in a bark of hoarse laughter. "I am glad to see you laughing, Evaline."

Reaching out, he pulled her to him and hugged her close. At first Evaline felt uncomfortable with the attention, as she was very unaccustomed to such actions, but eventually she relaxed into the hold. At the sound of movement behind her, Evaline stepped out of Gabriel's hold.

Miss Bennet seemed to be putting a kettle on to boil. Evaline hoped that there would soon be tea. The very thought of having something warm to drink made her shiver and realize just how cold she still was. Approaching her, Evaline asked, "Are we going to be able to have tea?"

"Well, I think so. We will, at the very least, have hot water as the pump is working for now. Though I think it would be best to fill several containers with water now just in case the pump freezes." Biting her lip, Miss Bennet leaned down and began looking in the cupboards, presumably for either tea or containers to put water in.

Looking around the kitchen, Evaline spotted another row of cupboards. Deciding to work her way around towards Miss Bennet, Evaline started poking about, searching for items that would be useful in their predicament. Meanwhile, her brother watched the lady like a mooncalf and then started to feed more wood into the stove. When that was finished to his satisfaction, he went to gather more wood to stack in the corner. It seemed to Evaline that the wood had been stacked near the door that led to the stables. At least he would not have to brave the storm.

While Evaline thought she may never feel truly warm again, she did seem to find a few useful items. Gathering the large pot and a teapot, Evaline brought them over. "I found these. Hopefully, they can be of use." When Miss Bennet took them with a smile, Evaline felt compelled to speak. With dropping shoulders and a defeated air about her, Evaline began, "Miss Bennet, I am sorry that I pushed your niece. It was uncalled for, no matter my concerns over the mud."

Putting down the pot that she had been filling, Miss Bennet turned and gave Evaline her full attention. "I am grateful for your apology, and I am happy that you see the error in your action. But I am sure that Ellie is fine. Children of her age are rather durable and always seem to be taking tumbles. My greater concern is over why you would feel the need to protect yourself in such a way. Can you remember what you were thinking when it happened?"

Rocking back and forth on her stocking clad feet, Evaline allowed herself a moment to reflect on her feelings from the moment in question. The only thing she could remember feeling was fear. She had been afraid to get dirty, afraid of the consequences of getting dirty. But how to explain that? Looking up at Miss Bennet's kind face, Evaline found that she could only tell the truth. "I was afraid of getting dirty. I was afraid of what my mother might say or do if I allowed it to happen."

Though Miss Bennet's eyes narrowed slightly for a moment, she did not lose her smile. "Well, I can see how that might worry you. Not all mothers are like Mrs. Darcy who delights in her children having a good time even if they get dirty."

"My mother is not at all like that." Tilting her head back in an imperious fashion, Evaline imitated her mother saying, "A young lady is never seen in soiled clothes, and there is never an excuse for allowing it to happen." Shrugging her shoulders, Evaline continued in her own voice, "Lately there have been so many new rules and new punishments to adjust to."

"What punishments?" asked Miss Bennet.

Hesitating, Evaline wondered if she was betraying her mother by explaining things, but she was feeling so at ease with Miss Bennet that she boldly forged on. "I have often missed dinner for my errors. My new governess is rather fond of having me walk with a book on my head to practice my posture. If she is not satisfied with how much I am progressing, I must stand in place with the book on my head for up to half an hour."

"Has your mother said why she is instituting all the changes?" Mary asked, her eyes compelling and compassionate at the same time.

"I am apparently beginning to prepare for my come out. Mother says that I may not have the best dowry, but I will be the most accomplished young lady Meryton will have ever seen. She expects for me to be leading Meryton society by the time I am seventeen. She expects me to make only the best match. I will need to catch someone titled and, failing that, they must be remarkably connected and wealthy."

"I have never spent much time with your mother, but it seems that she is trying to help you in the way that she knows." Pausing for a moment, Miss Bennet's nose wrinkled and to Evaline seemed to look conflicted. "I will not speak against your mother and how she wants to bring you up. However, I want you to know that I am here. I will listen to whatever you have to say. In fact, I want to listen to all of your worries and your thoughts. In fact, I would like for you to call me by my given name. Would you call me Mary?"

Evaline could do nothing but throw herself into the woman's side and cry. It seemed like she finally found someone that understood and cared about her on top of that.

# Chapter Fifteen

When Gabriel came into the room with another armful of wood to stack by the stove, he found his sister clinging to Mary's side, sobbing. "Hey now, what is all this? Is everyone well?" Dropping the wood, he rushed over to them and stood hovering in concern. On closer inspection, Mary had tears in her eyes as well.

Mary shook her head and, running her fingers through Evaline's hair, she hugged her tightly to her side. "Nothing for a man to concern himself with. We were just talking. Everyone is fine."

Gabriel found himself confused by the glib tone of Mary's comment. "How are you fine? You are both crying!"

Laughing and wiping at her eyes, Mary smiled down at Evaline before gazing back at him and saying, "Gabriel, you will just have to understand that women are mysterious. Sometimes we scold and sometimes we laugh and sometimes we cry. It is not for you to understand." This elicited an extra round of laughter from Evaline.

Glad that they were well enough, Gabriel took the subtle jibe and went back to stack the wood he had dropped. "I surrender to your superior manner of mystery. As long as you are both well, I am happy enough."

Mary went back to filling the containers they had found with water and placing them on the counter. While Evaline seemed to search for anything useful in the cupboards. They were all settling themselves into necessary tasks quietly and without speaking. Gabriel knew that there was a need for conversation. He had two ladies that he needed to apologize to but could not find the words or the moment.

"I found us some mugs, Mary, but unless we find tea somewhere, I am not eagerly anticipating hot water on its own." Bringing the mismatched cups over to Mary, she set them on the counter next to the various random things that she had found.

Gabriel noticed that they were all quite plain and chipped. Most likely they had been used by the servants at some point, but Gabriel was impressed at even they had survived. So much had been shattered by Mr. Bennet's wrath before their arrival. He also noticed that Evaline had started to call Miss Mary, Mary. When had that happened? Shaking his head in confusion, he sighed while moving to warm his hands by the stove. Suddenly, Gabriel remembered that Mary had not seen the changed contents of the pantry yet. The last that she had been to Longbourn, there had been a rodent problem, and they had just barely cleaned the kitchen. Things had much improved in the interim. "Mary, I never had the chance to tell you about the changes in the pantry. I think you might find some tea in there now."

"Changes?" Mary looked at him in confusion and then at his sister. When Evaline shrugged, they moved together to look into the nearby pantry.

Holding his breath, he waited for their reaction. He thought she might be happy with what she found, but he was starting to second guess his thought process where women were concerned. When he heard his sister's squeal of delight, he moved to stand in the open doorway.

His little sister was on her knees next to the little cat bed that had been placed on the ground beneath the lowest shelf. On the bed sat a less than regal looking cat that was receiving love none the less.

"When did we get a cat?" Mary inquired, her voice full of wonder.

"Well, Isaac knew that we were in need of one. He had observed the rodent problem firsthand when a mouse came out calm as could be and ate some of the lunch he left on the counter." Gabriel grinned when he heard Evaline's laugh. He realized he had never heard her laugh so happily. Evaline never laughed or smiled much at home. Looking at Mary, who he knew was somehow the cause of his sister's changed demeanor, he beamed. "To make a long and convoluted story short, he learned of a tenant farm that this gentleman had wandered on to and had been getting into territory disputes with the family's own cat. So, Isaac took the cat off their hands and brought him here. It turns out that he is a prodigious mouser. He has started to fill out quite nicely."

Leaning down, Mary ran her fingers against the gray fur on his head. "What have you been calling him?"

Gabriel gave a half shrug and a rueful grin. "You need to remember that it has been a group of men working on the house. We rarely name things as you women do. At most, we have been calling him Cat."

Smiling at Gabriel affectionately, Mary shook her head and said, "Oh, that will never do. This defender of the pantry must be granted a name worthy of the effort he puts forth on our behalf. What do you think, Evaline? Do you have any ideas about what we should name him?"

Twisting around, Evaline inspected him more thoroughly before responding. "Well, he is all gray except for his feet, which are white, so I thought maybe smoke. But that does not seem right. His attitude does not match something as cheery as that. Maybe something historical like a general or king? He seems very commanding, and he does protect the pantry from invading hoards, after all." Evaline tried to entice the cat to chase after her fingers, but he merely lay there batting his tail. The cat reclined regally, allowing their attention but not going out of his way to ingratiate himself on them. He was a noble beast, and he knew it. Of course, the humans gave him attention. It was only right.

Standing next to Gabriel, Mary placed her fingers on her chin and thought for a moment, biting her lip as she did so. "I found a kitten recently. She is too small to go after mice, so I did not bring her over to Longbourn to help with the mouse population. I named her Cleopatra. Maybe we could name him after one of the gentlemen from that era? Perhaps Caesar, Antony or even Octavius?"

When Mary spoke the last name on her list, the cat looked up at her and meowed sharply, seeming to incline his head. Gabriel watched the cat seem to accept his name with the grace of a ruler and nodded in agreement. "So, Octavius it is, then. I do believe that cat is only allowing us to name him out of some form of cat generosity."

Mary smiled at the cat, who was still accepting the attention from Evaline with a quiet dignity. "It is the cat way. They are not like dogs who always seem to love their people. Cats expect their people to love them, and whether or not they return that affection is irrelevant." Finally, looking around the pantry, Mary noticed some of the other changes that had come with acquiring a cat. "You have stocked some supplies, it seems."

"Yes, we were rather missing the ability to make tea, so we first brought tea to use at our leisure and then other random things seemed to follow." Gabriel looked around the shelves. It was not much really, but it would keep them from being too hungry. A variety of items were displayed, including apples, a well-wrapped wheel of cheese, several tins of tea, and inexplicably, a few bunches of dried herbs were hanging in the back. "Apparently, Jeremy's mother sent the herbs saying they would help the long empty house smell fresh and more like a home."

Grabbing a tin of tea, Mary seemed lost in thought for a moment before she grimaced and then said, "I will make some tea, and then we can all talk. Gabriel, do you think you can get two more chairs into the kitchen? Then we might have some semblance of normalcy while we take our tea." Smiling at the distracted Evaline, she said, "Evaline, do you think that Octavius might like a bowl with some water? We do not have any milk to offer him, but he might be thirsty." Having given everyone assignments, Mary moved into the kitchen to prepare the tea.

In short order, there were three mismatched chairs in a semblance of order around the large kitchen table. The cat had its saucer of water, and they were all drinking tea from their mugs. Taking another long sip of the warm tea, Gabriel allowed it to start warming him from the inside out, but understanding the need to talk, he said, "What did we need to discuss, Mary?"

Mary held her cup in her hands as if absorbing the warmth it offered her and looking to it for strength. "It will be impossible to return home tonight. With the weather being so temperamental, it would be dangerous to even consider returning to Netherfield. The possibility that you could make it to your estate is too low for comfort." Glancing up from her cup, Mary looked Gabriel in the eye. Her eyes were as serious as he had ever seen. "We will have to stay the night here, and more than that, I am uncertain of how much we can warm the bedrooms to make them habitable. Or if we even have the wood, we will need to do so. It would be best to decide what we will do for the night. It is hours away, but I think if we are to make the attempt to have the bedrooms habitable, we would have to start soon."

Gabriel did not know why he had not thought about the fact that they were stranded at Longbourn. He was so focused on survival that he had not looked to the next problem, which was getting back home.

Mary was right. Even getting to Netherfield at this point would be nearly impossible. If it was only himself, he might risk it, but he would not countenance trying to take Evaline and Mary out into the storm. "You are correct, there is no way to leave here safely before tomorrow, and that depends on how long the storm lasts tonight." Getting up, Gabriel looked out the window where the snow was still swirling. It seemed to have slowed down somewhat from when they made the mad dash into the building, but that could just be wishful thinking.

Mary smiled encouragingly at Evaline before asking, "I hesitate to sleep upstairs at all unless the floor has been repaired. I would hate to fall through a floor again."

Turning back to face Mary and his sister, he smiled, at least confident in that one situation. He had made sure the floors were safe. He had no desire to have anyone else fall through the floor and injure themselves. "No, the floors have been mended. The wood that was rotten has been replaced. The floorboards are currently unfinished and need to be sanded and stained, but for now, structurally, it is safe." Rubbing at his face, Gabriel worried over their situation. It was quite possible that this accident of events would ruin Mary in the eyes of society, but he hoped that they could mitigate some of the talk. "We have enough wood to warm one of the bedrooms. What do you think of having you ladies share a room together and I bed down here in the kitchen?"

Giving a small cough, Evaline then clearing her throat and after pausing said, "As long as I may stay with Mary, I do not care where we sleep." Have said her fill, Evaline took another sip of her tea, which Mary had managed to sweeten with the sugar she had found in a tin in the pantry.

"I think your plan works. It would be better for talk if we slept in different parts of the house." Looking down at her cup with a slight blush creeping across her cheeks, Mary continued, "There are enough blankets around the house to make you an adequate pallet, I think."

Gabriel liked it when Mary blushed. There was something about the way pink spread across her cheeks, trying to hide in her hairline, that intrigued him to no end. He couldn't help but suspect that the redness spreading across her cheeks was due to concern about the town's opinion. "I am sure I will be comfortable enough and I will have Octavius to keep me company."

"Do we have enough wood inside to heat the bedroom we will use? It will take some time, I think, to warm a bedroom to a comfortable level. I know it is not late, but it has been a long day for all of us and I think we will do well if we are ready to go to bed at an early hour. We can have a dinner of apples and cheese. At least we won't be hungry." Noticing that Evaline had nearly finished her tea, she poured her another cup and then added plenty of sugar to it for her.

"There is more wood outside along the wall to the stables. I will go out and get some more brought in and out of the snow so that it may dry. At least it is close and I can follow the line of the building." Pushing back from the table, Gabriel stood and went to the stove where all of their shoes had been lined up to dry from their journey in the snow. For a moment, he looked at Mary's shoes sitting next to his boots. Something about the sight caused him to pause. The simple sight made him smile unexpectedly. He looked down at his stocking-clad feet before his gaze moved back to where Mary sat. His smile grew larger just thinking about the fact that she wasn't wearing either.

Mary appeared unaware of the path his thoughts had taken, which was likely for the best. She picked up one of the blankets from a stack and brought it over to drape around Gabriel. "Thank you for going back out there to get the wood. You do not have a coat, so this will have to do to protect you from the cold and snow."

Reaching up, Gabriel clasped Mary's hand where it held the blanket tight around him. He could feel a faint tremble run through her hand, and he was eager to reassure her. "I will be quick. This blanket will be warm enough for my quick task. I will be back in no time. Do not worry." With that, Gabriel went out the door and into the storm to collect the wood.

EVALINE WATCHED MARY WATCH her brother go and knew with even more certainty that there was something there. She had half suspected something for all that he talked about her, but the looks that had been passing between them were unmistakable. It would be nice to have a sister that she knew loved and supported her. Clearing her sore throat again, Evaline asked, "So, how long have you loved my brother?"

Mary made an odd squeak as she turned around that made Evaline grin. Then, she suddenly became conscious of her mouth flailing, and Mary rapidly closed it, feeling her cheeks grow hot with embarrassment. "I... Who told you that I love your brother?"

Shrugging with an unconcerned attitude, Evaline came close to rolling her eyes. "I think it is rather obvious in how you look at each other. I am fairly certain that he loves you too, just so you know."

It was into this conversation that Gabriel returned, his arms loaded down with wood. Setting the stack of wood down, he looked between his sister and Mary, keenly aware that he was missing something. "Should I ask what has Mary redder than a strawberry, or should I finish getting the wood first?"

"Wood!" Mary's voice croaked, but then clearing her throat she said, "Get the wood, thank you!"

After looking back and forth between the obvious embarrassment radiating from Mary and the barely contained laughter evident in Evaline's composed demeanor, he said, "I will be back shortly, but once the wood is collected, I think I will have questions." Shaking his head, but willing to follow orders at the moment, Gabriel simply turned to go back out into the storm for more wood.

Evaline watched as Mary moved to collapse at the table, her blush still hot on her face despite the fact that the room was only just becoming warm enough to be comfortable. "My mother said I should not let things like emotions complicate my life." Walking over, Evaline sat down in the chair nearest Mary and turned to face her. She enjoyed having someone to talk to who did not simply lecture or belittle her. Mary was so different from the other woman in her life, and she wanted to know about those differences. "Mother said that emotions only get in the way of obtaining a good match and you are making me consider if it would be simpler to avoid looking for love. I certainly do not want to be caught becoming as flummoxed as you over some boy."

Rubbing her hand down her face, Mary seemed to find the line of thought she was looking for and frowned. "Some women do look at marriage as a transaction used to obtain the best possible living situation. They look for rank, prestige, and the comfort of the home they will live in. My sisters and I, however, have all agreed to look for other things in marriage."

Tilting her head, Evaline rubbed at her nose. "You are looking for emotions, for love. I heard Mother say that Mrs. Darcy was acting as if she had made a love match. She did not seem very impressed."

"Yes, my sisters and I saw firsthand what it was like to have a marriage where there was no love and respect to be found. We all used that knowledge to our advantage and chose to look for men who would be partners in our lives." Grimacing slightly as if remembering the unfortunate marriage she spoke of, Mary continued, "I will only marry someone who I know will love and respect me. I do not see that as a bad thing but rather something to aspire to, because if there is respect in a marriage, no matter where you live or who you know, you can find happiness. If you manage to find love as well, you are a person to be envied."

"And you love my brother?" Evaline leaned back in her chair, twirling a strand of hair around her finger. She found it reassuring that there seemed to be different ways of doing things than what her mother proposed was necessary. The things her mother talked about as goals for her life did not sound like anything she would enjoy.

Though she became four shades darker, Mary responded, "Yes, I love your brother."

"Are you hesitating because you do not think he respects you?" Leaning forward in her chair, Evaline tilted her head. "Gabriel is very respectful. I have never heard of him disrespecting a woman."

Screwing up her mouth for a moment, Mary seemed hesitant to speak, but then, after a pause, responded in a somber tone. "I cannot say what your brother feels, but it is very reassuring to know that you view him as respectful. I hope that he respects me."

Once more, Gabriel walked into the room with split logs in his hands and a smattering of snow in his hair. He put the wood down before walking over to the stove, where he picked up one of the towels that had been hanging nearby and began to dry his hair. Then he took off his boots and warmed his feet near the warmth that radiated from the fire. All of this he did in silence until he asked, "So what have you two been discussing in my absence? Mary is even pinker than before."

"I have confirmed that Mary loves you, but she will not tell me about what you feel for her. Have you not told her? When do you plan on telling her?" Tilting her head the other way, Evaline studied her brother, wondering what his reaction would be. Oddly enough, she found herself grateful for the storm as it had created a unique circumstance that allowed her to understand her brother better. She was thinking he was her favorite family member, though she was fairly certain that should he wed Mary, she would quickly become Evaline's favorite.

Gabriel's eyes widened and his mouth flopped open. His gaze darted quickly from Evaline to Mary, then back to Evaline, and he swallowed but was incapable of making much response at all. "Ahh?"

Her brother looked so funny, his face nearly identical to Mary's, who had suddenly become fascinated with the hem of her unfashionable dress. Evaline laughed at both of their reactions. Not maliciously as she might have in the past, but in a way of coming to understand that adults did not have it all together as they might like a child of almost thirteen to think. "I think you should talk to each other. I am going to the pantry to play with Octavius." Standing up from her chair, Evaline took her cup and poured herself more tea. Despite her efforts to soothe her throat with the warm beverage, the pain persisted, but she was grateful that they had tea to drink at all. Wrapping her blanket firmly around her shoulders, she took her cup and happily retreated to the pantry.

# Chapter Sixteen

Back at Netherfield, Kiernan, Bingley, and Darcy stood just outside the stable looking at the storm. Darcy turned and asked, "So Mary followed him to Longbourn? How long after she left did the storm blow in?"

Kiernan looked out at the swirling mass of snow with concern written clearly in the lines of his face and shoulders. Shaking his head, he said, "An hour? They would all have had plenty of time to reach Netherfield before the storm."

Bingley, his arms wrapped around his torso already fighting the cold, shook his head in concern. "As much as I worry for Mary, I do not think it is a good idea. I would hate to send out people to look for them in this storm when they most likely have taken shelter at Longbourn. It is unlikely anyone would even make it to Longbourn to check on them." Stepping back, he got out of the direct strength of the wind.

It was unsettling to be unable to assist Mary when she needed it. Kicking at the mounting pile of snow at his feet, Kiernan said, "I should have gone after her earlier."

Gripping Kiernan by the shoulder, Darcy tried to comfort the teenager. "If you had left when you intended, you would have been caught in the brunt of the storm before you made it to Longbourn. There is no telling if you could have made it there safely. You know Mary and Mr. Goulding are both clever enough to stay put when faced with this mess. We will hope and pray that they have taken shelter from the storm." Shepherding Kiernan back into the stable, Darcy reassured him, insisting, "We will go out at first light to check on them. The storm will have to have blown itself out by then."

Letting himself be escorted back into the waiting warmth of the stable, Kiernan fought his worry. Though a new thought drew him up short and a ghost of a smile drifted across his face. As long as they were all safe at Longbourn the situation might just turn out for the best. Mary and Mr. Golding being stuck at Longbourn together meant that they could no longer avoid facing their problems. Hopefully this blizzard would lead them to a greater appreciation for one another and the love that bound them both.

MARY STOOD AND WENT to the stove and began arranging things so that she could boil more water for tea as they had drunk all she had earlier prepared. Taking that moment to herself, Mary contemplated how embarrassed she was to consider that a twelve-year-old girl had so easily deciphered the Gordian knot that was her heart. Had it been that obvious to everyone? She knew her sisters knew, or at least suspected, but was she gossiped about? Was she pitied by her friends for her disappointed hopes?

When she finally turned away from the stove, Gabriel had hung the blanket he had used outside on the back of a chair to dry. He did not appear chilled, but she knew he had been out in the cold recently, so she retrieved the last blanket and gave it to him.

Taking the blanket, Gabriel looked her in the eye, his expression concerned. "I am sorry if my sister pestered you inappropriately."

Waving off his worry, Mary said, "She is at a hard age, and I am sorry, but I do not think your mother is making it any easier on her. Apparently, your mother recently began grooming her for her first season and is already filling her head with how she needs to become one of the leaders of local society." Returning to the stove, she carefully readied the teapot, eager to brew another pot of tea once the kettle started to boil. "She noticed the contrast between her mother's lectures on how to approach marriage, and how I did not reject emotion and even love the way her mother advised."

Standing, Gabriel began to pace the blanket around his shoulders, fluttering behind him like a cape. "She is not yet thirteen. Her first season will not be for what..." Gabriel seemed to consider his sister's age and, after some quick calculation, said, "at least four years or possibly even six. What is my mother thinking?"

Gathering her cup as well as Gabriel's Mary rinsed them out before filling them up with more warm tea. "She has told Evaline that she is expected to make a grand match without letting her emotions get in the way. So Evaline was interested, or rather thought it was humorous to see how we seem to be struggling with emotions. I do not mind reassuring your sister. She is a dear. In fact, she reminds me of myself in some ways. I was more uncomfortable with the fact that I was so easily read by a relative stranger than I was by any of her questions." Turning, Mary held out the steaming cup of tea to Gabriel, a wobbly smile on her face.

Accepting his cup from Mary, Gabriel gazed into the tea as if it could tell him what to say at that moment. "I know that feeling, actually. I had a very interesting talk with Kiernan the other day. He seemed as clear-sighted as my sister."

"Yes, Kiernan can be quite insightful. He was the one who prompted William to propose to Elizabeth." As Mary positioned herself at the table, she placed her cup down and clutched the blanket tightly around her shoulders, seeking comfort and warmth. Then, looking back at Gabriel, she shrugged. "Maybe it is just that younger people see through the complications of life that we adults seem to accumulate."

Gabriel moved to the seat across from Mary and put his cup down. Mary saw his serious look and instantly felt guilty. Her ultimate wish was for him to love her with such fervor that he would bear his heart, not because he was forced to do so. Rushing to reassure him somehow, she said, "You are under no compulsion to act on anything your sister said or prompted with her questions."

Nodding in acknowledgement, Gabriel looked down at his cup for a moment, saying, "I understand that." Peering up and into Mary's eyes, he continued, "But I *am* compelled to act by what my heart tells me."

Overwhelmed by how perfectly his speech aligned with her desires, Mary struggled to find her voice, whispering, "So what does your heart say?"

Not breaking eye contact, he declared, "It tells me that, yes, Evaline was right in her assumptions. I love you and I have loved you for some time."

Mary looked at Gabriel's hopeful face and found herself less moved by his declaration than she would have thought. She had half suspected, half known, that he loved her for some time. He had let enough things slip in his manner and the way he spoke to her that it was no grand revelation. "Though I am happy to hear you finally admit to it and I love you in return, I am realizing that love without action is not enough for me." Giving herself a moment, Mary took a sip of tea. Gabriel looked crestfallen, and she hated putting that look on his face, but she needed to get her point across. "Loving me but doing nothing about it is like expecting spring blossoms without the warmth of the sun to help them grow. I do not want some kind of courtly love where you admire me from afar and leave me to embroider in my tower. If you are unwilling to act on your love, I will find a way to move past my love for you and be happy without you in my life."

"Then Kiernan was right. I have hurt you with my hesitation." Dropping his head to the table, Gabriel groaned. Raising only his eyes, Gabriel looked at her without moving his head. "I am a fool, and I am sorry for any pain I have caused you."

"Thank you for being considerate enough to apologize. I will not deny that I have been hurt." Mary found herself unable to torment Gabriel. For all that she said she would move past him and find happiness on her own, she knew that it would take a while to get to that point. Right now, her love for him made viewing Gabriel brought so low hurt her deeply. Reaching out, she took his outstretched arm that he had been laying his head against. Squeezing his hand, she waited until his eyes found their way back to hers. "What do you want, Gabriel? This conversation is not all about me. I want you to be happy just as much as, if not more, than me."

Her last sentence seemed to act on Gabriel as if she had slapped him. The horror on his face made Mary recoil. What had she said to hurt him so? She had meant to be encouraging. She did not mean to hurt him as she obviously had.

SHOVING HIS CHAIR BACK, Gabriel got up and began to pace. Running his fingers through his hair and looking woebegone, it took him a moment to speak. "How could I ever want you to find a way to look past your love for me? I am incapable of wanting you to move on. That would never be what I want."

Wanting to soothe him but not knowing how to do it, Mary followed his erratic movements with her eyes. Eventually, Mary said the only thing she could come up with, "What *do* you want, Gabriel?"

In a startling move, Gabriel rushed to Mary and knelt before her, blocking her into the chair where she sat. Gabriel grabbed the arms of her chair, boxing her in. Then, looking at her with the most earnest expression she had ever seen him wear, Gabriel began. "I want to be married to you. I want to face all of life's problems together. I want us to act as we have weathered the storm at Longbourn, standing by your side and offering support to each other when we stumble. I want to watch you care for our children the way you have been caring for my sister. I want a child with your glorious, changing eyes to look up at me with the adoration the way Artie stares Darcy. I want so much, and it begins with getting you to marry me."

Mary gave a slight shake of her head, attempting to suppress the overwhelming surge of hope that had erupted within her upon hearing his words. Biting her lip, Mary whispered, "You do not have to say that. Please do not say such wonderful things if you do not mean them."

With a sigh, Gabriel reached out to run his hand along the side of Mary's face. Then, smoothing the wrinkles in her brow with his thumb, he responded. "I would never hurt you that way. It has been a long time since I knew it was what I wanted, but to my deep regret, I hesitated."

Mary knew that her forehead was screwed up despite Gabriel's effort to smooth the skin between her eyebrows. For a moment, she wanted to surrender to the tantalizing sensation of his touch, but she resolutely pressed on, even as she closed her eyes. Whispering, she asked, "Why would you hesitate if that was what you truly wanted?" Opening her eyes, Mary took in Gabriel, where he knelt before her, still trying to rub her worry away with his thumb. "Did you think I would deny you? I have tried to let you know how I felt in every way possible, and yet you did nothing! You never acted, never reassured me that my fears were baseless."

Falling back to sit on his heals Gabriel released her face and groaned. "I know, and I am a fool for it. I have nothing to offer you Mary, I am a second son. My family has made it very clear that I will get nothing for them. I was basically told that I would have to fend for myself." Running his hands through his hair in frustration, Gabriel growled. "Your sister just married an earl, Mary. He has so many estates that it might take them a year to visit them all and make sure that they are well handled. Darcy owns half of Derbyshire and the rumor that he had ten thousand pounds a year is greatly underestimating his income. Jane, of all your married sisters, married the least well off, and Bingley still owns an estate and has more income than your father ever did. How was I to ask for your hand when I have nothing to offer you?"

Slumping, Gabriel looked up at Mary with a saddened mien. Continuing his speech, Gabriel explained, "My allowance from my family is a pittance compared to your brothers-in-law's income, and I have been told that it will cease when I turn twenty-five. How can I ever support you in a manner to which you are accustomed?" Taking a moment to breathe deeply with his eyes closed and shoulders drooping, Gabriel sat nearly deflated. Then, reaching out, he took Mary's hand with a grim smile. "I say all of this and yet I still want to marry you, even knowing that our marriage would be seen as a degradation to you by many. What kind of man does that make me?"

Her tears silently trickling down, Mary clung to his hand, a flood of happiness washing over her as she finally embraced the reality of his sincere desire to marry her. "It makes you the man I love. Do you think I care about houses and wealth? We will find a way. I have a dowry that has grown to the point where I am sure we could live comfortably somewhere as long as we are careful."

Rising back to his knees, Gabriel looked at her with hope glimmering in his eyes. "I do not want you to have to be careful."

Shaking her head, Mary's voice held a firm resolve when she said, "I would rather be careful than heartbroken. You saw me roll up my sleeves and don an apron and clean right alongside the maids. I am not above hard work. The only thing that would make that work not worth it is if I did not have you by my side." In a mirror of the move Gabriel had earlier done, Mary rested her palm along his cheek, asking, "Will you allow me to be by your side?"

"I dream of our life together, one where our love will blossom and weave a tapestry of beautiful moments, regardless of where we live." Gabriel looked into her eyes smiling and asked, "Mary Bennet, will you marry me and fill our lives with beautiful memories no matter where we live? Will you stand by me, no matter the obstacle that life puts in our way?"

Leaning in, Mary hugged Gabriel around the neck. Her response was no less powerful for all that it was whispered, "Yes, Gabriel. A million times, yes!"

slowly from her embrace, Gabriel lowered his lips to hers, kissing her with an ardor that he was sure that Mary had never before guessed at if her startled squeak was anything to go by. It did not stay a one-sided kiss for long, as Mary soon became an eager participant. For a time, Gabriel forgot everything but how completely happy he was.

"So, are you getting married?" Evaline smiled at them, her arms full of Octavius in all his regal glory. The gray cat seemed to put up with her attentions in an odd sort of way. "Do you think you can convince Mother to let me stay with you sometimes?"

Laughing at the interruption and loving that Mary was once again bright pink, Gabriel smiled at Evaline. Sitting back in her chair, Mary pressed her palm over her heart and Gabriel wondered if it was beating as rapidly as his own. It took a moment for Mary to respond to Evaline's inquiry, and Gabriel, for his part was unable to find the words to  respond with. Laughingly she said, "We will see how much you can visit. We do not even know where we are going to live yet." Giggling, Mary looked at Gabriel.

He sat back on his heels, running his hands down his face in embarrassment at being caught by his little sister. After a moment, he peeked through his fingers at Mary, his shoulders shaking with laughter to accompany her continued laughter. He had completely forgotten that they were not alone.

"That makes sense, I suppose." Stroking the cat in her arms, Evaline continued to grin at catching the two so distracted by their kiss.

Reaching out, Mary smoothed the hair that he knew had been drying wildly on his head. She smiled at him as she continued to speak with Evaline. "Yes, well, your brother is going to see if he can find some bricks to warm our bed for later and we are going to go upstairs and explore the bedrooms. What do you say we go pick out where we want to sleep?"

Evaline sniffed. Her nose was still red from her time outside. Despite that, she smiled happily, replying, "Yes, that sounds like fun. We can pick the warmest one."

"Why don't you return Octavius to his throne room and we shall go see what we can find?" Looking back to Gabriel, she raised her eyebrows in question. "What do you think of the plan?"

Having dropped his hands from his face entirely, Gabriel looked deep into Mary's eyes. Now that he knew she loved him and wanted to be his wife, Gabriel found he did not want her to be out of his sight. Despite feeling inclined to pout, he said, "I think it is a brilliant plan, however I can see one flaw."

"Oh?" Eyes widening, Mary tracked Gabriel's movements as he deliberately moved closer, intruding upon her personal space.

He leaned in, their cheeks touching, and whispered into her ear, his voice barely audible. "It will take you away from me, and I do not want you ever gone from my side."

Mary smiled at him dreamily as he moved back and once again knelt before her. Resting her hand on his shoulder, she pushed at him playfully, saying, "You will have to learn patience, then. You know, I have read that patience is an excellent trait to practice." After she kissed Gabriel on the cheek, he quickly moved out of her way and extended his hand to help her to her feet. It was good timing as Evaline came out of the pantry, her blanket wrapped around her shoulders ready to go explore the upstairs.

MARY WAS SO HAPPY to know that Gabriel was ready to move forward with their relationship. In fact, she was an engaged woman. It was almost as if a weight he had been struggling under had finally lifted. She had come to Longbourn in order to determine whether she was wasting her time in her stubborn, irrepressible love for him, and she had succeeded in her quest, albeit not in the way that she had expected.

Looking into the various bedrooms with Evaline brought with it various memories from her less than happy childhood. Despite that, she had fun with Evaline in their exploration. They had taken the time to look at all the beds and the blankets that were still on the beds. The broken pieces of furniture had been removed and that was reassuring.

Evaline had started gathering the quilts that she liked and wrapping them around her like so many cloaks. She was trailing them with her as she moved. It was obvious that there had been no start on the cleaning on the second floor. There was far too much dust for Mary's liking and Evaline had started to sneeze repeatedly. The rooms still had some furniture that had survived Mr. Bennet's fits of temper, but it was all covered in a thick layer of dust, giving everything an abandoned feel. They cautiously removed the sheets from the beds to check the suitability of sleeping arrangements, but their actions only resulted in a cloud of dust filling the air.

Mary knew that there was not much she could do about the swirling dust particles, though she worried about Evaline and her incessant sneezing. She suspected that the warmest room would be the room directly over the kitchen, but that room would not necessarily be the best situated. Oddly enough, some of the beds were missing. Just what had her father done when they left?

After looking into quite a few rooms, Mary found one that looked like it might suit their purposes. "What do you think, Evaline? Will this do for tonight?"

"Ach...hoo." Evaline sniffed and grumbled, her nose becoming angrier from its recent ill use. "It is smaller than som' of the others?" It was obvious that she had a stuffy nose. She appeared increasingly miserable.

"Yes, but a smaller room will be easier to keep warm. I think this was one of our maid's rooms. It has a fireplace, and the bed seems to be in good order though small." Going over, Mary removed the sheet that had been in place over the bed, trying to be careful to keep the dust from flying over everything. The quilt on the bed seemed serviceable, if plain, and they had plenty more blankets to pile on top of the bed, curtesy of Evaline's collection. "If we take the extra blankets we found down to the kitchen with us, we can warm them by the stove while we eat. It will make for a warmer night. What do you think?"

After sneezing once more, Evaline looked at her sodden handkerchief with distaste. Rubbing at her face with her hand, Evaline looked at Mary and offered a ghost of a smile. "I am all for warmth. It is much colder up here than it is in the kitchen. Can we go back now?"

Looking at the poor girl with pity, Mary agreed. "Do you want me to help you carry the blankets? I do not want you to fall down the stairs."

Shrugging, Evaline only offered a quiet, "Sure."

Mary observed Evaline's drooping posture and diminishing energy. Was she just affected by the dust, or was this from being in the storm earlier? Eyebrows furrowed in unease, Mary gathered most of the quilts that had been wrapped around Evaline and then followed her down the stairs.

Her mind began searching for remedies that she had learned both from her mother and Jane. Arriving back in the kitchen, she set the blankets down and encouraged Evaline to sit in a chair. "Here, why don't you sit, and I will get you some more tea with sugar in it. Are you hungry? There is cheese and apples to be had."

Laying her head down on the table, cushioned on top of the blankets, Evaline closed her eyes. "Tea sounds wonderful."

Leaning down, Mary gave the girl a hug and used the opportunity to listen to her breathing. She had not noticed it earlier, but Evaline was faintly wheezing. Kissing her brow, Mary was relieved that she did not seem to have a fever, at least not yet. "I will get right on that tea." Going to the counter, Mary poured more water on the kettle that was resting on the stove before moving it to the warmest spot. Touching the side of the teapot with the back of her hand, she judged it to be warm enough, and she gathered Evaline's cup from the pantry to pour her some tea.

Gabriel had smiled at Mary when he saw their return, but it quickly turned into a frown when he saw her worry. Going over to her at the counter where she was filling a pot with water, he asked, his voice low, "What can I do to help?"

Gabriel's request reminded Mary of the deep affection she held for him. He did not pester her with questions about what was going on or what had happened. Gabriel merely offered to help. He really was a great man, and she would love spending her life with him. "Can you encourage her to drink the tea? I am going to get some water boiling and check the herbs to see if there is anything we can use to help her."

Nodding, Gabriel took the cup of tea from Mary, but not before kissing her temple. It was similar to what Mary had done with Evaline, but certainly did not produce the same reaction. Mary was forced to ignore the shiver that had swept down her neck and was working its way to her fingertips while she made her way to the pantry. Shaking her head at Gabriel's audacity, Mary greeted Octavius as he twined along her legs and left the room.

At the back, hanging from the ceiling, was what Mary looked for. She was happy to find rosemary. It was not the best solution, but Mary hoped that it would help. Moving back to the stove with rosemary in hand, she checked the small pot that she had set to boil on the stove. Finding a knife, Mary cut up half of the rosemary and dropped it into the boiling water. It was not long before the scent of rosemary filled the room.

Collecting a large bowl, she poured some of the steaming rosemary water into it very carefully and brought it over to the table where Evaline and Gabriel sat quietly. Amidst the stillness, the only sound that persisted was Evaline's coughing and sneezing. "Evaline, I want you to lean over the bowl and breathe in the steam for a while. I am going to cover you with the blanket so that the steam stays in there with you. Take deep breaths for me."

"If you think it will—achoo! Achoo!" Evaline groaned and then coughed repeatedly before she could find her voice again. "...it will help me stop sneezing and snuffling. I will try anything."

Gabriel helped Mary to settle the blanket over Evaline to trap in the steam. Then, stepping back, his worried gaze sought Mary's. "She seems to be getting quite unwell. She had seemed fine not an hour ago." Gabriel kept his voice low, probably hoping to not be overheard by his younger sister.

Wrinkling her nose, she asked, "Do you know if she has ever had a bad reaction to dust before?"

Looking off into the distance, Gabriel seemed to ponder for a moment before remarking, "Not that I know of, but I was away from home for most of the last ten or twelve years. I do not think I have ever seen dust on anything at home." With a shrug, he continued, "Despite our differences in beliefs and plans for my sister, one thing I cannot deny is my mother's meticulousness when it comes to cleaning. She demands that the maids always be on top of things. Heaven forbid my mother spots a speck of dirt or grime on anything."

Rubbing at her forehead, Mary snorted in reaction to Gabriel's response. "That explains more than it doesn't." Mary walked away, gesturing for Gabriel to follow as she went to the linen cupboard.

EVALINE WORKED AT INHALING the steam and taking the deep breaths that seemed to help the tightness in her chest. Feeling the snot run from her nose and down her chin made her cringe. Yet there was not much that she could easily do about it, unless she wanted to use her sleeve to wipe at her snot. She absolutely hated feeling ill.

Though it was nice to be well cared for while feeling unwell. Her mother avoided her at all costs when she was ill or feverish. Her nurse had soothed and clucked over her often when she was ill as a child, but it had been some time since she had experienced this level of care.

The thought of her brother marrying Mary filled her with joy, as she knew firsthand how genuinely nice Mary was. Her brother deserved nice and, hopefully, Evaline would get to visit them often.

Sneezing again, Evaline felt her upper lip curl in distaste at the annoyance of more snot. Folding the sodden handkerchief over, she tried to find a clear spot to wipe her sore nose, but was only moderately successful. At least the steam seemed to be helping her lungs, which had grown oddly tight and itchy.

STEPPING QUIETLY AFTER MARY, Gabriel asked, "What do you mean?"

Talking to Gabriel over her shoulder, Mary explained, "Everyone was surprised that Evaline would push little Ellie. But think, Gabriel—Ellie had been covered in mud. I know my family would never worry about such a thing, but what would your mother have done or said if Evaline had come home covered in mud, or even splattered with it?"

Gabriel shook his head as Mary searched through the linen cupboard for something. "That would not have been good. My mother would have been furious."

"Among the punishments your mother and governess apply to your sister is going to bed without supper and standing at attention with a book on her head for long periods of time. I think she was afraid of what else they might come up with if she came home dirty." Mary finally found what she was looking for in a bundle of handkerchiefs that had been wrapped and placed in the back of the cupboard. The only handkerchief they had between them was overused and soiled, and Evaline would definitely need more before the night was through.

# Chapter Seventeen

Gabriel's day had not gone at all how he was expecting. What had started out as a meeting with Darcy had somehow turned into a life-threatening adventure and a declaration of love. He had asked Mary to marry him, and she had said yes. He had had really no time to contemplate the day's outcome due to how his sister's condition had declined so rapidly.

As the evening progressed, he ended up taking turns with Mary to care for his ailing sister. While he had taken on the responsibility for things like starting the fire in the room, the girls would be staying in. Mary showed him how to best help Evaline to breathe freely. His sister had been quite happy to get more handkerchiefs, as she was constantly having to deal with sneezing. Mary had even gone as far as to dust the upstairs room, wiping everything down with damp cloths, hopefully to keep his sister from having such an adverse reaction overnight.

Evaline was feeling better, at least he presumed as much. He really did not know. She had said she was feeling better before she and

Mary had gone up to bed. He was lying on the floor next to the stove and staring up at the ceiling. He knew that Mary was somewhere above him, possibly asleep, but it was possible that she was thinking of him. While he was worn from having endured the storm, it was not enough to allow him to sleep. The mere thought of her presence made it impossible for him to fall into slumber.

How had he managed to find such a woman? She was willing to take him when he offered her nothing and nowhere to live. Not only that, but she had been willing to throw herself into caring for his sister. Despite the snot on her clothes and her tired appearance, she completed the task with a smile and kind words of comfort, and he couldn't help but adore her.

His mind was awash with thoughts of Mary and how her family might take his proposal. She seemed to think that all would be well. He knew, however, that his family would react badly if someone in his position approached them to marry his sister. The person who married his sister would be expected to bring wealth, land, and possibly a title to the union. Frankly, his family would be upset that he was marrying Mary. They wanted him to go find an heiress and more than that, they thought badly of her because of Mr. Bennet's behavior.

Of course, he thought badly of Mr. Bennet's behavior as well, but for different reasons. The man had been a poor excuse for a gentleman. Cruel to not only his tenants and servants, but his family as well. He did not deserve all that life had granted him. That did not mean, however, that his disapproval spilled over onto the rest of the family. No, he saw what they had done, what they had endured, and marveled at their strength and determination.

The weight of unanswered questions bore down on his mind, pulling him into an abyss of doubt and confusion. What was her family going to think? Where would they live? How could he support them? Mary said she had a dowery that had grown. What did that mean? How soon would they get married? He knew that technically Mary's reputation would be tarnished by their little... What could he call what had happened? Adventure, escapade, life altering experience? Whatever he called it, would it have any bearing on the speed at which they married?

Would he be able to explain things in a positive light? He knew people could be horrible about a woman's tarnished reputation. He had seen what the dowager countess of Matlock had attempted to do to prevent Miss Catherine from marrying her son. It had not been successful, but that did not mean Miss Catherine had not been hurt by the matter. Mary had been very upset for her sister. It was disheartening for him to see her so distraught, unable to provide the comfort he yearned to give by pulling her into a comforting embrace. It was not his place then, but it soon would be. He would soon be able to offer consolation and support whenever it was needed.

He knew those thoughts would not help him sleep any better than imagining Mary in the bed sleeping above him or worrying about the possibilities of the future. The knowledge that he should relax and find solace in sleep did little to calm his busy mind or provide any relief. It was going to be a long, sleepless night.

GABRIEL LOOKED UP, HEARING steps approaching from the direction of the stairs. He had been up for some time and had been staring out at the pristine snow-covered wonderland on the other side of the window. Turning eagerly, he brushed at the wrinkles in his clothes. He had changed back into his own outfit but though dry, it needed a good ironing.

Mary entered the room, her clothes slightly wrinkled, but her smile radiating warmth. "Good morning, Gabriel. Did you manage to sleep well enough on the floor?"

"I slept well enough once I was able to fall asleep." Making his way to the counter, he poured a cup of tea and handed it to her, his actions smooth and coordinated. Once he was done, he breathed a sigh of relief that he had not done something daft like spill the tea on her. How did one interact with their affianced when snowed in and isolated without a true chaperone and still behave as a gentleman? Would it be untoward to kiss her good morning? He knew what he wanted to do, but he refrained. Somehow, he found himself more nervous around her now that they were engaged. He did not want her to regret her confidence in him. "How did you and Evaline sleep?"

Mary grimaced and took a long sip of her tea. "I cannot tell if she merely had a reaction to the dust or something while we were exploring or if she succumbed to being in the storm for so long.

It could be some of both, actually. Either way, she is feverish this morning and coughing."

Gabriel looked at Mary with concern. He did not know how to care for his ill little sister. He clung to the hope that Mary would have a suggestion. Maybe his sister's illness was not overly serious. "Is there anything we can do for her here?"

Shaking her head, Mary looked at him with worry in her eyes. "Frankly, I am at a loss. We do not have the supplies to care for her as we should, and I am half worried that there is simply too much dust upstairs. If that is what is bothering her, we need to get her away for it."

Taking up his cup of tea, he checked out the window. As he looked up at the sky with a discerning eye, he couldn't help but question how much longer this clarity would remain. Though snowflakes weren't falling, the foreboding clouds served as a reminder that the storm could reignite at nature's whim. "It has cleared up for the moment, but I cannot be certain how long it will last. Even if it is not snowing, it is freezing out. Do you think it is wise to take Evaline out in this weather?"

Mary joined him at the window, and after sipping her tea, she held the cup close to her chest, allowing it to warm her. "I cannot say if it is wise to take her out in this weather. But I do know that I do not have what we need to care for her here. I can only hope if we bundle her up warmly enough and get to Netherfield swiftly that we may manage it and that hopefully the benefits will outweigh the risks."

Taking another sip of tea, Mary seemed to draw closer to Gabriel, hovering only a hairsbreadth away.

The warmth of Mary's body next to his provided a sense of security, and he could feel her shift and gently rest her head against his shoulder. They both looked out the window at the white snow-covered morning, feeling the warmth of each other's presence. Gabriel had trouble thinking for a moment. Eventually logic reasserted itself and he managed, "If we are going to do it, we should go soon. I would hate to get out there and have it storm again."

Finishing her tea with one last long gulp, Mary put her teacup down. Moving to the counter where her and Evaline's clothes had been laid out to dry, Mary gathered them. "I will get her ready to go out and we will come down shortly. Have you checked on the horses? Did they weather the storm well?"

Smiling at Mary's concern, Gabriel responded, "The horses are well. Fox seemed eager to get out and stretch his legs, though both mares were perfectly content to laze about."

"I am glad they managed the night. We will have to make sure they get treated when we return to Netherfield." With a last weary smile, Mary turned to go care for his sister.

EVALINE HAD WOKEN UP feeling groggy and sore for some reason. Blinking at the ceiling that looked unfamiliar, she remembered with time all that had occurred the day before. The little girl covered in mud, getting lost in the snow, Octavius and then Mary and Gabriel kissing.

She also recalled starting to feel unwell. What had started out as a sore throat and sniffles had progressed to a tightness in her chest and chills. She felt no better now and was, in fact, feeling worse. Looking around, she realized that Mary was no longer by her side, but she had no desire to go look for her. Despite the cheery fire in the fireplace, it was warmer beneath the covers, and she had no desire to move.

"Good morning, Evaline." Mary came into the room, her arms full of clothes.

It took more than one attempt for Evaline to croak her response. "Morning." Her throat had grown so sore. Shaking her head dizzily, she sat up, bringing the blankets with her.

"You poor dear, you are not doing well at all. I brought your clothes from yesterday up. They are dry and, in fact, warm because they had been sitting next to the stove." Coming over to the bed where Evaline lay, Mary laid out the clothes and smoothed the hair from her face. "What do you say we get you dressed in your own clothes?"

Evaline leaned into the comfort that Mary offered. "Alright, though I do not like the idea of changing. I am too cold." Evaline reached down to begin undoing her dress. "I doubt I will ever feel warm again."

Mary made quick work of helping Evaline into her warm clothes. "Yes, I think part of that is from your fever. It is colder in this room than I would like as well." Once Evaline was in her original dress, Mary moved to put a second pair of socks on her feet.

Evaline had no idea where she had found extra socks in the abandoned home, but she was grateful that she had. "Thank you, my feet feel like ice." Evaline broke off into a hacking cough that hurt somewhere deep in her chest.

Mary's eyes widened and her eyebrows drew together, but then her face calmed, and she asked, "Are you still cold? I think this dress you wore last night could fit over the one you are wearing now. We are going to try to get back to Netherfield today, so layers would be a good idea."

With a groan and a sniffle, Evaline nodded her head. "Let us put on the other dress as well. I will not be fashionable by any means, but I will be warmer." Once dressed in both layers, Evaline chose to lie down and rest her eyes while Mary changed as well.

"There is tea downstairs, and the stove makes the room much warmer. What do you say about relocating downstairs?" Mary's voice came from nearby.

Feeling too worn out from the rigors of changing her clothes, Evaline simply nodded her head and forced herself to leave the bed. Making the way down the stairs was only managed with the support of Mary and the sturdy railing. Shaking her head in frustration, Evaline fretted. If she was this weak and chilled inside, how would she ever manage to travel on horseback to Netherfield?

GABRIEL SAW HIS SISTER brought in supported by Mary and his concern for her grew tenfold. Her eyes were glazed slits in a flushed face. She had become much worse overnight. Mary was correct. They could not care for her here. She needed nourishing soups, medicine, and, if Mary was correct, an environment free from dust. But even if that was true, how would she handle even the fifteen or twenty minutes it would take to return to Netherfield?

Turning, he tried to school his features. He did not want Evaline to see him worried for her. Pouring fresh tea into her empty cup, he brought it to her as she slumped at the table. "You look as if you could use a nice cup of hot tea."

Watching her sip at the tea with little enthusiasm, Gabriel moved to Mary. Keeping his voice low, he commented, "She is much worse from last night."

Picking up her own cup of tea, Mary took a sip. Then gazing at Evaline slumped at the table now ignoring the warm tea after only a few sips, she frowned. "Yes. I hoped that when she got up and dressed that she would have more energy, but she seems to have been worn out by simply changing her clothes."

Watching his sister nod off to sleep with her head on the table, Gabriel allowed himself to frown. His voice still pitched low, he asked, "It is at all wise to bring her out into the cold?"

"Under normal circumstances, I would not tempt fate by bringing her out in this weather, but these are not normal circumstances. Along with medicine, she requires a dust-free room, freshly laundered bedding, piping hot broth, and soothing tea. She needs more than we can provide for her here. More than that, we are running out of tea and food for ourselves as well." Rubbing at her forehead, Mary sighed. "I suppose you could get what we need and bring it back, but we need so much that it just does not make sense to me."

"Well, I will put out the fires and we can leave as soon as may be. You are definitely correct about one thing - we finished all the food last night and there's nothing left for us to eat." Moving to the stove Gabriel set about making sure the house would not burn down after they left.

GABRIEL COULD NOT TELL if his sister was asleep or just silent. With determination, he urged Fox on through the snow-covered path, the icy wind biting at his cheeks. Mary had made sure that Evaline had been dressed in several layers and then wrapped in blankets. To ward off the cold, Mary placed a snugly wrapped warm brick in her lap. Her hacking cough rung out in the still morning. It was reassuring to know that she was at least alive. He could not see much of her at all beneath the blankets, but he could feel her move as she coughed or breathed.

Though he wanted to urge his horse faster, he was afraid that going too fast, Fox might slip on the icy ground. Looking back, he noted that the pony was handling the pace well. She was surefooted and was quite willing to follow wherever she was led. Further back, Mary was atop her mare. Her appearance was quite comical, but he chose not to say anything. Wrapped in blankets as much as possible, he could barely see her eyes.

Turning a bend that would have them on the last leg to Netherfield, Gabriel noticed that there were two riders approaching. As they got closer, he saw exactly who it was. He called out, "Hello! Have you come looking for us?"

Darcy, riding his beautiful giant of a horse, nodded. "Yes, I will say that you had the ladies rather concerned. I assured them you were all safe at Longbourn and that you would have done the wise thing and stayed until at least this morning." Urging Cadmus to go faster, Darcy offered a grim smile. "It seems I was right. Though we should get you to Netherfield as fast as may be you are not at all dressed for this weather."

As they met up in a little clearing, the difference in their two groups was glaringly evident. While Gabriel, Mary, and Evaline looked like homeless waifs wrapped in blankets and shawls, Darcy and his groom dressed for warmth in coats, scarves, and hats. Unable to do anything but agree, he urged Fox forward, not wanting to stop to chat when he should be getting his sister to Netherfield. "Just so."

Brows furrowed, Darcy leaned forward in his seat, examining what he could see of Evaline. Concerned, he asked, "Is Evaline well?"

Mary finally catching up with the group spoke up. "Not at all. I would not have taken her out in this weather for anything, but we were out of food, and we had nothing to treat her with at Longbourn."

Eyes wide, Darcy turned his gaze to Mary. His lips forming a grim line, he questioned her. "Are you well, Mary? To say your sisters are concerned about your wellbeing is an understatement."

Mary shrugged beneath the many layers that draped her form. "Well enough though, I would love a hot bath and something hot and filling."

Turning, Darcy spoke to his groom, "We will all proceed to Netherfield as swiftly as we can while staying safe. John, if you are able to get to Netherfield before me, do so and let them know that we are coming and we need them to ready hot baths. In addition, please let them know Evaline is ill and will require care."

Turning his horse around, the groom nodded and knuckled his cap. "Aye sir." Digging his heals into the sides of his horse, John urged him to return to Netherfield at speed.

Watching the man take off much faster than he was willing to go, Gabriel shook his head. Though he was conscious of speed, he was less certain about going that fast on the snow. Turning to Darcy who had come abreast of him on the road, he commented, "He is a rather confident rider."

Darcy nodded and said, "It is why I brought him with me. He was once in the dragoons with my cousin. He can ride anything, in any weather. That and his horse is one of my shire horses and is very used to inclement weather. They will get back to Netherfield safely and quickly."

It was, in fact, true that John would get to Netherfield in good condition and in good time. He also conveyed the message of their needs effectively enough that when their small group arrived at the front steps of Netherfield, a veritable army was there to greet them. Gabriel was glad to see the efficiency of the house.

It took a moment for Gabriel to realize that Bingley was there, arms reaching out to take Evaline from him. Finding his voice, he said, "Thank you."

Bingley offering his well-known grin freely despite the cold, he responded, "Do not worry, we will take care of her." Bingley went up the stairs with haste, getting the ill girl out of the frosty weather. His wife followed quickly, already calling out orders to the servants inside.

Sliding off his horse with a thump, Gabriel saw that Kiernan and Elizabeth were helping Mary from her horse and bringing her inside as well. While his habit was to see to his horse, grooms were there already taking him away with the other horses.

Darcy came to his side. Reaching out, he put his hand on his shoulder. "Come get out of the cold. I am sure you will do much better with some warmth and some food."

# Chapter Eighteen

Evaline looked up at the angelic lady in a fevered haze. "Why are you being so nice to me? I hurt your daughter. I am sorry about that, by the way."

Reaching over, Jane gathered the cloth from Evaline's forehead, then she smiled serenely at her before saying, "Everyone deserves kindness, Evaline." Turning, she took a moment to saturate the cloth with cool water in the nearby basin. With a gentle twist, Jane wrung out the cloth and then pressed it against Evaline's burning forehead. "I know you are sorry for your actions. Thank you for your sincere apology."

As her fever climbed and the woman who was kind enough to let her use her first name remained with her. Alternately trying to get her to drink the foul tea or plying her with cool, oddly scented cloths. Evaline repositioned herself again, not quite able to get completely comfortable. Even her mind was uncomfortable. Ideas ran in and out of her head so swiftly that she could not seem to complete a thought. "Is she well?"

"Do you mean Eleanor?" Watching the confusion on Evaline's face, Jane tutted over her for a moment before continuing, "Eleanor is fine. In fact, she is outside playing in the snow with her cousin Artie."

"I'm sorry." Evaline mumbled.

"I know, dear." Came Jane's response.

Rolling over once again, Evaline sighed. "Gabriel is happy. He loves her, you know."

Smoothing the hair back from Evaline's sweaty face, Jane grinned, "Yes, I know. Mary is quite in love with him as well. It is always lovely to see a sibling happy, isn't it?"

Evaline managed to think about happiness for a time, but then her mind circled back to the kindness she was experiencing. Was it just because of her fever that she felt so cared for in a way that seemed unfamiliar? "Why are you being so kind to me?"

Jane frowned for a moment before removing the blankets from Evaline's feet and starting to wash them in the odd smelling water. "I do believe Evaline, my girl, that you will soon be my newest little sister. If there is anything you may learn about the Bennet ladies, it is that we take care of our own. You are one of ours now."

Once her feet were dried and recovered by Jane, Evaline began to drift off. It was nice to think that she might have a sister, or was it sisters? So far, having a sister was proving to be better than having Jude for a brother, though Gabriel was not too bad. Wrapped in a cocoon of warm feelings and soft blankets, Evaline finally fell into a comfortable sleep.

MARY ALLOWED HER SISTER to shepherd her into the house. Even though it was not storming like the day before, the temperature must have still been below freezing. Riding outside without the proper winter wear was not ideal at all. Her boots were not designed for cold weather, and she had no gloves. While at first her hands and feet had felt like blocks of ice, she no longer felt much of anything at all.

Stumbling as she went up the steps, Mary felt Kiernan slide his arm around her waist to steady her as she went. It still astonished her sometimes that he had grown to such a height so quickly. Just the other day, he had been a fresh eyed boy eager to learn and now here he was practically her height and deceptively strong. "Thank you, Kiernan." She murmured.

Grinning, he shook his head. "I can't have my sister fall on the steps just as she is arriving home." Getting inside, he made sure she was steady before releasing her from his hold.

Elizabeth took up the spot in front of Mary, unwrapping her shivering form from the many layers of blankets. "Though you seemed wrapped up like a mummy, you are still shaking like a leaf." Elizabeth started chaffing Mary's hands, looking her worriedly in the eyes.

Mary looked around the hall for someone but became distracted by Elizabeth's actions. Wanting to reassure her sister, she tried to joke with her. "I think right now I might prefer to be a m-m-mummy. If I was in Egypt, I doubt I would be this c-c-cold."

With a sharp glance of assessment, Elizabeth's frown of worry turned into action. "Right, we are getting you into a hot bath." Wrapping up Mary in a one-armed embrace, she moved her towards the stairs.

To Mary, things seemed to move in a bit of a haze after that. She was ushered to a warm bath and forced to drink hot tea. Mary thought she remembered Elizabeth steadying her hands around the cup as she tried to drink with numb hands. Warm clothes were provided and in no time at all, Mary was being put to bed like a young child with warm bricks at her feet. Elizabeth sat beside her, smoothing her hair back from her brow in a soothing fashion.

With a start, Mary remembered what she had been forgetting. Struggling to sit up under the drowsy haze that had enveloped her, she spoke urgently to Elizabeth. "Evaline is quite ill."

Pushing her sister back down into the bed, Elizabeth shook her head. "Jane is caring for her. You are going to focus your attention on nothing more difficult than dozing and drinking hot tea. I might even tempt you with porridge in a few minutes. We will care for Evaline."

Slumping back in bed, Mary was glad that Evaline would be in excellent hands. Flexing her fingers, Mary fought a groan. The sensation in her fingers was coming back in annoying pins and needles. "I will not say no to porridge. Though I will expect there to be honey." Mary finally felt herself relaxing. Yawning, she closed her eyes. Evaline was being cared for by Jane, who knew all sorts of remedies. She was warm and Elizabeth was there to look after her. Opening her eyes to gaze at Elizabeth, she asked, "How are you feeling? I know your nausea has been bad most mornings."

Elizabeth screwed up her face and gave a slight laugh. "This morning has been bearable, and I am hoping that I am beyond the worst of it. I have my ginger tea right here and I managed my toast already, without a problem." As if to punctuate her earlier statement, Elizabeth reached out and took up her own teacup and took a sip.

Mary offered a commiserating smile. Elizabeth liked to always be active and useful and being held back from that because of illness was quite frustrating to her. "I will hope that the worst is behind you and that my niece or nephew will behave going forward. Do you think all this trouble means that this child will take more after you than William? I mean, really, I cannot see him behaving badly while you were quite wild to hear mother talk about it."

Laughing in the way that she was known for, Elizabeth grinned wryly. "It would be just my luck to carry a child so like me as to make me ill. Mother always said that she thought I would be the end of her the way I would get into things when her back was turned."

GABRIEL WATCHED MARY BE guided away by her sister, confident that she would be well cared for. Having completed the task he had set out to do that morning, namely, getting his sister and Mary back to Netherfield, he now felt at a loss as to what he should do next.

Darcy's commanding voice called out to various servants, making sure that all those in the house were being properly cared for. People were scurrying about seeing to his orders. Gabriel knew Darcy was an excellent master and all the servants respected him and Mrs. Darcy. They were so eager to help that they would probably bend over backwards to fulfill everyone's needs.

Hot water was being provided as well as tea and the like. Gabriel noted that there had been a request to make sure that the servant's quarters had enough wood to keep everyone warm. Was it any wonder that he so greatly respected the man? Gabriel knew some people were put off by his stern demeanor at gatherings, but once you got to know the man, he was a genuinely good person and a great friend.

Gabriel had been so lost in thought he had not realized that Kiernan had been talking with him until he reached out and grabbed his shoulder. "They have a room ready for you, Mr. Goulding. Let me show you the way. I am sure you can feel the icy chill all the way down to your bones. You need to get out of those clothes and into something warm."

"Thank you. It was a rather frigid ride." Gabriel followed Kiernan up the stairs and down the hall to a part of the house that he had never been in before. It occurred to him that they had thought to provide him a room in case he needed to take shelter. He would truly love to be part of this family. He only hoped they accepted him as he hoped they would.

"I suggested they might put you across from me," Kiernan spoke as he opened a door at the end of a hallway. "You seem to be of a size with Bingley. I am sure that someone will bring you some of his things to change into for the time being."

Gabriel looked around the cozy room as Kiernan stoked the fire and added another log to get it really roaring. Still too numb to really think or say much, Gabriel found himself nodding his head.

A maid entered the open door loaded with various items. "I have the tea, sir. As well as the clothes that Mr. Bingley has sent."

Rushing over to relieve her of some of her burden, Kiernan said, "Thank you, Millie."

Looking at Gabriel as she set up the tea, the maid said, "Mrs. Nichols, the housekeeper, wanted to send her apologies sir that we do not have the tub set up for you at the moment, but it will be provided as soon as can be."

Gabriel nodded his head in understanding. Somehow find his way to speak, he responded instinctively to thank the kind young woman. "Thank you. I am sure the tea will help me warm up for now." With a little bob, the maid made her way out of the room and Gabriel sunk into the chair by the fire.

Realizing that he had at some point divested himself of all the blankets he had wrapped around him, Gabriel held his hands out to the fire. The chill within him was bone deep and he could only barely feel his fingers. Looking over at the sound of rattling, he noticed Kiernan was pouring a cup of tea. Soon enough he had wordlessly brought the teacup over to him and, making sure he could hold the cup steady on his own, Kiernan retreated to the chair across from him. Taking a sip, Gabriel sighed as the heat from the tea seemed to melt the ice in his veins. Though Kiernan had added more sugar than he would have normally taken, Gabriel was grateful for the kind gesture. "Thank you for your assistance, Kiernan."

"Do not mention it. You took care of my sister. It is the least I could do." Kiernan settled more comfortably into his chair, an infectious grin settling across his face. It took Gabriel a moment to notice the glint in Kiernan's eyes that did not match the smile. "Of course, if you had allowed her to come to any harm, well then, things would be different. She arrived safe and sound and presumably happy enough, so we are fine."

Gabriel blinked at the implication of the young man's words. It was a stance he might have held if his sister had been caught in a storm with some gentleman. The bond Kiernan had with the Bennet ladies was akin to that of siblings and close siblings at that. He would do whatever he could to keep them out of harm's way, despite his tender age. "I would never allow Mary to come to any harm if it was within my power to prevent it."

"Good answer. Mary has collected a strong enough group of brothers. You would not fare well if you were to wish for anything but her happiness." Nodding, Kiernan got up and poured himself a cup of tea and then resettling this time with a more youthful mean. "So, did you and Mary come to any decisions while you were stuck at Longbourn?"

Gabriel saw the young man across from him in a new light. He was an old soul with flashes of maturity beyond his years, but he was still a teenager who was happy to have fun. Give him a decade or so and he would be able to accomplish anything. "Yes, while Mary was quite put out with me for a time, we spoke. You were right by the way she was hurt by my hesitation. And though I should really be speaking to Darcy about this first, I will let you know we are now engaged."

"Good." Finishing his cup of tea, Kiernan stood and, putting his cup of tea down, he stretched. He stretched in the way of all growing young men who always seemed to be finding extra bits of themselves that needed to be aligned with the rest. "I am going to see if I can scrounge up something for you to eat. While you wait for your bath. Can't have Mary's husband-to-be fading away before she has a chance to marry you. She would be quite unhappy."

MARY FELT ENTIRELY TOO coddled, laying abed when she strictly did not have to. Eating in bed was something she rarely indulged in, but she had taken porridge earlier and now after a brief nap she was having broth and bread, all while abed. If she was offered another cup of tea, she would probably float away.

At least, she had finally rid herself of the bone deep cold that she had earlier felt. She was glad to be warm and wondered that something so enjoyable was never noticed unless you had really been cold. Looking up from her nearly empty bowl, she saw Jane entering the room.

Jane smiled as she approached, asking, "How are you, dear?"

Putting her tray to the side, Mary attempted to sit up straighter and, seeing this, Jane helped to rearrange the pillows in a better fashion. Finally comfortable, Mary looked at Jane. "For a while I felt like I would never again be warm, but that has passed. I am well. I doubt there will be any lingering effects of my morning in the cold." Mary indulgently let Jane feel her brow. Jane had ever been a mother hen, especially when they were sick. So it was a familiar feeling to have Jane check her brow for fever. "I was hoping you would visit. They tell me that Gabriel is fine, but I know Evaline is sick. I had wanted to come find you and check on Evaline. However, Elizabeth was quite insistent that I stay in bed."

Sitting down in the bedside chair, Jane sighed. "You do not seem to have developed a fever, but I do not think taking it easy would be amiss. I agree with Elizabeth that staying in bed until tea later this afternoon is a good idea."

Mary watched her older sister carefully, it seemed that she was worn herself and could use some rest. "I will comply with your requests, but it looks as if you may need rest yourself. Is Evaline that bad that you have worn yourself out caring for her?"

Grimacing, Jane looked shook her head. "She is very unwell. Her fever had climbed quite high but seemed to come down when I started bathing her feet in vinegar water. Her cough seems to have settled in her chest. It's hard to believe that she was so healthy just two days ago. Sometimes I wonder how some people have such rapid declines in health. What all happened while you sheltered from the storm?"

Mary realized Gabriel must not have passed on any information about their experience. "I had decided to confront Gabriel about his intentions and found him chastising Evaline for her earlier actions."

Eyebrows raised, Jane cut in. "Gabriel, is it?"

Knowing she was blushing, Mary could do nothing but roll her eyes and confirm her sister's suspicion. "Yes, Gabriel. I will get that part of the story in a minute or two."

Leaning back in her chair, Jane propped her feet up on the footstool. Her eyes dancing, she waved Mary on in an encouraging gesture. "I will hear it all. Proceed."

"Anyway, Gabriel was chastising Evaline, and she ran off. I got off my horse and told him he should be more understanding of his sister. After that, we argued for a while, not noticing that the weather was growing steadily worse. When it started sleeting, we were both caught completely by surprise." Shaking her head, Mary remembered how he had wanted her to seek shelter while he looked for his sister alone. "We went searching for Evaline in the storm. It took some time before we found her and could bring her back to Longbourn. Between getting so thoroughly wet and cold, I think she was already at risk of getting sick, but then we had to dress in clothes from the attic and we were looking for blankets. Dust was everywhere. I think she might react strongly to dust. So much so that she started wheezing."

Understanding the situation, she nodded her head and remarked, "It sounds like the poor thing did not have a chance of staying healthy. I have a feeling that she will have to stay at Netherfield for some time. I would not risk her traveling home in this weather."

Nodding at the news Mary, said, "I think she will be happy for an escape from her home environment for a while."

Jane's normally serene expression hardened slightly, her lips thinning. "I had a feeling that might have influenced her earlier inappropriate behavior."

Finding herself becoming angry at the woman's manipulations of her young and impressionable daughter, Mary wanted to growl. "Would you believe that Mrs. Goulding is already preparing her daughter for her to come out? Apparently, she will accept nothing less than the best. Her daughter must be the leading lady in society by the time she is seventeen. The poor girl's head is full of all of her mother's sayings." With a pointed look Mary continued, "Among which is 'a lady doesn't allow herself to become dirty on any occasion for any reason or there will be consequence'."

Shaking her head, a frown flitted across Jane's face before being replaced by a grim visage. "I had a feeling it might be something like that. Society is full of mothers like that. Is it no wonder we avoid it as much as we can?"

"Too true. Look what happened during poor Kitty's first season. I will be perfectly content to never attend a society gathering again." Mary had been upset when the petty tabbies had gone after her younger and more vulnerable sister. Even now, with her sister so happily married, Mary was still put out with those women.

Jane stood as a maid entered the room with tea. "Thank you. Can you set it over there?" Moving to pour the tea for her sister and herself, Jane smiled back at her sister. "Do not think that you will be able to get out of telling me about what happened between you and *Gabriel*. What exactly did you argue about, and did you finally agree on something?" Handing Mary her cup with that look that older sisters seem to do so well. With a raised eyebrow, a slight head tilt, and a knowing smile, she silently communicated her superior understanding compared to her younger sibling. Moving back to her seat with her own teacup in hand, Jane sat and then waited for the story to continue.

Giving a little huff, Mary sat for a moment contemplating and staring at the steam coming off of her tea. Finally, she looked up and said, "I demanded that he tell me what his intentions were. While he was eager to assure me of his love, I realized that it was not enough for me. I told him I wanted more than just his love. I told Gabriel that love without action is not enough for me to be happy."

"How very brave of you." Taking a sip from her cup, Jane said, "How did he respond to that?"

"We spoke of matters for some time. You were right, by the way. He was concerned about his ability to provide for me. I think he feels inferior when compared to Bingley, William, and Colonel Theodore."

"It seems that pride is something that most men struggle with. Though to be fair, he is correct to worry about things like where you shall live," Jane commented in her normally serene way.

"I simply want to be part of the decision about how we will live. Worrying about it by himself was not helping matters." Mary took a sip of her tea, knowing that she was already beginning to blush. "Yes, well, after some back and forth and some rather romantic statements on his part. He proposed, and I accepted. We may not know where we are going to live yet or what we shall do exactly, but we will do it together."

Putting down her cup, Jane leaned in and gave Mary a big hug. "I am so happy for you, Mary. I know how much you love each other." With her arm draped around Mary, Jane sat on the edge of the bed and chuckled. "I do not envy you, your mother-in-law. Though I am sure you and Kitty shall have plenty of stories to share with each other. I suppose in some ways, Elizabeth and I are lucky that our husbands came to us as orphans."

Leaning into her sister's hug, Mary grinned. Despite the intervening issues, her joy shone through brightly. "Yes, well, I doubt Mrs. Goulding can ever be as bad as Lady Matlock. She simply does not have the connections to try and have me harmed." Laughing momentarily with her sister, Mary enjoyed the sisterly moment before sobering slightly and saying, "I am sure that it will be a long engagement. It will be some time before we can come up with living arrangements and the like, but I am content."

Jane smiled kindly at her sister once again. The happy light that appeared in Jane's eyes when Mary had spoken about living arrangements made Mary suspicious. It was a look that said Jane knew something that Mary did not, but was choosing not to share the information. Mary began to feel a slight unease. What was it that her sister or, more likely, sisters were plotting? When, after waiting a moment, Jane still did not speak of whatever she was thinking, Mary shrugged inwardly. Her sister would share, eventually. Besides, Jane was a kind soul who would only withhold something if she wanted it to be a good surprise. The only question in Mary's mind was—would she enjoy the surprise as much as Jane seemed to?

# Chapter Nineteen

After his warm bath and the copious amounts of tea and porridge that Kiernan insisted he have, Gabriel searched out Darcy. He found him in his study looking over papers, but the man greeted him warmly when Gabriel knocked at the door. "Darcy, did you have a minute? I was hoping to talk to you."

"Come in, come in. Sit over here by the fire. How are you doing, Goulding? Have you warmed up enough from this morning?" Gesturing to the pair of chairs near a cheery fire, Darcy encouraged him to sit.

As he sat down, he could not help but hold his hands out to the warm blaze. Turning his gaze from the flickering flames to Darcy, he answered, "Yes, I am doing much better now. Have you heard of how my sister and Mary are doing?"

"While I hear from my wife that Mary is doing quite well, your sister seems to be fighting a high fever and a persistent cough." Pausing, Darcy seemed to realize that he may have misspoken and quickly added, "Jane is confident that she will recover with time and care, though, so you should not worry."

"Thank you, that is good to hear, though I will admit I am happy to leave the caring for my sister in Mrs. Bingley's capable hands. I have not the first notion of caring for a ill person. I will visit her after we finish speaking." Stopping to gather his thoughts, Gabriel looked back at the flames. How did you ask permission to marry someone? Was Darcy even the man he should speak to? Feeling his jaw pop in protest at how tightly he had been holding it, Gabriel forced himself to relax and plunge forward to speak about what he knew he must. "I... Well, I suppose you must know that I have long had feelings for Mary."

Grinning, Darcy sat back in his chair. "Yes, and if I had been unable to decipher it, my dear Elizabeth would long ago have bludgeoned me over the head with her hints."

"Well... Well, while Mary and I were stranded due to the storm, we had the time to have quite the discussion. At first, it was more like an argument, but eventually we came to an agreement." Fidgeting in his chair, he tugged at his borrowed cravat. "Darcy, I know I do not have much. I am not a first son, so I do not have an estate to offer her, or even wealth. Even fine clothes and jewels are not something I have at my disposal, but I love her, and I want to live my life with her. She has assured me *most adamantly* that she is not happy simply waiting around until I am able to support her in the manner to which she is accustomed to before becoming engaged." Rubbing his hands on his trousers, Gabriel tried to rid himself of the anxiety that was creeping up before continuing. "I have asked Mary to marry me, and she has accepted. I know she is of legal age and may marry where she chooses, but I would like her family's blessing. So, I am asking you, will you approve of our marriage?"

Shaking his head, Darcy's lips curved into a smile before he said, "Your feelings for my sister have not been well hidden, Goulding. We have long known which way the wind blew between the two of you and have mostly been waiting for it to all come to a head." Getting up, Darcy went to his sideboard and produced two glasses and a snifter of brandy. "If we had been unhappy with your suite, we would have done something about the way you were pining after one long ago."

"I had not realized that I was so obvious in my affection." Fighting the need to tug at his cravat again, Gabriel sighed.

"I would tell you to think nothing of it, but I can remember being in your shoes and I know how hard that advice will be to follow. As for your statements about being a second son. I found myself unconcerned with the issue." Pouring a measure of the amber liquid into a glass, he offered it to Gabriel. "Look at me. The love and affection that I share with my wife is a precious gift that I cherish every day. That is all I want and care for in my match with Elizabeth. It is the same with all the Bennet ladies. They do not seek out position or wealth, they seek love."

Accepting the drink, he savored the taste of the top-notch brandy, feeling the pleasant burn as it slid down his throat, bringing a cozy warmth to his body. He had been half afraid that Darcy would be upset about his audacity to want to marry Mary. That fear was dissolving like so much snow before a fire. He did, however, have another fear, and it peeked out as he looked around the room. Gabriel's eyes were drawn to the beautiful things he lacked, knowing he would be unable to present them to the woman he adored. "They may not have sought wealth, but they all seem to have found it. I never want Mary to feel ashamed of what I can't provide for her."

Gesturing with glass in hand, Darcy replied, "Goulding, take this piece of advice from a man older than you, your future brother, in fact. The Bennet women's pride doesn't hinge on their outfits or the furniture's appearance; rather, it stems from their commitment to love, respect, and facing the world as a united front. You have more to offer her than you think."

Maybe it was the alcohol, or maybe it was the reassurance, but Gabriel started to realize that he had more to offer Mary than a lack of home. He had more than enough love and respect for her and, as for facing the world as a united front, it was something he would do with her any day of the week. "You are right. I love and respect her, and we have proven with how we worked together in the storm how well we can get on during life's trials." Taking another sip of the brandy, Gabriel smiled. "You know that still doesn't solve the whole where to live problem."

"Do not worry, Between Theo, Bingley, and I we have nine estates. I am completely confident that you will have somewhere to live." Darcy smiled confidently, unaware of just how flabbergasted Gabriel had become.

Nine estates, yes. Gabriel was sure that they could find somewhere to live. "You do not seem to do anything by halves, do you, Darcy?"

Darcy had the decency to look abashed before replying, "No, I suppose I do not." Their laughter could be heard from the next room.

GABRIEL STOOD AT THE morning room window watching the children play in the acuminated snow. They were having such unabashed fun. Little Eleanor was not coordinated enough to throw a snowball, but she could certainly throw handfuls of the stuff in every direction. Artie seemed determined to build a snowman, and he was doing a good job with the help of ever-loyal Kiernan. Had he or any of his siblings had that much unrestrained fun in their young lives? He thought not.

Their merry faces triggered a deep ache within him, as he yearned for children of his own, the image of them gleefully playing in the snow haunting his thoughts. Children that would have Mary's amazing eyes and the love and confidence that he realized that he never had. It was a happy realization that he was that much closer to having that dream come true. He was engaged to Mary and soon enough, they would be married. Children would follow and one day he would make sure that they had fun playing in the snow.

He wished his sister had the opportunity to play with the others in the snow, but perhaps she would get the chance to join in on the fun later in the winter. There was bound to be plenty of snow in the coming months. His sister was sleeping above stairs and though she still appeared to have a fever, it was not high enough to worry him too much. Mrs. Bingley and Mrs. Darcy seemed to have it all in hand. He knew they were borrowing clothes for her from some of the younger servants, who had gladly lent items of her size, but he did not want to deprive them of their possessions for longer than necessary.

Turning from the window with a smile full of longing. Gabriel went off to see about borrowing some outerwear. It was clear enough and warm enough that he thought he could make the trip home and back to retrieve some of his and Evaline's things. He also wanted to let his parents know about his engagement. He had a feeling that it would not be well received.

COMING DOWN OFF OF Fox, Gabriel looked to see John there with his own sturdy horse, happy and unfazed. They both seemed suited to action, none the worse for the trip from Netherfield. "Thank you for coming with me, John."

Coming down from the horse with ease. Which was saying something as his horse was larger than Darcy's Cadmus. "I never mind a good jaunt and Sampson here gets frustrated when he gets stuck in the stalls too long." Running his hand along the horse's long mane, Johns seemed to speak to the giant animal.

"I should not be too long, I do not think. I just want to speak with my parents and gather a few things for Evaline and I." When it looked like John was not going to follow him in the building, he turned back to John and said, Would you like to wait in the kitchen? I am sure Mrs. Humphrey would love to ply you with tea or hot apple cider and biscuits."

"I am partial to hot apple cider. Let me just see to the horses and then I will come in." Nodding his head in thanks, he turned to speak to the approaching groom.

Entering the kitchen, Gabriel could already smell the delights that Mrs. Humphry was working on. If he was not wrong, there was ham and biscuits somewhere in the works as well as the hot apple cider that she always had going in the kitchen on wintry days. She swore by the healthful properties of the stuff, but he sometimes wondered if she just knew how much everyone enjoyed it. His mother adamantly refused to allow it to be served to the family, deeming it unfashionable.  Gabriel went down to the kitchen and drank a cup with Mrs. Humphrey whenever he was in the mood.

"Oh, my boy!" Mrs. Humphrey's form enveloped Gabriel in a rush, nearly knocking the air out of him.

Returning her hug with affection, Gabriel patted her back reassuringly. She was deceptively strong for a woman of her age. Maybe it was all those heavy pots and pans she worked wonders with? "I am whole and hardy, merely waylaid by the storm."

"When you did not come back, I hoped that you had stayed at Netherfield. But I worry. You know how I worry." Stepping back from the hug, she searched the pockets in her apron for her handkerchief and dabbed at her watery eyes.

Giving a rueful grin and rubbing the back of his neck Gabriel disclosed the truth. "I wish I had been stranded at Netherfield. Evaline and I were at Longbourn when the storm rolled in."

Shaking her head, Mrs. Humphrey said, "That place is barely fit to house a house cat. You poor dear, but you seem alright. How is the young miss?"

"Not well. She had been exploring the garden when the storm blew in and became lost. We had to search for her. She is at Netherfield now but is ill with a fever and a cough." Gabriel hoped that his sister would recover from her ordeal with speed, but knew she was in safe hands.

Brow wrinkled with worry, she exclaimed, "Oh my, the poor thing. She would have been so scared. If she is sick though, there are no better hands for her to be in than those Bennet girls. They all know how to care for the sick. Just like their great grandmother Catherine, they are."

"Yes, I have seen with my own eyes how competent they all were when caring for Evaline." Gabriel remembered how Mary was able to aid Evaline with practically nothing at her disposal. She had been efficient and caring, doting on his ill sister with the utmost care.

Leaning back, Mrs. Humphrey looked up at Gabriel, her gaze searching. "Did you say we?" Her grin spread across her face, plumping her cheeks with joy.

Gabriel wondered how it was that she had realized what he hadn't said. "Mary Bennet also had to take shelter at Longbourn. And before you ask, yes, in the course of our time there, we came to an understanding. We are engaged." Gabriel knew that Mrs. Humphrey had long been aware of his affection for Mary. She often encouraged him to act, and he did not know why he had never followed her advice. He had doubted himself, but never his love for Mary, for that was sure.

"I knew it! I am so happy for you, my boy. She will be the making of you!" Reaching out, she patted his cheek like she always had when he was a child.

Gabriel's smile radiated warmth and kindness as he gently patted the hand on his cheek. "Yes, I believe she will. Let's just hope my family feels the same way." Pulling back, Gabriel looked around the kitchen, realizing how much he would miss the place once he and Mary married and moved somewhere else. "I am going to pack some things for myself and Evaline before I speak with my parents. John, the groom who came with me, may come inside in a moment. I promised him cider." Gabriel's mind shifted to what he needed to accomplish and how to do it swiftly. He was planning for a swift exit once he delivered the news to his parents about his engagement.

"Ugh! Your family! Really, you should take nothing your family says to heart. The family you choose means more than blood sometimes. And meaning no insult, but your blood family does not merit much attention. There are better people you can fill your life with." Nodding her head decisively at the end of her speech, Mrs. Humphrey looked at Gabriel with clear eyes that spoke of wisdom.

Gabriel looked at Mrs. Humphrey in shock, wondering briefly if she was somehow related to the oracles of Delphi. She was right; he did not have to fill his life with his family's pettiness. He could choose to spend time that he enjoyed and that would not make him disrespectful or ungrateful. Swooping down, he kissed her weathered cheek and grinned, "Thank you for your support, Mrs. Humphrey. I will come back through when I leave."

"You do that, my boy. I will see to John, and I will make up something for you to take back with you to tempt your sister to get to feeling better." Turning back to her table covered with various odds and ends, she called out to one of the scullery maids to look after the stew before it burned.

Gabriel watched her go about her work for a moment before turning and returning to his rooms. He would make sure to pack enough to last him a while. He did not know how long his sister would need to recuperate at Netherfield. Surely his valet would know how to get some of Evaline's things.

LOOKING AROUND THE PARLOR, Gabriel could instantly sense the difference between his family and Mary's. While his family was in the room, none of them had anything to do with one another. There was no talking, no kindness, no joy, and certainly not love.

He had been standing at the entrance to the room for some time, with no one noticing or caring. His mother sat in a chair near the window, her feet propped on a footstool, flipping through a fashion magazine. His father sat across the room reading a London paper. Jude was not present. He was probably off somewhere wreaking havoc or shooting small birds. Clearing his throat, he attempted to get his parents' attention.

"Oh, Gabriel, I was wondering where you had been." Mrs. Goulding barely glanced up before looking back down at the magazine in her lap. "Where have you been hiding?"

Rolling his eyes, Gabriel replied, "I was caught in the storm Mother, I had to take shelter at Longbourn."

His mother's impeccable face twisted into a revolted expression. "That place." Wrinkling her nose, she continued, "I told you, that place is not worth your time. Look what happened, you get stranded."

Already tired of his mother's attitude, Gabriel could not help but say, "I would not have wanted to weather the storm without the building."

Not even bothering to look up while she chastised him, she turned the page of her magazine and said, "Do not be sarcastic, Gabriel. It is beneath you."

It was no use trying to get her to change her mind, so Gabriel responded the only way he could. "Yes, Mother."

Looking up at him finally, she said, "You know, I was implying that you should not have been wasting your time helping to repair that place for those people. You should be in London or maybe Bath looking for an heiress. If you are not going to become a cleric or soldier, then it really is the only option open to you." Looking back down at her magazine, she turned the page.

"I am not ashamed of working, mother, but that is not the conversation I have come to have with you and father." Looking over to see his father still looking at the same page of his paper, Gabriel shook his head. Was he even awake? "I was stuck in a snowstorm with Evaline and had to take shelter at Longbourn. Mary Bennet was also there, thank goodness, because when Evaline became sick, Mary was able to help."

Looking at him in confusion, she asked, "You had Evaline with you?"

It astounded him at the lack of care she had for her daughter. Had she really not realized her daughter was away from the home for more than a day? She had allowed him to bring her with him to visit Netherfield. Then again, she had not been paying much attention to him when he spoke to her about it. "Yes, she came with me. I wanted to introduce her to Mrs. Darcy and Mrs. Bingley."

"Oh, that is right." Looking at the next page, his mother tilted her head, examining the dress on the page. "You say she became ill. Did you bring her back?"

"No, she is far too ill to travel. The ladies at Netherfield are caring for her at the moment. Mrs. Bingley suspects it will be some days or possibly weeks before she is fully recovered." Would his mother finally react appropriately to hear the seriousness of her child's illness?

"I suppose that is just as well. I am not one for having *illness* in the house." Mrs. Goulding's nose wrinkled once more.

Gabriel took several calming breaths. It was no use. He might as well just plunge in with the news and be gone. "Mother and Father, I have come back from Netherfield to gather some things for myself and Evaline. I plan to stay there while she recovers, so that she is not alone. Before I go, I wanted you to know that Mary and I are engaged. We have not set a date, but I am thrilled that she has accepted me."

The magazine in his mother's hands snapped shut. "What?"

That had certainly grabbed her attention. Gabriel waited while she seemed to struggle to form words. Her mouth twitched in a comical fashion, opening and closing repeatedly. It would not do to laugh at her, but she would have to speak soon, or he might lose his struggle to remain composed.

Finally finding the ability to form words, his mother finally protested, "If you are getting engaged because of having to take shelter with her unchaperoned, do not worry so. Everyone in town knows of her father's problems and machinations. I am sure that we can manage things. Just because she is crying, compromise does not mean you must comply."

Gabriel's entire body tensed up, his fists clenching involuntarily at his mother's horrible words and attitude. Taking a deep breath, Gabriel struggled to be able to open his mouth without raising his voice. He finally managed to say, "Mother, I would be very careful of how you speak of the woman I love. Yes, we are engaged, but it is not because of any supposed compromise."

"Gregory! Are you listening to this?" Looking over at her husband across the room in irritation, she waited a moment and then screeched. "Gregory!"

Gabriel's father jerked in place behind the paper and Gabriel was able to confirm that his father had, in fact, been asleep. "Hmm...what now?" Looking at his wife, he blinked repeatedly, as if trying to get his bearings.

Frowning, Mrs. Goulding gestured at Gabriel. "Your son has engaged himself to a Bennet chit!"

Mr. Goulding folded his paper and set it aside, looking confused. "I thought those girls were married?"

All but rolling her eyes, Mrs. Goulding responded, "Only three of them."

Tilting his head, Mr. Goulding asked his wife, "How many of them are there?"

"Five," she answered with a harrumph.

"Five is entirely too many daughters in my opinion," shaking his head Mr. Goulding looked from his wife to his son asking, "and you are engaged to one, Gabriel?"

Gabriel had watched the back and forth between his parents with grim distaste. It was a pattern he had seen repeated throughout his life. His parents lived in their own separate worlds that merely overlapped in physical space. They only came together to do something when forced to. If his father had been the one to start the conversation, it would have run the same course. Rubbing at the side of his nose to try to stem his aggravation, he replied. "Yes, father," he answered, his heart beating with joy despite the circumstances. It still thrilled him to be so connected to Mary. "Miss Mary Bennet has done me the honor of accepting my hand, and I am officially betrothed to her. I realize you won't care to listen, but I have long been in love with her, and I am overwhelmingly happy about how everything has turned out."

His mother made a sound akin to a cat before beginning her tirade. "Feelings! Really? Maybe I should have spent more time explaining the world to you. I thought I would have to focus on Evaline. I knew that I would have to train such idiotic notions out of her. Young girls are always foolish, but I never suspected I would have to worry about my son." Throwing her hands up in frustration, she stood and paced through the room.

His father looked at his wife and then his son. "Are you sure that you wish to proceed with this, my son? Mr. Bennet was not well liked in these parts. Do you want to be so connected to such an infamous man?"

Looking at his father with his eyebrows drawn into a hard line, Gabriel responded by saying, "Father, while Mr. Bennet was a horrible man, his widow and daughters are nothing but the best women I have ever known. Besides Mr. Thomas Bennet, the entire Bennet family line has been known for their kindness and generosity."

"Really, Gabriel, the thought of the Goulding name being connected to a dissolute bankrupt man is beyond baring." Huffing, his mother punctuated her statement with a stomp of her foot.

Gabriel forced himself not to roll his eyes. His mother could be very theatrical when she wanted to be. Knowing that he could not open his mouth without being disrespectful, he waited to speak until questioned directly.

Beginning to look ponderous, Mr. Goulding Sr. cleared his throat. Then, looking at his disgruntled wife, he addressed her, "Maybe you are looking at this the wrong way, my dear. Didn't you say that one of the girls had married an earl this last season?"

Freezing in the middle of her most recent round of pacing, she said, "Yes, I will never understand how she managed it. I suspect some very underhanded plot to compromise him or something of the like." She then continued her pacing, albeit slower than before.

"With our son married into the family, we will then have connections to the earl. Think of what you can say to your friends." He cajoled.

His mother halted in her tracks. "That is true. If Gabriel were to become a brother-in-law to an earl, it would be something we would not have to be embarrassed about. That sounds much better than being connected to a Bennet. You are right, my dear. I can spin this so that we may save face. You may marry the chit, Gabriel. I am sure that I can teach her how to run a household properly." Moving back to her chair, his mother sat and took the magazine in her hand, reopening it and dismissing him from her attention.

Looking at his father, Gabriel waited to see if he had anything else to say. Part of Gabriel wanted to refute what his mother had been going on about, but he knew from experience that he was incapable of changing her mind.

His father grinned as if he had solved some great problem. "Well there, you may marry your Bennet girl, though I would suggest not having five girls. It is not at all the thing, my son." Then, opening his paper again, his father returned his attention to whatever he had been pretending to read before he had been awakened.

Seeing that he had been basically dismissed, Gabriel left the room and went down to the kitchen. He had asked for his things to be taken there by his valet. Pearson would come to Netherfield in a day or so with more items. Gabriel really would rather spend his time at Netherfield with Mary than at his family's home. At Netherfield, there would be warmth and joy and a loving atmosphere. Why would he stay elsewhere?

In the kitchen, Mrs. Humphrey was just wrapping up something and putting it in a saddlebag. "You look as if you have been in a bit of a battle, my boy."

"It certainly feels as if I have. At least they have now decided that I may marry Mary. Not that I would do anything else." Shaking his head, Gabriel raked his fingers through his hair. "I let them talk, but I was not happy about the way they talked about Mary and her family. I cannot understand why my mother is so set against the Bennets."

"Didn't you know that your mother used the fact that Mr. Bennet lost Longbourn to crow about the fact that she now is mistress of the biggest estate around Meryton? Longbourn and Netherfield are both larger than Oakhill, but with them empty, it put her at the top of the local pecking order." Picking up a dirty bowl, she put it into a stack with others that would be washed later. Tucking another item into the saddlebag, she hefted it up and gave it to him. "With Longbourn being redone, I think she fears losing her status in her circle of friends. By badmouthing the Bennets, she may think she can hold her position, but too many people know what those girls did for the people of Longbourn. The town will not be fooled."

Moving the saddlebag over his shoulder, Gabriel frowned. "I never would have thought anyone would be unhappy to see Longbourn brought back to its previous standing. You are glad that I am working to rebuild Longbourn, right?"

Cleaning up around her as she spoke, Mrs. Humphrey said, "I am glad that Longbourn will be restored to its former grandeur. For well over two centuries, Longbourn served as the cherished family home of the Bennets, earning the utmost respect and admiration from all who beheld it." Pausing in her clearing of the counter, she looked up and said, "Though I think that it is a pity that there will be no more Bennets to uphold its good traditions."

As Gabriel said goodbye and then mounted his horse to return to Netherfield, he could not get the things Mrs. Humphrey said out of his mind. It was not a long journey back to Netherfield, but he thought the whole way. By the time he arrived, he had a vague outline of a plan in mind. Smiling, he went into the building, eager for dinner to arrive. He had something he wanted to say.

# Chapter Twenty

Glad to be finally released from her room by her well-meaning sisters, Mary went in search of Evaline. She had learned from a maid that Evaline had been placed in a room near to the nursery. Mary was eager to see how she fared.

Finding the room, Mary peeked inside, not wanting to disturb Evaline if she was asleep. The girl seemed to be awake and looking out the nearby window, so Mary knocked softly and entered the room. Turning at the sound, Evaline spotted Mary and smiled before bursting into a fit of coughing.

Rushing to her side, Mary helped the girl to sit up, soothing her as best she could. As soon as the fit passed, Mary arranged the pillows so that she could lean back while remaining upright. "You poor thing. Would you like a sip of water?" Reaching for the nearby glass, she held it to Evaline's trembling lips while she took a measured sip. "There you go, slowly now." Feeling Evaline's forehead, Mary realized that she still suffered from a fever, but it was not what it had been.

"Thank you, Mary." Evaline spoke, her voice raspy from coughing. Smiling wanly, she squeezed Mary's hand in gratitude.

Looking around, Mary realized that there was no one in the room with Evaline. She was under the impression that a maid had been asked to sit with her. "Are you alone Evaline? I thought someone would have been in here with you."

Clearing her throat, Evaline smiled at Mary's concern. "The maid wanted to see about getting me some broth now that I am awake. She only just left."

Nodding in understanding. "I am sorry you are so very ill. Is there anything I could do for you? Would you like a book or something to help pass the time?"

"I am too tired to focus, but maybe later." Reaching out, she grasped Mary's wrist, squeezing it. Her countenance shifted, her glassy eyes betraying a heightened sense of eagerness. "You know, I dreamt of you and Gabriel."

"Really? Was it a pleasant dream?" Moving to the bedside table, Mary took up the rag that was in the basin and ringing it out, placed it on Evaline's fevered brow.

Settling more comfortably into the pillows at her back, Evaline explained, "Yes, it was. We were all living at Longbourn. You and my brother were there, and it was nicer and clean and warm. We were having a fun time and laughing." Grinning despite herself, she giggled softly.

"That does sound like a delightful dream." Mary smoothed Evaline's hair away from her face, smiling in response to the joy.

Brows drawing together, Evaline shook her head slightly before continuing. "Then it became very odd. Octavius invited all his cat friends and then he started wearing Roman armor and they began making plans to declare war on another cat family. It was very odd."

Mary felt her shoulders shaking in restrained mirth at the image that Evaline depicted. "Yes, well, sometimes when you have a fever, you can have odd dreams. Did Octavius end up fighting the other cats?"

Scrunching her face slightly, Evaline said, "No, I woke up."

A slight knock on the door had Mary looking to see that Jane was there with two little forms in tow. "Hello, Mary, I was wondering if you would be in here. Hello Evaline, how are you feeling?"

Swallowing back a cough, Evaline smiled faintly. "Fine, I think."

Mary eyed Artie, who was standing slightly in front of Jane. Always so protective, Artie kept glancing at Evaline and then back at Jane and Ellie as if he might have to defend them.

"We were going to go down and spend time with the family before dinner and I wanted to say hello," Jane smoothed Artie's hair in a reassuring fashion. Ellie was settled comfortably on her mother's hip, looking down at Evaline with wide eyes. While Artie was protective, Ellie was proving to have her mother's soothing disposition.

When Evaline sneezed several times in a row, Mary and Jane looked at her in concern. Ellie struggled to get down, which Jane allowed. Mary was curious to see what Ellie wanted to do. Standing in front of her mother, she patted Jane's pocket, prompting Jane to remove the handkerchiefs she kept there. Artie stepped closer to Ellie and maintained his position between her and Evaline. Meanwhile, Ellie picked one of the handkerchiefs and took it over to the side of the bed and held her arms out to Mary. Her small voice asking one of the few things she could. "Up".

Pulling Ellie up on her lap, Mary watched with wonder as Ellie leaned over and offered Evaline the handkerchief. Artie, eager to continue his guard duties, positioned himself next to the bed as close as he could to his small cousin.

Taking the handkerchief with tears in her eyes, Evaline looked at them all in wonder before looking at Ellie again. "Thank you, Ellie. I am sorry I pushed you before. I promise to do better."

Ellie patted Evaline's hand and smiled before leaning back and snuggling into Mary's comforting embrace. Artie, on the other hand stayed there looking at Evaline, his brow pensive and very like his father's dark stares. After a moment he said, "Thank you for pologizng. It was good. But why you push Ellie?"

Blushing despite her sickly pallor, Evaline looked the small boy in the face and responded honestly. "I was afraid of the mud."

Artie seemed astounded by her honest reply, questioning, "You 'fraid of mud?"

Responding with a simple nod and a shrug, Evaline offered no other explanation.

Seeming to think hard, Artie straitened his shoulders, "I will protect you from mud next time. You feel better we play with no mud."

"Thank you. Artie, that would mean a lot to me."

"Feel better. See you later." Turning, Artie went back to Jane's side, ready to go.

Seeing that the exchange was over, Mary kissed Ellie's rosy cheek, and stood handing her back to her mother. "Well, I was going to stay with Evaline until the maid comes back with her broth. I will meet you downstairs."

"I will come visit again after dinner, Evaline. Rest if you can. Sleep is some of the best medicine." With a last warm smile, nodded and then holding Ellie securely ushered Artie from the sickroom.

Shaking her head, Evaline stated, "I did not expect that at all. Even baby Ellie is kind."

"Yes, it is a bit of a rule in our family. Kindness is a must." Mary thought about all the examples of kindness she had seen displayed by her family and smiled. Though it was not always easy to be kind to those who had been cruel to you, being kind had its rewards. Continuing, Mary said, "It is rarely ever very hard. In fact, you do not need to be able to speak much to show compassion, as Ellie so adequately demonstrated."

Glancing at Mary with a hopeful glimmer in her eyes, Evaline whispered, "Jane told me earlier that I am to be one of you."

"Yes, I do believe you are one of us. You are to be our little sister. I think Lydia will be thrilled to meet you. She has always been the youngest and will be glad to hand the position over to you." Mary grinned at the joyful look that came over Evaline's face. The poor girl really needed some kindness and sisterly love in her life.

The maid bustled in carrying a tray loaded down with broth and bread as well as a few other odds and ends. "I am sorry I was gone so long, miss." The maid seemed a bit frazzled, trying to bob a curtsy with her hands full.

Standing away from the bed so that the maid could put the tray down on the bedside table, Mary said, "Do not worry yourself, Clare, we are fine."

"Yes, thank you for bringing the broth." Looking at both the surprised maid and Mary, Evaline offered a wry grin. "If I am to master kindness, I will need to start practicing."

WHEN IT WAS TIME for dinner and the children were yawning, their nurses came to collect them. They would most likely fall asleep shortly after returning to the nursery with all the busy fun they had had that day. Between snow fights and exploring the various parts of the house with Kiernan, they had walked what must have seemed like miles on their little feet. They had also played for a time with all the adults before dinner, of course.

Unlike many adults of means, all the adults present had taken part in the fun and games that the children presided over. Artie was happy that his uncle Bingley and his father were available to play with his blocks as he confided to them that Ellie was not good at the game of building castles. Kiernan was his chief architect, and he was even kind enough to allow Gabriel to join in the fun, providing he was careful not to knock the tower in the corner down. The girls, on the other hand were content to look at the dolly that Ellie wanted to show off. They even helped change her into her night clothes so that she would be prepared for bed.

The dinner was a bit of a special one and Elizabeth had made sure that the cook would have something that everyone would find delectable. The table buzzed with lively discussions and bursts of laughter as everyone enthusiastically engaged in conversation. They spoke of everything from the latest news of Theodore and Kitty, who had chosen to weather the winter in Scotland to the Luddite movement to progress at Longbourn and plans for the upcoming spring planting at the various estates. It was a lively gathering where no one, not even Kiernan or Gabriel, felt left out, as everyone made an effort to ensure their full participation.

When dessert was brought out, Gabriel stood and waited for everyone's attention. Taking Mary's hand in his own, he looked at everyone at the table. "Before we all partake of our splendid looking dessert, I wanted to make an announcement. Some of you might already know, but while we were stranded at Longbourn, I asked Mary to marry me, and she said yes." Looking at Mary, he smiled and kissed the knuckles of her hand before looking back at her family. "What none of you know is that I made a decision today after visiting my family. Though I will always respect my parents for giving me life and providing for me in the way that they knew how, they have my older brother to carry on their legacy. I realized after speaking to them that theirs is not a legacy I want to uphold." Gesturing to the warm smiles at the table around him, Gabriel continued, "This legacy of joy, kindness, and closeness is what I want to uphold. I want to help represent this family. This family that was brought together and formed around some very remarkable woman of whom my Mary counts herself part of. So I have decided that rather than have Mary become a Goulding, I would like to become a Bennet." Looking around at all the wide-eyed expressions, Gabriel began to feel uneasy. Was he explaining his feelings well enough? "Except for one man, the Bennets have been a respected name in these parts for centuries. People still talk about your great grandmother with respect and gratitude. That is not something I want to be lost. I want to take up that mantle if you will let me."

Silence reigned in the room for a handful of heartbeats before Mary stood and, throwing her arms around him, hugged him with a strength that he had not expected. As she was not speaking, in fact, no one was speaking. He was starting to wonder if they liked the idea at all.

"I suppose you will do." It was Kiernan's laconic response that set everyone off talking at once. Their shock at Gabriel's suggestion quickly wore off, and everyone was saying how it was a wonderful idea.

As Mary held him tightly, she whispered her thanks, her words barely audible above the sounds of their surroundings. "Thank you for seeing us, for seeing me. For seeing what we are and for respecting that. That you want to do that means so much." Finally pulling back, she reached up and kissed his cheek.

Standing up, Jane approached Gabriel, her eyes teary but her smile radiant. Taking his hand in both of her own, she said, "I remember Grandmother Catherine and I know that Lizzie and Mary have some slight memories of her as well. She died shortly before Kitty was born. Mama once told me about grandmother's concern that her grandson would tarnish the reputation of the Bennet family and overshadow their long history of doing good. That you want to ensure that the good things, the good people of our family are remembered and represented, means more than you will ever know."

Eventually, everyone settled back into their seats and began eating the treats that had been served. When they were all nearly finished, Darcy cleared his throat and, looking slightly uncomfortable, spoke to everyone. "There has already been an announcement, but I have something I would like to say that now seems even more fitting. When Theo, Bingley and I purchased Longbourn, it was because we, like Goulding, did not want the Bennet legacy to fall by the wayside. We never intended to keep it for ourselves. Bingley and I had been trying to find a way to make sure Longbourn could remain for the Bennet ladies. Theo was the one who saw how it would be for Mary and Gabriel. His suggestion was so remarkable that we swiftly put things in motion." Rubbing at the back of his neck, Darcy clasped Elizabeth's hand and with her smiling encouragement, he continued. "Longbourn is Mary's estate granted to her on her marriage. The only stipulation in place is an entailment of sorts, that any Bennet daughter will have a home provided at Longbourn if she finds herself in need. So with Gabriel's earlier announcement, it looks like there will be Bennets at Longbourn once again."

Reaching under the table, Gabriel gripped Mary's hand in his own. She was once again tearful, looking at him in wonder. Gabriel looked around the table. Everyone was smiling and happy, not surprised at all, it seemed that he and Mary might be the only ones unaware of the plan. They were gifting them an estate. It was too much. "I had thought to ask if I could work at one of your estates or manage something for you somewhere. I would have never dreamed that you would give us an estate. It is too much!"

Elizabeth looked at him, her smile never slipping, though her tone was nearly hard. "It will not be easy. This will be work, but it is a work that you are both capable of. You both have the ability and the drive to make sure Longbourn is better than it ever was. I know you will care for the tenants and the people in the town with grace and compassion." Looking over at Jane, Elizabeth saw her nod. "Jane and I are happy in our homes. We do not need to worry about another estate. Kitty just became a countess, and her hands are more than full. Mama has her new life and I fear Longbourn has too many bad memories for her to ever be truly happy here. This estate is for you and Mary."

Mary spoke up, her voice full of wonder. "What about Lydia?"

Jane tilted her head as she questioned, "Would you ever turn her away if she wanted to live with you?"

"Of course not!" Both Gabriel and Mary spoke up in unison.

Elizabeth took up the conversation at that point. "Then the estate is yours. Besides, I think she is happy visiting around to all her sisters and eventually she will find her own husband." She tilted her head in apparent contemplation before waving her hand dismissively, as if to brush away a worry. "I am just hoping that we can get it livable so that you may move into your home once you marry, but that's just details."

The rest of the evening was a merry time of plans and dream weaving. Of course, they would not marry without all of Mary's sisters present, so they would have to wait until Kitty came down from Scotland in the early spring. The time that they would wait would help them work at making Longbourn livable for the new couple.

Eventually they moved into the sitting room, still discussing plans for Longbourn and the wedding. Gabriel sat next to Mary, her hand in his, the joy clearly written on her face making his heart leap within his chest. How long had he told himself that he had to wait to claim her? He had worried for so long that he had to find a way to support her when, in reality, he had only needed to follow his heart and things had fallen into place as if by magic.

Gabriel appreciated that Mrs. Darcy had pointed out that he would have to work for the gift of Longbourn. He would hate to have his pride get in the way of his happiness. She was right; it was going to be hard to build Longbourn up into a profitable estate, but he knew that it could be done. He had hoped for a place for him and

Mary to start their lives together for such a long time and now, finally, it was in their grasp.

Leaning over, Gabriel could not help but kiss Mary's rosy cheek. Their hopes and dreams were coming true, and better yet, they were together.

THE TIME LEADING UP to Mary's much anticipated wedding seemed to both pass by in a flash and crawl. She had a mountain of work on her hands, with countless tasks demanding her attention. The physical work left her happy but tired and sore at the end of the day, though she was not too exhausted to dream and plan. Mary's dreams were not for the wedding or wedding breakfast, but for Longbourn. She was far more concerned about getting Longbourn livable than with what food and decorations would be had when she married. Frankly, she did not much care about the wedding, she just wanted to be married.

Because of Elizabeth's difficult pregnancy, Elizabeth and William had decided to stay at Netherfield longer than expected. They would not return to Pemberley until after the marriage. Mary had been happy about the decision, as it meant she could also stay at Netherfield and continue to work on bringing Longbourn to a livable state.

They were waiting to marry until Kitty and her husband arrived safely from Scotland. No one wanted them to travel when it was unsafe, so the wedding had been planned for early spring. This gave Mary the opportunity to work at Longbourn with Gabriel, well chaperoned, of course, so they would have somewhere to live once they wed.

Mary and Gabriel both believed they were not going to have so much company that necessitated ten guest rooms. Eventually they might need those rooms for their children once they left the schoolroom, but that was what a minimum of fifteen years down the line. So the plan was to scrub and clean Longbourn from top to bottom and make sure it was safe to inhabit. Not a speck of dust would be allowed to remain in the house from the kitchen to the servants' quarters. Then they would pick two rooms to be made over into guest rooms. They would redo more rooms as the need arose, and the funds were available.

Looking over at Nellie who worked alongside her, Mary smiled. She had asked Nellie to be her lady's maid, which had delighted the girl. Nellie dedicated herself to learning all she could to be a proper lady's maid, but she wasn't hesitant to get her hands dirty and contribute to the ambitious project that was Longbourn. At that moment, they were cleaning one of the upstairs rooms. At one time it had belonged to Kitty, and it had fared no better than any of the others when it came to destruction and dirt. Everything from the linens on the bed to scrubbing the floors and walls needed to be taken care of. It would take them quite some time, but Nellie was a kind workmate who helped Mary work more effectively.

Mary paused from scrubbing the floor and glanced up, surprised to see Gabriel standing in the doorway. She watched him grin at her for a moment, wondering just how long he had been watching her. Feeling confident and playful, she tilted her head and greeted him with a question, "Do you need my help with something, Mr. Goulding?"

Gabriel grinned, saying, "Do you have a moment to come see something, Miss Bennet?"

Scrunching her nose, Mary pretended to think for a moment before saying, "I have tea with a duchess in a few hours, but I suppose I do have a moment to see something with you." Standing, Mary dusted off the skirt of her dress, taking note of the wet spots, but deciding it was a small price to pay for getting her future home in shape.

Walking to Gabriel, she giggled when he offered his arm as if they were at some grand ball and not in their rattiest clothes and both coated in dust and grime. It was a short walk down to one of the more put together sitting rooms. There was not much there, but there were a few chairs and a little table in case anyone needed a break and wanted to sit and drink some tea.

Gesturing for her to sit, Gabriel looked slightly nervous. Once she was sitting, Mary noticed there was a plain box on the table that hadn't been there the last time she had come through the room. Interest piqued, she slid her gaze from the box back to Gabriel, waiting for an explanation. She did not have to wait long.

Picking up the box, Gabriel handed it to her, saying, "It isn't much, but I thought... Well, open it, and I will see if I can explain."

Mary's fingers hesitated only a moment before prying open the lid of the box and looking inside. At first, all she saw was packing material, but then she noticed a flash of porcelain shining through. Ignoring the wood shavings, she reached in and carefully plucked out the mysterious item and froze.

It was a fragile porcelain figurine, reminiscent of the ones her mother used to scatter around the house as decorative accents. Painted with soft, delicate hues, the figurine showcased a cheerful young lady walking with a gentleman. The detailing was amazing, Mary could even depict a small kitten peeking out of the basket on the woman's arm. Glancing up at Gabriel, Mary blinked tears out of her eyes.

Rubbing at the back of his neck, obviously slightly embarrassed, he said, "I know your father destroyed all the little breakable things that you cherished from your childhood. Although the figurine may not hold sentimental value, it symbolizes the beginning of creating the warm and joyful home I aspire to provide for you. It is not much, but I wanted you to have something pretty and delicate in your home."

For a moment, Mary could not stop the tears that leaked out of the corners of her eyes. The memory of finding her mother's broken shepherdess amidst the destruction of Longbourn weeks ago lingered in her mind as she reflected on the passage of time. So much had changed for the better. She was confident in the love of a wonderful man, and she was working with him to build their future together. Running her finger down one of the delicate lines of the figurine, Mary smiled. Things were only looking up. Where her father had destroyed and degraded, Gabriel upbuilt and encouraged. Longbourn would never be the same, and for that she was eternally grateful.

Dashing at her tears, Mary held the figurine to her heart and said, "Not just my home, *our home*, and it is perfect! We are rebuilding this home together and we are going to fill it with our hopes and dreams and happy memories. I love the idea of starting it with this."

Gabriel leaned in to wipe her wet cheek with his thumb. "You know, I would not be opposed to filling our home with children, too. I only mention it because you know we have been coming up with lists of projects we need to work on, and I was thinking we should add it to the list."

Laughing at his audacity, Mary replied, "That is one project that will have to wait until after our wedding." With one last loving caress, Mary began putting the little figurine back in its box. It was too precious to leave out during all the remodeling.

"Speaking of weddings, do you need help making any of the arrangements? I would hate for it to be delayed unnecessarily."

Mary couldn't resist the magnetic pull of his exuberant gaze as she met his eyes, a smile spreading across her face. It seemed that he was just as eager as she was to be married. "My sisters have it all in hand. Frankly, I could not care less what goes into the event. I just want to be married to you."

# Chapter Twenty-One

**Four months later**

"I believe you were correct in wanting to keep everything simple for your wedding. You were such a beautiful bride, Mary. The minimalism of your wedding made it all the more special, emphasizing the true essence of love and commitment." This came from Jane, a large smile on her face.

Mary remembered her lovely wedding not two weeks ago, and she felt a warm tug on her heart. "Really, I could not be bothered with all the useless fripperies that brides normally want. It wasn't about the act of getting married for me, it was about embracing the commitment and status of being married. I just wanted to be done with it, so I could fully dedicate myself to my new home and embracing my role as a wife."

Jane smiled at her comment and exchanged a look with Elizabeth who giggled. The joy of having older sisters that Mary would not give up for anything. All of her sisters were there with her. The only one missing from their gathering was her mother. Though she missed her presence, Mary understood why she had gone back to her estate with her new husband so soon after the wedding. Her mother had apologized for the short visit, but Mary understood the weight of painful memories that her mother carried. It was one of the reasons why Mary was working so hard to transform Longbourn.

Mary looked around the sitting room and smiled. If you had not seen Longbourn at its worst, you would have never known that a few short months previously there had been holes in the walls and the furniture had laid in broken ruins. A fresh coat of paint in a soothing sage green had helped to transform the space. Among the few little pieces of bric-à-brac, there was one that stood out - a sentimental figurine gifted to her by Gabriel.

The furniture was all new to her but had, for the most part, been gifts from her sisters. Kitty and Lizzie had the attics in their estates searched through for suitable pieces to supplement her empty house. It was enough that between them and a few select purchases from her uncle's warehouses; they were comfortable. She and Gabriel had left what rooms they did not need to use empty. They saw no need to refurbish the entire estate when they should really focus on the tenant homes and ensuring that they could have a good planting season.

In fact, they had managed to provide tenant cottages for four families so far. Two were newlywed couples looking for a good start to their married lives and two were actually families that had lived at Longbourn previously. By the end of the month, they would have another two tenant homes ready to be moved in to by waiting families. It was a lot of work, but Mary was happy. She had never liked being idle.

"It seems that married life suits you." Lydia's energetic voice drew Mary back to the conversation she should have been attending.

"Yes, I believe it does." Mary said joyfully, smiling at Lydia and then at the rest of her sisters. She had been the only one to have been married from Meryton's chapel, though her wedding breakfast had been at Netherfield, not Longbourn.

Shifting in her seat to accommodate her burgeoning belly more comfortably, Elizabeth studied the little side table that seemed to pull the room together. Looking at Mary, she said, "I love what you have done with this room, but that is no surprise you always had wonderful taste."

"That is kind of you to say, but Kitty helped me pick out the coordinating colors." Mary beamed. It was nice to be able to preside over her own sitting room with all of her sisters present. As time passed, it was becoming increasingly rare to be able to manage it.

Shaking her head, Kitty refuted her sister's claim. "Oh, do not say it was all my doing. I just let you know what colors I thought best go with that lovely green you liked so much." Kitty took a sip of her tea and propped her feet up on the footstool that Lizzie was already using.

"I am still astounded that this tea service survived." Looking at the teacup in her hand, Jane blinked away the tears that seemed to creep up on her.

"Yes, it is quite remarkable that somehow grandmother's cherished tea set has survived when so much else didn't." Mary examined the teapot with delicate little flowers adoring its surface. Standing, she went to the tea service and, glancing at her sisters, she asked, "Would anyone like some more tea?"

Pouring more tea for Lydia and herself, she regarded her sisters. Jane and Lydia sat on one of the settees chatting together about upcoming plans. Mary had told Lydia that she was always welcome to stay at Longbourn. They all were, but Mary wanted to make sure Lydia felt as though she had a home anywhere she chose. Lydia had hugged her and thanked her, but said she was eager to return to Pemberley with Lizzie. Mary understood Lydia was eager to go wherever the children were. With Artie at Pemberley and another babe soon to arrive, she would be content. Their niece Ellie and their little brother Mathew both lived on estates that were just a morning's journey away, which was incredibly convenient.

There was still a debate about whether Lydia would be having a season that year. Lydia had seen how Kitty's season had gone and was not overly enthusiastic about the idea. Her sisters knew that she would rather be holding a baby than dealing with the cats in society sitting rooms. With new babies on the way, it would be hard to drag her from them. Perhaps she could attend the little season or have an abbreviated season. They had time to decide.

Turning her head, Mary watched how Kitty and Lizzie snuggled into one another on the settee they shared. While it was now glaringly obvious that Lizzie was far into the middle of her second pregnancy, Mary suspected Kitty was also with child. Though Mary knew she was not yet pregnant, she was unworried, as it had been less than a month since her wedding after all. It seemed they were all soaking in the simple joy of being together. It was the last gathering of the sisters before everyone would go their separate ways to their own estates. William was eager to get Lizzie to Pemberley before she was too far along in her pregnancy. Of course, everyone would need to work on spring planting and the like.

"And here we have them all!" Mary knew that the booming voice was Colonel Theodore Fitzwilliam's and, with a smile, she glanced up and saw all the gentlemen of the family in the doorway. They had been out checking on the tenant farms, making sure things were in order for the new tenants as well as the two farms that were about to be moved into.

Mary only really had eyes for her own husband, who, though tired and dirty, still made her heart flutter. Walking to her side, Gabriel leaned down and kissed her cheek. Knowing she was blushing wildly at his open display of affection, Mary asked, "How did the day go? Is the Harris family settling in well?"

"They are doing marvelously. Mrs. Harris thanks you for the basket again and Mr. Harris was thrilled with the help setting up his milking barn." Grabbing a biscuit off the tray, Gabriel popped it in his mouth and after chewing it, he smiled and said, "Where is Evaline?"

"She is with Georgiana in the music room. She has been thrilled to learn a few new pieces while she was here to take painting lessons from Kitty."

Shaking his head, Gabriel laughed. "My mother could not give her permission to stay fast enough when she learned she might get painting lessons from a countess."

Kitty spoke up from where she sat next to Lizzie. "Your sister is a dear little thing. It has been a pleasure showing her some of what I know."

Mary looked at Kitty. Theodore stood behind her, his hand on her shoulder and a grin on his face. When they had come back from their trip to Scotland, they were both happier than Mary had ever seen them. They said that they had loved the countryside, and the estate was in good keeping with a wonderful steward and his wife looking after the tenants well, but the winter had been harsh. They wanted to winter at Matlock, but the early onset of winter and unpredictable weather deterred them from traveling.

"I am just happy that I am not the youngest sister anymore," Lydia laughed. "We will have to pair up and embrace all of you condoling couples."

Mary was worried about how Lydia might feel now that she was the only sister without someone in her life. It was so evident when they were all together like this. William, always concerned, knelt next to his wife and placed his hand on her belly. Bingley was talking softly with Jane and Theodore was leaning over, whispering something to Kitty that had made her blush. Maybe Lydia would find someone to love this year. Though she was still young, after all. She had time.

THAT NIGHT, MARY SAT on her stool by her mirror, brushing her hair when her husband came in. Sitting on the bed, Gabriel pulled off one of his boots. Mary smiled at him as she watched him in the mirror. "I already sent Nellie to bed. She was dead on her feet. It has been a long day for everyone."

Nodding his head, Gabriel acknowledged Mary's statement and knew too well how right she was. It had been a long day. Nellie had been so happy when Mary asked her to train to be her lady's maid. She was very understanding that they would not have as much staff as Mr. Darcy or even Mr. Bingley, and therefore would have more responsibilities than the typical lady's maid. A dedicated worker, Nellie had woken up early that morning to help with preparation for the special dinner they had put together to see everyone off. It was good that she would get some rest.

All the visitors would leave Hertfordshire at first light, going off to their various destinations. The large family dinner had been the biggest gathering they had had at Longbourn thus far, but it had gone very well. They had talked well into the evening, despite the knowledge that it would be an early morning. It was only when both Mrs. Darcy and Lady Matlock had fallen asleep curled into their husbands' sides did the party break up and everyone left for Netherfield. Pausing with his hands on his remaining boot, Gabriel asked, "Are you going to be all right with all of your sisters leaving tomorrow?"

Shaking her head, she turned on her stool and faced him. "I will miss them, but we will write, and they will be back at some point. Then, too, we have plans to gather again at the end of summer for a few weeks before harvest. I think we will meet up at Matlock this year. Theodore and Kitty certainly have the room for our burgeoning families." Turning back around, she set down her brush and began to plait her hair.

"I am glad. You know I hate to see you miss them." Gabriel looked around the room that was so very *them*. The master and mistress chambers had been thoroughly redone in order to accommodate the couple and remove any last vestiges of Mr. Bennet. Like her sisters, Mary saw no need to sleep separately from her husband, and Gabriel had been rather happy with the idea as well. So they adapted the master suite to their needs and turned the mistress suite into an office and library with space for both of them to be about their tasks. Gabriel had said he always wanted to be as close to his wife as could be, even if he had to work.

Old Mr. Bennet's study had been converted into the housekeeper's office and sitting room. Most of the bookshelves had been removed and dispersed about the house. Gabriel had been thrilled when they had offered the housekeeper's position to Mrs. Humphrey, and she accepted. She still helped in the kitchen occasionally when she wished to, but her efficiency in all things had transferred well in the way that she ran Longbourn. She also got along famously with Mary, which was a bonus. They had, in effect, created the perfect little home for themselves. It would not have suited many, but it suited them.

Even Evaline spending time with them was so very suitable. Mary was able to shower her with affection, adopting her as a true sister, especially when her own sisters were not nearby. Evaline visited often and his new sisters had managed to bring his mother around to the idea of allowing the countess to arrange Evaline's come out with a certain amount of training beforehand. The arrangement was proving beneficial to his sister, and not in any of the ways his mother had hoped for. In just a few months, she had begun to understand true kindness and the importance of finding love and making it a priority in your life.

Returning to the moment, Gabriel watched the woman who had brought love into his own life. He could not help but be mesmerized by the way her fingers moved through the splendid strands of bronze and gold in the candlelight. While Gabriel loved her hair down and wild around her face, he also understood it would tangle while she slept. So he refrained from undoing it as he wished. At least he refrained from undoing it *sometimes*.

Narrowing her eyes as she tied off her braid, she attempted to glare at him in the mirror. "I have come to know that look, Gabriel Bennet."

"What look, my love?" Gabriel replied innocently.

"I can see you calculating how best to get my hair out of its confinement."

Finishing with his second boot, Gabriel stood and put them away, then slowly stalked back to his wife. "I admitted to you amid that snowstorm that I was thoroughly in love with your hair. You came into this marriage well aware. I still can see no reason why you would be so put out by my habit."

Gabriel watched the blush suffuse Mary's face and run down her neck and under her collar. It had been enchanting to find out just how far down her blush went when she was embarrassed. Huffing and rolling her eyes, he could tell Mary saw the direction of gaze. She had quickly caught on about his fascination. Gabriel had been thrilled to learn that, though she tried to act annoyed by his behavior, she was rather flattered.

Facing him while attempting to maintain her frown, albeit unsuccessfully, she said, "You are not the one who wakes in the middle of the night with hair seeming to have gained a mind of its own and trying to strangle you. I should make you braid it every time you take it down."

Closing the distance, Gabriel leaned in and whispered, "It would be my pleasure to braid your hair for you. You only need to teach me." Kissing the hollow behind her ear, Gabriel grinned as he heard her breath catch.

It was some time before braids reentered either of their minds, yet neither of them was disappointed with the outcome.

# Epilogue

Gabriel retrieved the mittens that had fallen in the snow and put them back on his son's tiny hands. "There you go, Danny. Go have fun but be careful."

"Yes, Papa!" Daniel called back as he scooped up some snow, attempting to form it into a ball like some of the older kids.

Watching his three-year-old boy run off to play with his cousins warmed Gabriel's heart despite the chilly air. How many years ago had it been since he watched Artie and Ellie play in the snow and he wanted the same for his own children? It seemed like yesterday, but with how all the children had grown, he knew that not to be true.

Had it only been four years since the surprise blizzard at Longbourn had changed his life so irrevocably? Looking back at the man he had been leading up to that event, he was almost ashamed of his previous stupidity and presumptuous attitude. Driven by his foolish pride and misguided intentions, he ended up deeply hurting the woman he loved by waiting to declare his intentions. He would forever be grateful that she had found the courage to confront him.

She had been so right in her statement that love without action was not enough. The last five years had certainly been proof of that. Love was not the jewelry and fine things that he had thought she deserved—it was the joy of working together day after day to create a life they both cherished. It was quiet nights when he read aloud and she worked on sewing baby clothes. It was struggling in a flooded field to help their tenants knowing that Mary would be waiting for him at home with a warm cup of tea and that soft smile he had grown to know so well.

Not everything was easy. There had been a very poor harvest the year before last that had set them back, and his relationship with his parents and brother would probably always be rocky at best. Rebuilding Longbourn took sacrifice and hours of planning, but no matter how things progressed, they worked together to build it into a home full of love and kindness. Their efforts extended to providing everything necessary for the families in the tenant cottages to be comfortable, well-fed, and happy. They had even built a small schoolhouse on Longbourn land near the manor house so Mary could pursue her love of teaching the local children to read and write well enough to thrive. Yes, he had a lot to be grateful for, and it was all thanks to his wonderful Mary's courage.

Amidst the chaos unfolding before him, Gabriel's heart swelled with happiness as he took in the joyful energy that filled the air. There were squeals and laughter from all over the lawn. An overnight snowstorm had surprised the family that had converged at Pemberley for a reunion of sorts. The fresh snow had been begging to be played in, so mittens and coats were supplied, and the children were having a ball.

Artie was with his brother Gil, trying to build a snowman. Kiernan, home from school and as tall as could be, was patiently helping some of the smaller children form snowballs. Ellie was with some of the other girls making snow angels. Somehow, all the Bennet sisters had managed to come this year and resulting in quite a few children playing in the yard. Even his own sister, Evaline, was out there playing. His mother had allowed him to take Evaline to visit with everyone because, of course, the countess and earl would be in attendance.

Now that he paid closer attention, he noticed there were more young people playing in the snow than just the Bennet cousins. Some were like his sister, who, although not officially a Bennet, still held a place within the family. It was such a fortunate thing to witness so much joy from so many cheerful and deserving people. Anyone who would turn up their nose to playing in the snow was certainly missing out.

CROUCHED IN THE SNOW with the two of the youngest children, Kiernan helped their clumsy hands pack the snow together. Benedict, with black hair and blue eyes, was the spitting image of his father, yet he was full of Lydia's mischievous personality. Adelaide was Benedict's twin sister, and despite her small size and age, was just as intrepid as any of the Bennet women and refused to be outdone. Lydia may have gone about finding the love of her life in a manner that no one had expected, but she had proven herself just as happy with the results. Adelaide and Benedict were certainly proof of that. Kiernan thought that if he could experience even half the happiness she seemed to radiate in a marriage of his own, it would be sufficient.

Eventually, the two little ones transitioned from snowball construction to rolling around in the frigid powder. Kiernan scanned the group of children as they happily shrieked and played. He was fairly certain he was the oldest person on the field, and he felt a responsibility to help make sure everyone stayed safe. A huddle of fathers stood on the side, ready to help, but for the moment they were all chatting. While they were not playing in the snow, they seemed just as cheerful as their many children.

Kiernan's survey of the snowy reunion was interrupted when he saw one of the older girls fall on a slick patch of ice. He hurried over to help her up, but upon reaching her, found himself momentarily frozen in place. There in the snow was an angel staring up at him. He quickly realized that his previous assumption was incorrect—she was not a child but rather a young lady in her late teens. The sight of her auburn curls tumbling around her shoulders was matched only by the radiance in her bright green eyes as she laughed at her fall. It took a moment for Kiernan's brain to function enough to remember the task at hand and help her to stand. Holding her elbow to make sure she was steady, he asked, "Are you all right?"

Dusting off the snow, she smiled, and her left cheek revealed an alarmingly cute dimple. "Despite being clumsy, I am fine. You are Kiernan, right?"

"Kiernan Anderson at your service." Offering a bow, he tilted his head, unable to remember who she was. "I am sorry, but I cannot remember who you are."

Her grin never faltered as she replied, "That is all right. I do not believe we have been formally introduced. I am Marianne Gardiner. Elizabeth is my cousin, and my mother thought Elizabeth might need some help with all the children and people. I was happy to come, as I love spending time with children, and I always enjoy my time with my cousins." Looking around at the jubilant chaos, she laughed. When a little body catapulted into her at speed, she nearly went down again. Had it not been for Kiernan, who swiftly braced her, they both would have taken a tumble. Giggling at the collision, little Lord Cedric Fitzwilliam bowed and apologized before taking off again, still being chased by Danny. Glancing up at Kiernan, her eyes dancing, she whispered, "Though sometimes it feels as though I have willingly offered myself as prey to the wolves."

Kiernan found himself swiftly losing all reason and possibly his heart as he got lost in the playful warmth of her verdant gaze. Eventually he said, "Do not worry, I am an expert wolf wrangler. I shall protect you." Then, realizing how ridiculous he must have sounded, he withdrew his hand from her shoulder and nervously rubbed the back of his neck instead.

With eyes still dancing, Marianne said, "Well, good sir, I shall count on your aid should I find myself in peril again."

LYDIA WATCHED THE ANTICS of everyone playing in the snow, but upon noticing Kiernan, she giggled and said, "Would you look at that? It seems that the next round of courting may have started sooner than we expected."

Shaking her head, Elizabeth gave a rueful grin. "Yes, poor Kiernan looks as if he was poleaxed. I wonder if William has noticed. I have a feeling he will relish watching that relationship develop."

Mary had seen the look on Kiernan's face and had to agree with her sisters—he was lost to love and only time would tell if he had stumbled upon the real thing. Tilting her head, she thought for a moment. If she was not mistaken, Marianne was almost seventeen and Kiernan was eighteen, going on nineteen. They were young still, leaving plenty of time for both of them to see what came of it.

Returning her attention to her circle of sisters, Mary was blissfully content. Her mother had gone inside saying it was too cold for her, but Mary knew that she just wanted to spend time with her husband, away from all the chaos. Mathew, her little brother, was happily running around with his many nieces and nephews. Unlike most of the others, the Bennet sisters were all bundled up and sitting in chairs in the sun. Among them, three were at various stages of pregnancy, so it was fortunate they were all happy enough to sit around a cheery fire and talk.

Her sister Jane was finally pregnant again. Unlike her rather fertile sisters, Jane had struggled to fall with child after her daughter Eleanor. To Mary's eye, she looked as if she had lost weight with the way her clothes were hanging on her. "How are you feeling, Jane? How has the nausea been?"

Jane scrunched her nose and sighed. "I am just so glad to be with child again that I would suffer it all gladly. I almost thought I would be unable to make it to Pemberley this year. I had been so ill, but things are finally improving." Placing her hand on her slightly rounded stomach, she smiled. "I will admit that when I finally felt the babe move, I cried. It terrified Charles something horrible to find me crying like that, but he managed to get over it."

Lydia began rubbing her own swollen abdomen and winced. "I swear if I am not having another pair of twins, it is triplets, and they all seem to be wrestling."

Kitty laughed at her younger sister's comment. "Theodore always said Cedric was practicing archery."

"He would. He still calls you Artemis," Lydia replied with a snort.

Mary watched as Kitty glared at her sister, knowing full well it far from malicious. "And don't you tell him to stop!" That set all the sisters laughing.

Once she caught her breath, Mary asked Elizabeth, "Have the boys adjusted to having a sister yet?" Mary knew her young niece was sleeping up in the nursery. Though not much younger than Lydia's twins, she was too small to play in the snow.

"They were both hesitant at first, but now that she is becoming more mobile and walking, they have begun realizing that they can play with her." Elizabeth sighed as if remembering something. "Artie has taken to trying to get her to improve her vocabulary. He is already reading simple books and has started reading them to her, trying to get her to say all the words."

Jane grinned. "He is certainly your and William's son."

Mary suppressed a laugh knowing Elizabeth could not argue with that. She was grateful that despite their growing families, they were able to have such a happy day together. The Bennet sisters had certainly come a long way, and they had all found such happiness. Each of them had faced their own challenges to find their path, but in the end, they had all found love, and no one could deny the happiness that had brought each of them.

Her own happiness still felt so fresh and new even after the years that she had with Gabriel at Longbourn. Not only had they grown close as a married couple, but they had practically transformed the place they called home. It no longer held the weight of tragic memories; instead, love and kindness permeated every nook and cranny.

It helped that everyone who lived at the manor or on the estate property no longer did so under her father's oppressive shadow. Without that shadow, there was a brightness about the place that had been lost for quite some time. Even the maids went about their tasks humming. Mary liked to think that her Grandmother Catherine would have been happy to see the improvements.

Mary worked hard to nurture deep connections with all the tenant wives and their children, and it was truly a joy to be able to help as the need arose. Having a husband who was equally committed to creating a wonderful place to live had made a significant impact on Longbourn. That was not to say that everything had been easy. They had had their arguments over time, especially when he worried about her during her pregnancy.

It had been an adjustment to adapt to being a wife and then a mother. The birth of her son had brought new responsibilities, requiring her to shuffle things around and make necessary adjustments to maintain the school she had created. In that she was grateful for all of Evaline's help, as whenever she was able to, her young sister-in-law came to Longbourn and helped with teaching. The girl was truly blossoming into a kind woman who cared about others.

Looking up, Mary caught sight of Evaline as she played with the smaller children. She had little Daniel with her, and they were laughing merrily in the snow. It was a beautiful thing to see how close the two were. As she scanned the crowd for her husband, she had a sudden realization that he was actually watching her. Locking eyes with the man she loved so much, she could not help but beam at the adoration she saw there.

MARY WAS GRATEFUL FOR Gabriel's strong hands at her waist as he helped her down from the carriage. Descending from a carriage with her arms full of their sleeping toddler would not have been easy otherwise. After days of traveling back from Pemberley, they were finally home at Longbourn. She would miss her sisters and extended family, but Mary was glad to be home.

Daniel's nursemaid rushed over to them, eager to help despite the darkening twilight. "I can take him up to the nursery for you, Mrs. Bennet."

With a shake of her head, Mary replied, "I can carry him up. I would hate for him to wake now."

"Are you hungry, my dear?" Gabriel asked, his hand at the small of her back as they walked into their home together.

"Surprisingly, I am more hungry than tired. More than anything, I am just happy to be home."

They walked through their home together, their footsteps creating a gentle rhythm of harmony. Gabriel opened the door to the nursery and after some delicate maneuvering, they successfully settled Daniel into his small bed. To their amazement, he stayed fast asleep.

As was part of their evening routine, they took a moment to look down on their sleeping son together. Mary caressed his sleeping face for a moment before leaning over and kissing his flushed cherub cheek. This was followed up by Gabriel kissing Daniel's cheek as well, and then Mary settled into Gabriel's muscular form. Resting her head on his shoulder, she sighed happily as they continued to watch their son together.

He whispered, "You made a beautiful little boy, Mary."

Mary smiled softly to herself, not taking her eyes off the precious boy who represented the beautiful life she and Gabriel had created together. "If I remember correctly, you had something to do with it."

Gabriel laughed softly as they turned to leave their son's room. With a nod to his nurse, they continued on their way through the house. Mary smiled as she took note of all the small changes she had made over the years—a new side table here, a painting by Kitty there. Their home, for the most part, was modest, but cozy. She didn't want to bankrupt the estate, especially when there were more pressing needs, like repairing and expanding Longbourn.

By the time their little Daniel was grown and ready to take over, she and Gabriel were determined he would have a prosperous estate as his inheritance and any younger brothers and sisters would be just as provided for. Finally making it to their own little library, Mary was happy to see a maid delivering a tea tray with a hearty snack of bread, cheese, and cold meats.

Settling into her favorite chair, she watched as Gabriel tore off a hunk of bread and slathered it in the ginger marmalade she had recently taken a liking to. Holding the morsel up to her lips, he watched her intently as she took a bite and hummed under her breath, very happy as the flavor burst on her tongue. Once she could speak after swallowing, she said, "You know you do not have to go so far as to feed me. I can feed myself."

Wiping a smudge of jam off her lip and licking his finger, Gabriel smiled smugly at the expression on her face. "My pregnant wife was just jostled over rough roads for three days. Let me pamper her as I wish to."

Holding his gaze, Mary murmured, "You know that I have not felt the quickening yet. We cannot say for sure that I am carrying our next baby."

"And you know that I know your body well enough to detect your pregnancy, even without feeling the baby move." Leaning in, he kissed her deeply.

As Gabriel finally broke the kiss, Mary's lips curved into a smile, savoring the sensation of his presence against her mouth. "Oh, all right, feed me if you must." Who was she to complain about her husband's desire to spoil her?

Mary accepted another bite of food from Gabriel, savoring the flavors as she chewed contemplatively. She couldn't help but feel a sense of gratitude for having taken the leap and asking Gabriel to act on his love for her. How else could she have arrived at this state of complete and utter happiness?

# Acknowledgements

Before you go, I'd like to express my gratitude to all those who assisted me in bringing the Bennet sisters' stories to the world. I'd like to start by acknowledging and thanking the people closest to me. It was thanks to my sister Megan's encouragement that I began writing. Then there is my mother, who serves as my alpha reader and sounding board for fresh ideas. My sister Chelsea's support is invaluable, just like the inspiration I find in my nieces and nephew for my younger characters. If you haven't had the pleasure of debating with a one-year-old who can articulate their thoughts in complete sentences, you're missing out. It is an absolute delight!

Additionally, I would like to extend my appreciation to my Beta readers and the people who show support through my newsletter. Doris, Debra, Carol, and Frankie, working with you to bring my stories to the world has been an honor. The encouragement and feedback I get from you helps me more than you know.

Lastly, it has been an utter pleasure working with my editor, Tayler. Your feedback not only helps me ensure that my story flows and my characters shine, but I also thoroughly enjoy reading your comments. I always love seeing your emojis in the comments, especially the ones with heart eyes!

Most importantly, I would like to thank you. It's been a joy to create this work of love, but without readers, it would be an exercise in futility. The fact that you chose my book to read is an honor. Thank you for taking the time to finish my book, I hope the characters and their stories resonated with you.

If you enjoyed reading this book, please consider leaving an honest review on your favorite site. It does not have to be very long, but I would really appreciate the feedback.

# About the Author

My journey with words started out as a painful one. The letters on the page seemed to taunt me, and I spent countless hours with my mother trying to decipher their meaning. Our reading journey started with Little House on the Prairie and continued with other books, mostly in the historical fiction genre. Slowly but surely, I started reading independently, advancing from historical fiction to fantasy and science fiction.

The stories I found in the books I read held me captive, and I often lost track of time. The realization of the true power of the written word inspired me to pursue writing. Unfortunately, I had to put it on the back burner in order to deal with pesky things like paying for food and housing. Then a dare from my sister brought back memories of my passion for writing in high school. It was a passion that I was determined to rekindle.

When I got back into writing, I turned to my latest reading addiction for inspiration, Pride and Prejudice Variations. My mind was fixated on the regency era and the romance of Elizabeth and

Darcy, making it hard to write anything else. So I went with it and here we are.

**Visit jaimemariewrites.com to delve into my world of words, or find me on Instagram @jaimemariewrites for a glimpse into my creative process.**

# Books by Jaime Marie Lang

## The Bennet Ladies Liberation Series

Darcy's Gallant Gambit

Kitty Catches Kismet

Mary's Daring Demand

Jane's Fragile Façade

Lydia Acquires Adoration

## Other Novels

Murdered on a Wednesday: A Pride and Prejudice Mystery